THE ALEXANDER MA[illegible] CHRONICLES BOOK 1

L. D. ALBANO

Edited by Michael Waitz (https://sticksandstonesediting.net/)
Cover design by Deranged Doctor Design (https://derangeddoctordesign.com)
Formatting by Polgarus Studio (https://polgarusstudio.com)

ISBN: 978-1-7362791-1-3

# Dedication

For everyone in my family (Liz, Ainsley, Mom, and Tammy) who encouraged me to pursue writing this book...even if the content really wasn't their thing.

Special thanks go out to Aimee Brayman, the only soul brave enough to give me honest feedback when she Beta-read this story. This book wouldn't exist in its current form without you.

And to editor extraordinaire Michael Waitz, who saw something in the semi-coherent ramblings of a first-time author. You rock.

# About the author

L. D. Albano is as surprised as anyone else that he had the opportunity to write this. He is an IT professional who has worked in the field since 1997, performing duties ranging from service desk, to network engineering, and management. The five years prior to that were spent in Germany, Colorado Springs, and assorted other places while serving in the US Army.

He lives in the Pacific Northwest with his wife, daughter, and a cinnamon-colored Siberian Husky named Ronin. He will give you one guess as to who runs the household....

# Prologue

**Outside Taos, New Mexico, July 1903**

Alexander Titus Matthews could hardly believe what he was seeing. Nearly perfectly preserved within the hot and dusty confines of the cavern he was currently exploring, and partially buried under millennia of detritus, was the carcass of one of the Pleistocene's great carnivores. Its size and the shape of the head and muzzle made identification easy. *Canis Dirus*, better known as the dire wolf, had roamed much of the Americas for tens of thousands of years during the last ice age, and earlier. This specimen was abnormally large, upon cursory inspection, and some rough estimations indicated that the animal would have been almost seven feet long, the top of its head reaching armpit high on Alexander himself, and weighed in at around two-hundred-sixty pounds.

Any *Smilodon*, more commonly known as a saber-toothed tiger, would think twice about taking on a wolf this size, much less a pack of them. Granted, the outcome would favor the feline in any one-on-one battle. Still, it wouldn't be a *sure* thing, and it would definitely result in severe injuries, even for the winner. Both species were top predators during the Pleistocene, but the cats were most likely solo hunters and would be at a disadvantage if they came across a pack of dires. Realistically, they were probably on each other's prey menu, and encounters would have been frequent.

Alexander placed the lantern carefully on a small ledge near the jumble of rock, wood, and other items that had accumulated in the back of the now-collapsed limestone cavern. He had stumbled upon the sinkhole while searching the area for artifacts that could be studied and incorporated into his doctoral thesis on ice age fauna of North America. Scrambling through dusty and dangerous places was all in a day's work when one wanted to find fossils. Carefully scraping away and removing the litter that the remains were semi-buried in took time, but was well worth it when he finally was able to view it in its entirety.

This was a spectacular find, especially since most dire wolf fossils were found as fragments, or wholly disassociated, just a bone here and there. The La Brea tar pits were currently the best source for dire wolf fossils, but even that location had not provided actual tissue samples. This *mummy*, for lack of a better term, was as unlikely as finding the Holy Grail. Alexander's future career in archaeology was set with this discovery. Still, his hands weren't trembling because of that; rather, it was the sheer excitement of seeing and touching something no other modern man had ever experienced. Not only was the body intact, but much of the tissue had survived, as had much of the pelt. While time had taken its toll, and the pelt was a bit sparse in places, patchy in spots, the vast majority was still present. The dry environment of the cave had leached the moisture from the carcass rather than letting it decompose. Even the eyes, though shriveled and sunken into the sockets, were there. In fact, the remains seemed eerily similar to Egyptian mummies he had seen pictures of, the skin stretched taut over the bone structure itself.

His eye was drawn to a metallic glint that reflected the lantern light. This was odd because there shouldn't have been any modern materials associated with the remains of a Pleistocene animal. Had someone already been here? Did a scrap of metal wash into the site during a rainstorm? He leaned closer to get a better look and was surprised to see that it appeared to be a chain of some sort…a necklace perhaps, and that it led into the jaws of the wolf, almost as if the creature had taken it into its mouth before dying. Alexander tugged gently on the chain, but it was firmly lodged and would not come free. With both hands, he slowly worked the body loose and pulled it farther into the light. Alexander took a knee and grabbed the muzzle, one hand on top and one on the bottom, then tried to gently pry open the mouth without damaging it. Carefully applying pressure yielded the desired results, and he saw that a pendant of some sort rested upon the desiccated remains of the tongue. His right hand reached in to dislodge the item, but before he could do so, the jaws slammed shut. Alexander cried out in pain as the sharp teeth of the animal quickly pierced the skin of his hand. Something stung his palm in multiple places where it rested against the object that he held wrapped in his hand. Seconds later, a burning sensation crawled up his arm and quickly spread throughout his body, his panicked breathing was loud within the confines of the cavern, and his vision faded out as he lost consciousness.

Most of a day passed while Alexander was caught up in fever dreams. The sights and sounds that were experienced granted him knowledge of an unknown history that humanity had either forgotten, or that had been deliberately stripped from its collective memory. Mankind's origins were both far older and much more complex than anyone had imagined. The gods of pre-history were real, but they weren't gods at all. Aliens had enslaved humanity and used mankind for their own selfish purposes.

# Chapter 1

*"....After I recovered from the transformation that the virus-laden bite and the amulet had imparted, I made my way back to Taos, where I hid in my room at the boarding house and thought about what my plans should be. I knew without a doubt that I would never curse another person by turning them into a monster like I had become...and that is an oath that I have never broken. This was also the time when I lost what little religion I had left. How do you believe in a god, when your memories show you hundreds of gods, each and every one flawed by hubris and a condescending conceitedness that allowed them to treat humanity with such total disdain...."*

**An excerpt from the diary of Alexander Matthews**

**February 1980, Temple of Seti, Abydos, Egypt**

*Maria shivered in the cold desert air, the light jacket not nearly enough to insulate her body as the heat rapidly dissipated from the rock and sand. She and Alexander had come to this temple to study curious carvings that could only be found here. Of course, she hadn't realized that breaking and entering were going to be part of the evening fun, but then again, Maria was finding that her boss was a man of many talents. Not all of them legal.*

*He was standing near the top of the ladder, which he had purchased earlier in the day, currently shining a flashlight onto the hieroglyphs carved into the sandstone lintel and attempting to take photos. She might not be any kind of expert on Egypt or even history in general, but those definitely looked like flying machines to her. A helicopter, a plane, and other less recognizable figures jumped out at her.*

*Why Alexander would be so interested in them was also a mystery. Yet, it was readily apparent that he found them fascinating...and was willing to go to great lengths to study them.*

*He turned his excited face her way. "I'm almost positive this stone was recycled from an earlier structure. How* much *earlier is the question. And where was it located?"*

*"What are you implying, Alexander?"*

*"You'll think I'm crazy." His cheeks bulged until he expelled the air in a rush. "Let's just say that I suspect an earlier advanced culture occupied the Nile River Valley prior to the Egyptians."*

*She scrunched her face in confusion. "What, like Atlantis or something?"*

*He descended the ladder quickly. "Or something. It's not important, and we need to get out of here before we get busted."*

*A high-pitched howl, and barking yips, shattered the silence of the desert night. Alexander's head elevated, and he scanned the area around them alertly, seemingly sniffing the air. His broad shoulders tensed, and his fists clenched as he took two quick steps forward. His demeanor changed, becoming more aggressive and predatory, prepared for violence.*

*"Maria, I need you to pay very close attention to what I am about to say." When he looked at her, his expression was severe, almost clinically cold. His eyes, though, burned with anger that was palpable in the air. She could practically see the humanity drift away on a seething current of self-loathing, hatred, and excitement, all somehow rolled into one overpowering emotion that was barely restrained.*

*"I had hoped to shield you from what you are about to experience, but it would appear that I can no longer do so." He quickly crossed to where she was standing. "We are going to be attacked...soon." His words were harsh, almost staccato sounding as he spoke them.*

*Her eyes opened wide in shock, and she stammered, "What are you talking about, Alexander? Who is going to attack us?"*

*His hands grasped her upper arms, and he pushed her gently back against the wall. "Not important. I need you to trust me, OK? No harm will come to you, I promise, but you need to stay right here. If you run, I will have a harder time protecting you."*

*Loud growling was coming from the entrance to the temple, and she could see gleaming red eyes reflecting the light at her. She shook her head in denial. "I don't understand. . . ."*

*Her boss was unbuttoning his shirt. "I know you don't. This is going to get very ugly, and you are going to see things that you believe to be impossible. Frightening things. No matter what, though, you need to understand that I* will *protect you. Can you do that?"*

*She turned frightened eyes to him and jerked her head in a sharp nod, noticing for the first time that he wore a thick chain around his neck that supported a sizeable disk-shaped piece of jewelry, and he had a half-sleeve tattoo of some kind of animal. The ink covered part of his chest and his arm from shoulder to elbow.*

*"Good. If you need to, you can close your eyes—that way you will miss everything, good and bad." He had removed his boots as he was talking, and quickly pulled his pants off, standing naked before her. The growling was closer now, and she could hear claws scratching against the stone floor.*

*Alexander turned to face whatever was coming, and crouched down into an aggressive arms-wide stance. Suddenly, two indistinct forms rocketed at him, and he surged forward to meet them. Now she saw the animals were thin, graceful, and more resembled coyotes than wolves. A large black-backed jackal latched onto his calf and began to worry it with the razor-sharp teeth in its maw. In the meantime, Alexander had caught the other by the throat and was beating it to death with his free hand.*

*She heard vertebrae break as Alex twisted the head sharply, then tossed the carcass against the wall, where it fell limply to the stone floor. Even as he reached down for the jackal that was attached to his calf, a more substantial form approached. There was something wrong about it, though. For one thing, it was much larger than the others, and it was on two feet, clawed hands stretched out toward her boss.*

*Alexander spotted the creature and glanced back at Maria, and an apologetic look crossed his face, quickly followed by anger. His fist smashed down onto the skull of the jackal that was trying to hamstring him. Brains and blood flew from the impact, and the animal released its hold on him, collapsing bonelessly to the floor. Alexander straightened to his full height and…changed. She blinked her eyes, not believing what they were telling her.*

*Where a man had stood just moments ago was a very, very angry werewolf. He leaned forward aggressively and roared out a challenge that reverberated throughout the temple. The jackal-headed creature that had been stalking him paused, reevaluating what had become a much more dangerous situation. Maria couldn't believe her eyes. The thing facing off against Alexander looked almost exactly like the illustrations of Anubis she had seen since their arrival in Egypt. Additional jackals peeked around his legs, growling at Alex, but not yet attacking.*

*Evidently, her boss wasn't willing to wait for them to make up their minds—he leapt into their midst and began methodically killing them all. Soon, only the werewolf and the werejackal stood on the field of battle. Claws had scored Alexander's chest, and blood ran freely down his fur-covered torso. Other wounds, including his savagely mauled calf, marred his body, but if they bothered him, there was no sign of it. The jackal was limping heavily from an obviously broken leg, and one arm hung limply, the shoulder mangled from the bite that had savaged it.*

*Maria almost felt sorry for the Anubis lookalike; Alexander towered over him, the muscles in his body tensed and ready to end this.*

*But rather than continue the fight as she expected, her boss stepped back and changed into the naked man who had assured her that she would be safe.*

*Still glaring at the jackal, he said, "There has been enough death tonight. Take any remaining members of your Pack and go."*

*His opponent cocked his head in confusion, whining as he licked his snout. Finally, he dipped his head in acknowledgment and limped off into the night, leaving Alexander and Maria alone with the bodies of the dead.*

*Alexander took a deep, shuddering breath and turned to face her. She almost burst out laughing because he looked more afraid of what her reaction would be, than the curiously muted terror she felt. He made no attempt to approach, merely hung his head, and waited.*

*"I'll understand if you decide you don't want to work with me anymore. What you saw tonight was never supposed to be part of the job, and I'm truly sorry it happened," he said softly.*

*Shivering uncontrollably, Maria replied through chattering teeth, "What are you? What were* they?*"*

*His head rose slowly, mournful eyes meeting hers steadily. "We are the things that go bump in the night. The monsters that tales are made of. Not many normal people even know we exist."*

*Maria found herself calming down, which was strange, considering that her boss was a werewolf. Still, she sensed no danger from him, only a great sorrow and vulnerability. For some reason, he didn't frighten her, even though he should have.*

*"Alexander?"*

*"Yes?" he whispered.*

*"You should come over here, so I can tend to your wounds."*

***

Maria Ferrante was having an increasingly difficult time hiding her amusement at the antics of her soon-to-be-former employer on this sunny June day. He was pacing in front of his large mahogany desk, frantically waving his arms about, and rapid-firing questions in her direction.

"Are you absolutely sure about this, Maria?" he asked plaintively. "You could retire in a couple of years instead."

"Alexander, we've talked about this already," she replied patiently, much as one would to a small child. "I'm not getting any younger, and God knows all of the travel has begun to take its toll on my body. It takes longer and longer for me to recover from jetlag these days." Her expression softened as she continued, "The spirit is willing, as it always was, but I'm a realist. I'm 58 years old, and I want to enjoy the years I have left doing small things like normal people do. I own a house that I've barely spent any time in, and I want to putter around in the garden doing nothing more than working on a tan while drinking iced tea."

He stopped abruptly, turned to her, and snorted rudely. "Ha! You and I both know that you'll be bored to tears within a month. Then what?"

Sighing loudly, Maria brushed a hand through her still dark but grey-streaked hair. "I have no idea, I'll just have to figure something out though. Putting this off won't change any of that, Alexander, as you of all people should know." He looked away briefly, then nodded reluctantly.

Alexander glanced with a doubtful expression over her shoulder into the other office that was visible through the open door, at a beautiful twenty-something woman who bore a striking resemblance to Maria. "Maybe I should just do everything myself again...."

Maria crossed her arms over her chest and sarcastically said, "Oh, really? Are you telling me that you want to answer calls, respond to email, balance the books, manage all of the various investments, *and* take care of your own travel arrangements?"

Maria's skeptical look and raised brow spoke volumes to what she thought of that. In the face of her compelling argument, he seemed to wilt, asking, "Is she ready? More importantly, can I trust her? What happens when she figures it all out, Maria?" Collapsing into the leather chair behind his expansive wooden desk, he murmured, "I'm afraid of what her reaction will be; not everyone will, or can, take it as well as you did."

She walked around his desk and put her hand on his shoulder, then looked deep into his mismatched blue and amber eyes, a sad smile on her face. "I won't promise you she will not be shocked at your secret, but Tina is a very, very smart and strong young woman. She inherited a lot of what I am, much to the consternation of the rest of the family. I may be the only *acknowledged* black sheep right now, but I predict I won't be the only one soon enough." A devilish grin lit up her face as she watched her niece pack up what few personal belongings Maria had left in her desk. "Tina is the daughter I never had, the family I always wanted, and I'm afraid I may have been a bad influence on her."

Glancing back at the man who was obviously struggling with his emotions, she continued, "I'm old, Alexander...old and tired. You need someone who is capable of maintaining the fast-paced lifestyle you lead. We both know that what I'm saying is true." She told herself that her words were valid, but Maria also knew that part of it was that she just didn't want him to bear the burden of watching her grow older and die.

A ghost of sadness passed across his features as he looked up at Maria. "I'm going to miss you, my friend," was a whisper just for her ears. "How shall I make it through the coming days without you here to rein in my tendency to rash action?"

Sudden tears flooded her eyes. "And I, you. Working here with you has been my whole life. Frankly, I'm barely holding it together right now. How sad is that?" Alexander handed Maria a tissue and glanced doubtfully once again in the direction of her niece. His eyes flicked back to her at the sound of her sniffle and the tissue gliding across her eyes, removing the moisture that had accumulated there. She was fully aware that allowing her the time, and privacy, to take care of this, let him consider that this was the start of a new era. Maria had been with him for thirty-eight years, and he was used to her presence. It was obvious that he wasn't sure he was ready for this change, and though they had indeed discussed this scenario several times over the last few years, she suspected he'd never really believed this day would come.

Smacking him in the chest, she growled, "You better take care of her, mister. None of your shenanigans." Alexander scowled up at Maria with a *who me?* expression, and she burst out laughing. "Yes, you. Seriously though, be nice to her. I think she needs you almost as much as you need her."

A confused expression greeted her words, so she elaborated, "Trust me on this, Alexander, that girl is just as introverted as you are and *almost* as combative, but unlike you, she carries a ton of insecurities to go along with that. She was a complete tomboy when she was younger, and had no time for what she called *girly things*. Of course, she eventually outgrew that stage, but there are still a few rough edges that have survived even to this day. That young woman is smarter than I ever will be, Alexander, and yet ...she lacks people skills. Tina can be an extremely tough customer and has the tongue of a viper when she's pissed, so be forewarned."

Through lidded eyes, he nodded almost imperceptibly at her words. "I don't want to hurt her, Maria...like I did you." They had talked about this in the past, how this was one of his greatest regrets in life, the fact that she had given up so much for him and the work they did here. "Are you absolutely certain about this?"

"Not really, Alexander," she said, "but she has no one right now, and neither do you. Just promise me that you will be kind and gentle with her.

That's all I can ask. The rest will be up to her when she discovers the truth." Maria shrugged and nodded to her niece. "I think she's almost finished, which means it's time for me to say goodbye."

Alexander stood and took her into his arms and hugged her tightly. She melted into his embrace as she struggled to hold back more tears, then resolutely straightened up and pushed him away. Without a backward glance, she strode out of his office and closed the door firmly behind her.

***

Alexander watched Maria walk away, competing emotions washing through him as he thought back on all the years they had worked together. It was hard to believe it had been thirty-eight years since that fateful night in Egypt when he had been forced to reveal his curse. The courage she had exhibited in the face of the horrors she had witnessed still amazed him, and the fact that she had not only stayed with him after that but had embraced the job, was nothing less than miraculous as far as he was concerned.

The still-slim figure, in her always fashionable clothing, was walking out of his life and taking a massive bite out of his heart as she did so. The wavy, long hair that had always fascinated him swayed back and forth as she strode purposefully out of his office, her heels clicking loudly on the office floor.

Alexander smiled in amusement as he followed her with his eyes. Clothes, and in particular, shoes, had been one of the few things Maria had accumulated over the years. In fact, she had always somehow managed to fit in time for shopping on every trip she had arranged for them. Truthfully, he never begrudged her the time as she dragged him from one fashion designer to another. Maria had more than earned her obsession.

The door closed with a soft *click*, leaving him alone in his office with just his thoughts and memories.

***

Tina Ferrante glanced up as she heard the *click* of a door being closed. Her Aunt Maria smiled blearily at her through the tears that were threatening to stream down her face. A scowl broke out as she quickly crossed the three steps to grab Maria by the shoulders. "What did he do?" she demanded with narrowed and suspicious eyes. "I swear to God I will kick him in the junk if he was mean to you!" Maria knew she meant it too. The woman in front of her had been a significant influence in Tina's life, more mother to her than aunt, and *no one* was allowed to hurt her in any way.

"I believe you would, Tina, I believe you would indeed," her aunt laughed through her tears. "However, you can safely leave his *junk* alone; he was a complete gentleman. I'm crying because I'm really going to miss this job…going to miss Alexander. Sadness sort of goes with the territory, I guess." She shrugged wryly and scrubbed her face to get rid of the wetness. Maria looked around at what used to be her domain, taking in the conference room and the short hallway that led to the restrooms, and her desk that sat like a battleship in the large foyer that was the only entry into the antiquities dealer workspace. "I can think of no one else I'd want to pass the torch to."

Tina sniffed at that and protested, "Come on, Aunt Maria, it's just a job." Looking disdainfully at the closed door, behind which her new boss resided, she continued, "If you ask me, he's just another trust-fund baby, spoiled rotten by money he never had to earn."

Maria gave Tina a sharp look, then pushed her forcefully into the chair behind the desk and stood menacingly over her. "You listen to me, young lady, that is the finest man I have ever known. Alexander has never been anything other than kind and respectful to me, and without a doubt is the best friend I have ever had." Stabbing at her niece with her index finger, she went on, "You *will* show him respect. You *will* try to be pleasant, hard as that may be for you. And you *will* do your job to the best of your ability. Am I perfectly clear?" There was nothing friendly about Maria's icy stare, anger quickly suffusing her face.

"He already has some doubts about my bringing you in to take my place in his company, but he trusts *my* judgment implicitly. I've earned that trust over the years, and because I vouch for your abilities, he is willing to take a chance on an unknown…an unknown with no real experience, an unknown with a degree so new the ink still hasn't dried yet." Leaning in close, she hissed, "You *will not* make a liar out of me. Do you understand?"

Clearly startled by the vehemence in her aunt's voice, Tina stammered out, "Yes, ma'am. Duly noted." Maria had seldom displayed anger in Tina's presence, and certainly not anger directed at her as it now was.

Gazing deep into Tina's eyes, Maria finally nodded and said, "Good."

Maria leaned against the desk, took a calming breath, then held her niece's hand in her own. "This is an incredible opportunity, and I want you to seize it with both hands and never let go." A wistful note was in her voice as she continued, "I have traveled the world, dined at the finest restaurants, gone to operas in the grandest venues imaginable, attended the ballet in Moscow, and directly experienced so many other wonderful things I can't even begin to tell you about all of them. Some things I probably never *will* be able to tell you, as they shall go to my grave with me. And none of that would have been possible without that man and his father before him."

A calculating look crossed Maria's face, then she asked, "How much money do you think I have saved for my retirement since I started working here?"

Tina thought about it for a moment, shrugged, then said, "No idea. A million dollars?"

Her aunt grinned and replied, "Nope. Not even close. I have ten million and some change." Holding up a hand to stall Tina's disbelieving response, she said, "Think about it. Part of your contract is an apartment with all utilities paid, and a leased car. A BMW at that. How much a month would you say that was worth?"

"I don't know, maybe a couple thousand?"

Maria shook her head at that. "The apartment alone, which more accurately is a loft in one of the most exclusive buildings in downtown Spokane, would rent out at thirty-five hundred dollars a month all by itself. The lease on the BMW M4 is another thousand. And if I am not mistaken, and I'm not because I wrote up your contract myself, you also get a monthly stipend for clothing and the other incidentals necessary for the continued upkeep of your person so that you can adequately represent the company that employs you. Additionally, all travel expenses are covered by the company, so no out-of-pocket there."

A moment later, she continued ticking items off a mental list: "Top-of-the-line company cell, laptop, and tablet. All insurance completely paid for by the company—medical, dental, and vision. A four-day workweek when not traveling, six weeks of paid vacation per year, and the list goes on." Finally, she smirked and said, "Oh, and let's not forget the seventy thousand a year salary, which will go up every year if you don't step on your dick and get fired."

Tina burst out laughing at that and silently mouthed, *don't step on your dick* to herself. A few seconds later, she nodded her head in acknowledgment and said, "I understand. But how? How can a company with one owner and one employee afford to offer so much?"

Maria smiled at her. "The antiquities business is very, very profitable, my dear. Plus, Alexander is an extremely generous person. He knows how much of the burden he offloads onto his assistant, and is willing to show that he values that help. The only thing he asks in return is loyalty. You will manage a large portion of his empire for him...millions and millions of dollars are at stake."

Tina just stared at her aunt with a shocked look, and started to hyperventilate as the magnitude of it all set in.

Chuckling, Maria continued, "So, as you can see, you will *earn* all those perks and salary. But it is also a fascinating and enjoyable life. Accumulating money when you barely spend any is pretty easy. That and investing wisely."

Maria's expression hardened again. "Finally, a word of advice. Don't take it personally if Alexander growls at you occasionally. He is a tough person to get to know, very private and insular. He hasn't had the easiest of lives, and trusting in anyone is hard for him."

A skeptical Tina replied, "Oh sure, poor little rich boy. Boohoo." The sound of the slap from her aunt reverberated around the room, and Tina's hand covered the reddened cheek that had been its target, her eyes wide with shock. Maria had never gotten physical with her before, not even during her teen years when raging hormones made her already-smart mouth so much worse.

"If you ever say such a thing again, I will beat the snottiness right out of you, favorite niece or not," Maria ground out between gritted teeth. "You don't get it, do you? Put yourself into Alexander's shoes for a minute. How do you trust that people like *you* for who you are, and not for the money or the advantages that knowing a person like Alexander can bring? After the first time or two getting burned, would you continue to be open to others? Or would you close yourself up and keep the world at arm's length? The man behind that door is the loneliest person I have ever known, maybe the loneliest person in the whole world, and *you* don't get to judge that which you know nothing about." Her chest continued to heave, and Maria's hands were fisted as she glared down at her niece. *I need to nip this in the bud now before her attitude gets her into trouble*, Maria thought, irate at having to defend her friend. *She's so young and inexperienced, but this has to stop before it becomes an issue.*

Maria studied Tina silently, watching the younger woman try to absorb what her aunt had just said. It was clear she still didn't get why her words had upset her aunt so much. After a minute, she nodded sheepishly. "I apologize for what I said, but in my defense, I've known many other trust-fund babies who were complete douchebags while I was going to school at Gonzaga."

The unwavering glare on Maria's face finally gave way to something else. Something that looked an awful lot like melancholy. "Please promise me you will give him a chance. Promise me you will be kind to him. He *needs* you, Tina, and I think you might need him too. The problem is that you are very similar people in so many ways. You must step in for me and provide the stability and friendship I no longer can." *This would be so much easier if I could just tell her the truth*, ran through her head.

Her niece gasped as comprehension dawned. "This wasn't just a job for you. It was much more," she whispered.

Maria sighed, wondering just how much she could reveal. "Yes, Tina, it was my whole life. Did you never wonder why I remained single all these years?" Her voice cracked as she continued. "There isn't really room for anything else, a personal life separate from what you do here. Oh, don't get me wrong, there were plenty of one-night stands and short flings, but my heart always belonged to the Matthews men and the work we did. I don't expect you to understand, but perhaps someday you might."

She grabbed the box of her personal belongings and strode to the door that led to the elevators. Maria paused on the threshold and said over her shoulder, "Remember my words, Tina, and take care of Alexander for me."

"I will, Aunt Maria."

# Chapter 2

*"....I am plagued by dreams and nightmares. Each evening, I fear to lay my head down lest I be shown more of the unknown history of this world. Visions of thousands of slaves building grandiose palaces, temples, and other structures for our so-called masters. The senseless cruelty and murder of innocents for no other reason than boredom. And the steady decline of a once-great civilization. All these, and more, parade before my inner eyes, burning themselves into my consciousness...."*

**An excerpt from the diary of Alexander Matthews**

**March 1904, Just outside Cheyenne, Wyoming**

*The wind howled and battered at the shutters protecting the windows of the small, isolated cabin. A late-season blizzard had hit last night and showed no signs of ending any time soon. The restless, sweating man who occupied the bed near the fireplace seemed to be oblivious to nature's wrath. A particularly violent kick of his leg deposited the woolen blanket onto the rough wood-plank floor, and he was mumbling what were surely words, but not in any language a modern person would understand.*

*Alexander remained unaware of the outside world. He was trapped in the memories he had inherited when bitten, somehow passed to him by the amulet he now wore. The life he was experiencing was not his own but was inexorably tied to him as surely as if he had lived it, part and parcel of who he had become....*

*His Master, the god En, was screaming at him in proto-Sumerian, spittle flying from his lips with each word. "You have failed me, you worthless, miserable dog!*

*The task was a simple one, attack the city of that bitch, Nin, and destroy it."*

*The general of the army lay prostrate before the Anunna, not uttering a word for fear he would only make matters worse. He had learned at an early age that it was best to let his master vent his anger with no excuses or interruptions.*

*"I should end your useless life and see if another can do as I ask." The tirade continued. "Even now she consolidates her armies and prepares to strike back, and while you did manage to hurt her badly, it is not enough. Not nearly enough."*

*En used his staff to mercilessly cane the back of the man who lay before him, the heavy strikes raising bloody welts with each blow. The general suffered this abuse in silence, knowing that to show any sign of weakness would only lead to more pain and possibly death.*

*When the god had exhausted his anger on the helpless figure that lay before him, he walked the few steps necessary to collapse onto his throne, his hooded eyes burning with satisfaction as they surveyed the damage he had inflicted.*

*"No. Your death would only provide an easy escape from my righteous wrath. Instead, you will continue to lead my armies. But know this, you miserable worm, fail me again, and there is no punishment too harsh for me to levy onto your head." He threw a highly decorated clay drinking bowl full of wine at the man still sprawled out on the floor. "Get out of my sight. You sicken me."*

***

The following morning, Alexander cautiously stepped out of the private elevator that connected his office to his personal quarters above. Unbeknownst to virtually anyone, he owned this entire building, leasing out all but the top two floors, which were reserved for his use only. When he had purchased the building, which had been constructed in the 1920s, it had needed a lot of renovation. The penthouse occupied the entire rectangular seventh floor, and while the space required for operating *Destination Unknown Antiquities* was just a portion of the sixth, he had reserved the remainder for future needs and storage.

Crossing the vast expanse of oaken flooring and the tasteful area rug, to stand in front of the large double-paned tinted windows that dominated the back and right side of his office, he gazed out at downtown Spokane. Many would question why he would choose to base his operations out of such a small town rather than Seattle or Portland, Oregon, but he loved this city. A glimmer of humor shone in his eyes as he admitted if only to himself, that he really, *really* hated rain. It wasn't like he'd chosen to live in the back-woods—Spokane had around 250,000 people who called it home, and if you counted the surrounding areas, you could probably push that number closer to half a million. Besides, you could get to almost anywhere within city limits in no longer than twenty to thirty minutes, something that could not be said for more substantial metropolitan areas. He shuddered, thinking of the I-5 commute in Seattle.

He could hear Tina in the front office, which until yesterday had been the domain of his closest friend, Maria. Sighing deeply, Alexander walked over to the espresso machine that sat on the wet bar along one wall of his CEO suite. He took a few minutes and made a doppio espresso for both himself and his newest employee. As he hesitated, he could hear Maria's voice in his head, '*Stop being a pussy and just get it over with*'. He grinned, and strolled out to where Tina was reorganizing things to her liking.

She looked up as he set the saucer and cup on the polished wooden surface of her desk, a quizzical look on her face. Tina knelt next to the open bottom drawer on the right side of the desk, the chair pushed back to give her room to maneuver.

"It's black because I wasn't sure how you take your espresso." He pursed his lips in thought. "There's cream and sugar if you want?"

"Black is fine," she replied while pushing from her eyes a strand of brunette hair that had fallen forward. Then she grinned impishly up at him. "I thought I would be getting *your* coffee since you're the boss. Isn't that how it's normally supposed to work?"

His face took on a sheepish look, along with a slight blush she found endearing. "Ummm, I'm kind of anal about my coffee…among other things. So, I tend to make my own, and it's not that much harder to make it for two." Shrugging that off, he continued, "Did you get moved into the loft, OK? If there's anything you need or want to change, just let me know."

As she stood, he noticed for the first time that she was taller than he had expected. Maria had topped out at 5'5", but Tina appeared to be about 5'10". Given that he stood 6'3", that meant he didn't have to look down as far while they chatted. He decided that he liked that.

"Oh, everything is perfect. I feel like a pea rattling around in a pod, though. My last apartment was barely 800 square feet." Her cheeks dimpled as she smiled at him, distracting him momentarily.

Alexander took a good look at her for the first time. Her brown eyes sparkled with excitement as she regaled him with additional detail. Still, truthfully, he didn't hear a thing she said. Long, wavy brunette locks that cascaded to the middle of her back made him want to run his fingers through them. The white blouse she was wearing did little to conceal the fact that she was very well-endowed, and her slim, athletic waist and the long legs that emerged from her grey pencil-skirt were consuming all his attention. Mentally slapping himself for acting like a teenage school-boy, he tuned back in to what she was saying.

"...and the car is fantastic. I've never driven anything so responsive or powerful. There's no way I would ever have been able to get something like that straight out of school." Her hands were waving around erratically as she spoke, and he could swear that the floor was vibrating from her enthusiasm.

He cleared his throat, nervously. "Excellent. I'm glad you like it. Your aunt was pushing for something more sedate...like a MINI Cooper." He smiled slyly. "But I overruled her on that. Executive privilege, don't you know." The resulting smile took his breath away, and he decided to make a strategic retreat before he did something stupid.

***

Sitting behind the broad flat surface of his desk, Alexander silently panicked. *What. In. The. Actual. Fuck* had just happened? He needed to get his shit together because he *could not* fuck this up. His reaction to Tina was wrong on so many levels, and not only because he was her boss. He fired up some music and closed his eyes as he tried to purge his mind of inappropriate thoughts. Unfortunately, the song that was playing didn't help matters, Foreigner's *Spellbinder* was probably not the best choice given his current circumstances.

He quickly pushed the button on the controller to go to the next random song in his library, then sighed deeply in defeat as Black Sabbath's *Country Girl* began playing. Even his electronics were conspiring against him.

Making up his mind, he decided to remove himself from the situation entirely; a workout was just what the doctor ordered. Calling out, he said, "I'll be upstairs working out. If you need anything, please call my cell." Tina just waved in response, and he hurried to the elevator and escaped upstairs.

***

Sweat streamed down his naked torso, and he desperately forced himself through kata after kata. His retreat—and he was honest enough with himself to acknowledge that he had, in fact, retreated from Tina's distractions—had not worked out nearly as well as he had hoped.

Alexander came to a stop, breathing heavily, and knelt on the padded surface of the dojo, legs tucked beneath him, trying to calm his racing mind. After a minute, he gave up on any hope of centering himself and grabbed a towel to dry off, then cracked open a cold bottle of water and chugged half of its contents.

His troubled gaze slid to the windows. Early afternoon sunlight streamed through and dappled the interior of his apartment. The attraction he felt for Tina, while typical for any healthy male in the presence of a beautiful woman, was something he needed to throttle *now*. Not only was it inappropriate in the professional sense—workplace romances were *always* a bad idea—but it was even worse when it was between a boss and an employee. Or a monster and a Normal.

Alexander had lived by his own Golden Rule over the years, and that rule was '*You never, ever, shit in your own pool.*' Allowing any hint of his feelings, much less encouraging any sort of non-professional interaction with her, would only lead to trouble...trouble he could ill afford.

He had managed to walk that tightrope with Maria for nearly forty years. Surely, he could continue to do so with her niece? Alexander sighed, frustrated with the whole situation.

All the usual reasons still applied. Tina was a Normal...and he was a monster. It was bad enough that he would outlive her by centuries, but inevitably, as she aged and he didn't, she would grow resentful. Maria had managed to navigate that particular thorny issue, although not entirely successfully, but could Tina? No. It was far better that it never even reach that point, and getting romantically involved would only hasten such a confrontation.

Besides, not getting mired in relationships with the people around him had served him well over the years, and likely had kept him sane. Regular humans just didn't live very long in comparison with his kind, and to make matters worse, they were all too observant and noticed that he wasn't aging as they did, nor was he prone to any of the diseases or disabilities that seemed to plague humanity. And it was too damn hard when someone he had gotten close to died.

Having made up his mind, or at least attempting to steer clear of any complications arising from his new hire, Alexander finished his water and headed to the shower.

# Chapter 3

*"….Feeling as if I was losing my mind, I decided to go back to the University and bury myself in the work of getting my degree. Over time, the visions slowed to a trickle and eventually stopped…more or less. Determined to retain as much of this stolen knowledge as possible, I began to keep a diary, a journal if you will, that would contain everything I knew or could learn about the Anunna and their world.*

*I had a new mission. I would travel the globe searching for clues and artifacts. Doctorate in archaeology in hand, I set about learning languages that might assist in my efforts. Oddly enough, the changes that had been made to my body seemed to make this significantly more straightforward than it would have been otherwise. I also tackled a second degree in anthropology…."*

**An excerpt from the diary of Alexander Matthews**

**September 1922, Spokane railyards across the river from Gonzaga University**

*Alexander eased the Colt M1911 out of the shoulder holster snugged under his left armpit. He raised his nose into the air and took a quiet but deep breath. The vampire was close. He could smell her…and the blood of her victim. His eyes peered suspiciously into the deep shadows that dominated this part of the railyard, actively seeking movement.*

*He was seriously pissed off. It seemed he had only just cleaned his city up and gotten rid of all the undesirables, and now this. When would they learn? The large*

*Covens and Packs from Seattle and Portland seemed determined to keep pushing the limits, trying to see just how far they could probe before he inevitably snapped. He had purposefully shipped the last few mangled bodies back to their masters as warnings, but it would appear that they had not heeded them.*

*His ears caught furtive movement off to the left, and he shifted his body to face that direction. The gleam of fangs gave her position away, and Alexander cautiously advanced toward her. She clutched a torn and dirty figure in her clawed hands as she hissed at him in warning from where she crouched over the body. The vampire wasn't much cleaner than the hobo she had just fed on. Her blonde hair was filthy and matted, the clothes draped loosely around her body more holes than fabric, and she was barefoot.*

*He considered her disheveled state and then holstered his pistol. The young woman before him, her apparent age around twenty-one, was definitely not from an established Coven.*

*Alexander shook his head sadly. "Who are you?"*

*Her eyes darted around anxiously, looking for an escape route that didn't exist.*

*"Look, you can talk to me willingly…or I can put a bullet in your head. The choice is yours." He crossed his arms over his chest and waited.*

*She seemed to deflate when she realized he meant it. "Melinda," she mumbled.*

*"Melinda." He tried the name on for size. "And where is Melinda from? I can tell by looking at you, not to mention the horrible stench that surrounds you, that you are not from a Coven. So, what's your story?" His wrinkled nose and pursed lips showed precisely what he thought of her hygiene.*

*The vampire stood slowly, her hands self-consciously trying to smooth out her tattered clothing. "I'm from Seattle…or I was. I am a trained typist and worked at a law firm for a while, but then I got attacked and turned one night."*

*"And?"*

*"When the Coven found out, they labeled me as having been turned by a rogue, and they forced me out of the city. I've been on my own ever since, and as you can see," Her hands gestured at her body disdainfully. "I haven't done too well."*

*"How long have you been in my town, Melinda?"*

*"A couple of days. I rode one of the trains in and hid."*

*Alexander looked at her curiously. "Why did you hide?"*

*The vampire looked at him like he was crazy. "Because of the monster. It's all anyone talks about on the West side of the state. He's supposed to be ten feet tall, has skin like an alligator, and eats vampires." She shivered in horror as she recounted the story.*

*He burst out laughing, which only got louder when he saw her outraged look. When he finally was able to stop, he grinned at her. "I'm only 6'3", and my skin is the same as yours...except cleaner. And, in fact, I haven't eaten a vampire in years. You all are far too gamy for my tastes."*

*Melinda was looking at him skeptically.* "You *are the monster?"*

*His eyes narrowed, and all the humanity they had contained drained away in a fraction of a second, then he shifted into his Battle form. A deep rumble rattled from his chest, and his fanged maw moved down to within an inch of her now-terrified face.*

*Tears were running down her cheeks, and she closed her eyes, waiting for the end. She heard a loud* chuff, *and then his tongue gently licked the tears from her left cheek. Her eyes popped open in shock, and he shifted back to a now-mostly naked human. "Here's how it's going to work, Melinda...."*

***

It had been a month since Tina had started working for Alexander, and she was...conflicted. She absolutely loved the job and the challenge it presented. There was far more to running this operation than she had initially believed, but she was fairly certain that once she had performed the tasks enough, she would find a rhythm that simplified everything. No, that wasn't the issue at all. The fact that she found herself strangely attracted to her boss *was.*

Sighing quietly, she looked through the door to find him staring out the windows of his office, and as usual, listening to music. This morning it sounded like hair metal from the '80s, but it was a band she was unfamiliar with. Tina acknowledged that he was an attractive man, taller than her, but not excessively so, and very well-built. He moved with a grace that she had seldom seen, and while muscular, he didn't have a gym-rat's physique. No, he was powerful, but like a swimmer or a gymnast, perhaps.

What really bothered her, though, was the fact that she was even having these thoughts. He was her *boss*, and if she was honest with herself, definitely out of her league. Tina decided she needed to schedule lunch with her Aunt Maria, so she could apologize. The slap Maria had delivered when Tina had denigrated Alexander had been well-deserved...she could finally acknowledge that. He was not at all like her preconceptions of him. His demeanor to her had been nothing less than entirely correct...and *that* bothered her greatly.

Tina didn't date much. Dating usually ended in messy disasters. She knew she was attractive enough, but she just couldn't keep her mouth shut. Her waspish personality chased away most men, and for the most part, she was OK with that. If they couldn't handle it, then *fuck* them. She had been raised in an Italian family, and strong personalities were not just normal, they were essential. The difficulty was that she was even more abrasive than anyone else, except possibly her grandmother. And...she had a temper. Deep inside, she knew it would take a strong man to not only put up with her shit, but to see past the prickly exterior to the lonely woman inside. So far, she was batting zero in that regard.

Alexander was nothing less than a complete gentleman with her, and kept everything on a professional level, reserved even...and she wished he wouldn't. Tina had gone so far as to push the limits of what would be considered acceptable business attire, but he hadn't seemed to notice. One time, she had asked if he wanted to get a drink with her after work, but he had graciously declined. She knew there was a different personality that he mostly kept well-hidden, but on occasion, she would get a glimpse of it when he slipped up. Like yesterday. He had surprised her by asking her to meet him in the conference room. When she walked in, he was serving up salad and lasagna, and to be fair, it was the best lasagna she had ever eaten. When she told him that, he just shrugged and said he had been working on the sauce recipe for a very long time. That man deflected better than most people she had ever known, and actually seemed embarrassed when complimented. While this was an endearing trait, it was also highly frustrating.

In desperation, she had asked a couple of friends over to her place, and after several glasses of wine, vented her frustrations at them. While sympathetic with her plight, they also thought dating the boss might not be such a good idea. So *not* what she wanted to hear, and less than helpful. Both opined that if she ever decided to quit, she should hook them up because the perks were freaking amazing.

Thus, she found herself in the current situation. Her brain agreed that staying strictly professional was the best thing to do, but somehow, she just couldn't let it go. There was *something* about the man that drew her to him, but she couldn't pin it down. It had almost become a game for her...a dangerous game, to be sure, but a game nonetheless.

The door to the hallway and the elevators opened, surprising her. Not once since she had been hired had anyone actually come by the office. In fact, Tina wasn't even sure why they *had* a conference room, since it never got used. The woman who walked through the door was...hot. Annoyingly so. A petite, 5'6" tall blonde, with streaks of crimson in her straight collar-length hair, flounced in and stopped in front of Tina's desk. Snug black leather pants, stylish short boots, and a tight tank that emphasized her lack of a bra, all packaged up with a healthy dose of attitude. Tribal tattoos peeked out from the minimal coverage her shirt provided, and she was smacking gum like she was trying to chew through a wall. Tina instantly disliked her, knew she was just being a bitch, and totally felt justified in her appraisal.

"Can I help you?" She sniffed down her nose loftily. "I'm fairly certain that Planned Parenthood is on the second floor."

The waif in front of her stopped chewing for a moment, sneered, and said, "Aren't you just the cutest thing? Where's Maria?"

"Retired."

"Oh?" and a raised eyebrow was the only response. "Is Alex here? He and I need to chat." The trollop batted her long and perfect lashes at Tina.

"I'm sorry, but do you have an appointment with Mr. Matthews? What was your name?" Tina pretended to search for a calendar entry, knowing full well there was nothing scheduled for today.

The woman across from her leaned over the desk, resting on her forearms, grinned, and said, "My name's Melinda, sweetness, and Alex will *definitely* want to see me once he knows I'm here." A pop of her gum punctuated her statement.

Grinding her teeth and wearing a smile that was more of a grimace, Tina dialed Alexander's desk phone to let him know he had a visitor. Seconds later, he stalked out of his office door and with a huge smile, waved Melinda in. With a snarky glance at Tina, she flounced over to him and jumped up and into his arms, wrapping her legs around his waist and resting her head on his chest so she could wink a blue eye back at Tina. With a laugh, he swiveled in place and closed the door behind him as he reentered his office.

Tina could hear giggling and laughter through the door, and she silently fumed as she imagined just what was going on in there. As it turned out, she was utterly wrong.

***

Alexander peeled Melinda off and dropped her ass onto the dark-leather couch in the sitting area of his office, then turned down the volume on the sound system. Y&T's *Breaking Away* faded into the background and finally disappeared altogether. He was bemused by her actions. While she was always a bit of a wildcard, she usually didn't throw herself at him that way. "OK, Mel, what gives?"

She giggled and kicked her feet as she responded, "That was absolutely delicious. Did you see the look on her face?" and burst into laughter.

"Why are you tormenting my staff, Mel? Just what has she ever done to you?"

Pulling her legs up under her, she grinned devilishly. "Because I *can*, dear. Do I really need any other reason? Besides, she was snotty, and you know how that gets under my skin."

Shaking his head and chuckling at Melinda's antics, he asked, "Would you like something to drink?"

"Do you still have any of that 37-year-old Lagavulin?"

"Yup. So, talk to me. To what exactly do I owe the pleasure of your company on this fine July day?" he asked over his shoulder as he poured their drinks at the wet bar that resided along the wall near his private elevator.

Batting her eyes at him provocatively, she said, "Can't a girl just drop in on an old friend? Does there *have* to be an ulterior motive?"

He snorted in amusement as he handed her the crystal tumbler of scotch whisky. "Uh-huh. Come on, spill."

"Fine," she sighed theatrically. "Be that way." Taking a small sip of the water of life, she closed her eyes in appreciation and leaned back on the couch, crossing her legs. "We may have a problem. I'm hearing rumors of a possible rogue moving into town, and thought you should know. It's been a while, and I had really thought the retards on the West side would have gotten the memo by now that Spokane is off-limits. Or at least seriously unhealthy for them."

"Anything specific? Or just rumors?" he rumbled contemplatively. "If the Seattle or Portland organizations are making a move, it's really, *really* going to piss me off."

"Oh, I know, dear, I know. That's why I came to see you as soon as I had any indications there might be validity to it, and truthfully, I've got nothing solid for you. I was asked if I had met the new guy in town, and of course, I haven't." Leaning forward and gesturing with her glass, she asked, "When was the last time you went on patrol?"

He shrugged indifferently. "A couple of months, I guess. Sounds like maybe it's been too long. You'd think after all this time, they would understand that this is *my* town."

Melinda smiled at him. "No rest for the wicked, dear, no rest for the wicked." With that, she slammed back the remaining whisky and stood up. Alexander winced at the desecration of such an excellent vintage, and escorted her to the door.

"Thanks, Mel, I appreciate the heads-up."

Giggling again, she flicked her fingers at him and said, "My work here is done. Ta Ta, Love."

Through the open door, Alexander could see Tina scowling at both of them. *What the hell is wrong with her?* he thought, as he turned away and went back to his desk.

***

Tina poked her head into Alexander's office, but he wasn't there. She wanted to let him know she had an appointment at her salon and was leaving early.

Grumbling under her breath, she headed to his private elevator after determining he must be upstairs. She had never actually been to his apartment, and admitted to a deep curiosity as to what she would find.

The lift itself was understated and more functional than elaborately decorated. Obviously, it was well-maintained, however; she barely felt the device begin to move, and unlike many elevators, it was almost silent. Tina noticed that other than the button for the office, there was only one other destination that was serviced. She assumed the "B" meant the basement.

When the elevator doors opened, she stepped into his private domain and glanced around. Music, at a moderate volume for a change, drifted over the speakers that were scattered around the space, mounted near the ceiling. Tina smiled at the song that was currently playing…*I Will Follow* by U2.

It was an open floorplan that stretched over the entire interior space. Windows dominated all four outer walls, bright spots breaking up the brick façade, and sunlight speared in from the west as the sun began its descent for the evening. The ceiling towered high over the room and was covered in Art Deco tin tiles. There was an open space on the north side that could only be termed as a dojo and included racks for various weapons, most of which she couldn't even name. His gigantic bed, and what she assumed was a walk-in closet, commanded part of the south side of the room, and what must be the master bath enclosed some of the remainder. There was a home theater set up along the east wall, as well as a sitting area with room for several people. Surprisingly, there was an actual kitchen, including a large island topped by a stainless-steel grill. A small dining table and chairs sat not far from the kitchen. Paintings were scattered in between windows, and Tina was reasonably sure she recognized some of them. She assumed they would not be copies, but originals. Mostly full bookshelves ruled the remaining wall. Light-colored bamboo flooring off-set by dark tile covered most of the space, but large Persian rugs also had their place. The apartment felt homey despite being somewhat spartan overall. She smiled as she took it all in; clutter was apparently *not allowed.*

Just as her appraisal finished, she heard a door open, and Alexander walked out toweling his hair dry. Unfortunately, he wasn't wearing any clothes, and it was apparent he had just finished showering. The involuntary squeak she emitted alerted him to the fact that he wasn't alone, and he pulled the towel around his neck as he glanced up. Tina was sure her face couldn't possibly get any redder, and she thought she was going to die from embarrassment. However, that didn't stop her from getting an eyeful of his body. *Oh. My. God, yum*, she thought as he grinned at her. The smug bastard didn't even *try* to cover up. He pushed his long dark hair back, and it framed his face nicely, revealing the mismatched eyes. She had been curious about them ever since she had taken the job, but couldn't bring herself to ask about them. The right eye was a watery turquoise blue, but the left had a golden tint, almost amber-colored. Tina had never met anyone else with this condition. Additionally, it would seem that he manscaped regularly, as his body was completely hairless from the neck down. A realistic black tattoo of a wolf covered his right pectoral muscle and ran down his arm to where a short-sleeved shirt would just cover it.

He smirked at her and asked, "Are you done? Or do I need to spin around so you can see the back-side too?"

If possible, her face flushed even more crimson, and she was having trouble breathing. She quickly turned away from his nakedness and managed to mumble, "I just wanted to let you know I was leaving for the day. I have a hair appointment."

She could hear him chuckle behind her, "No problem. Have fun."

"Oh my God, oh my God," she whispered to herself. Tina almost fell in her mad scramble for the elevator, and escape, as his laughter chased her departing figure.

# Chapter 4

*"....Earth, and the Solar System, were accidentally discovered by the Anunna, whose civilization originated on planets located in the direction of what is known by humanity as the constellation of Orion. A jump drive malfunction nearly destroyed a research ship before dumping the badly damaged vessel into our solar system at a point near Mars. The ship's crew managed to get it into a stable orbit around the red planet and decided to determine what, if any, repairs could be made. It was quickly determined that any sort of fix for the jump drive was impossible. The technology to do so simply didn't exist on the ship, nor could it be built from scratch. They were stranded in this planetary system and would have to make do...."*

**Excerpt from the diary of Alexander Matthews**

**June 1993, Kettle River, near the Canadian border, Washington State**

*Alexander was dozing in the late afternoon sun. His clothes and personal items were stashed in the backpack that leaned against the back wall of the rock shelf that his wolf form was stretched out on. The Kettle River burbled below, and he was enjoying the natural beauty that surrounded his perch. A contented sigh escaped him as he stretched out and flopped over onto his side.*

*His ear twitched as he heard a twig snap and the sound of small rocks tumbling down the slope. Not long afterward, he scented a female grizzly, and she was headed his way. Reluctantly, he sat up and waited for her to make an appearance, and she did not disappoint.*

*The bear rushed at him, rearing up at the last moment, roaring and slashing her claws at him. Alexander yawned and licked one of his paws delicately, holding it up to his face. The bear dropped to her feet and looked confused. She shook her head quickly from side to side, huffed at him, and sat as well. A low growl rumbled from her throat, but it seemed less like any real threat, and more because she hadn't gotten the reaction she expected.*

*The wolf grinned happily at her and wagged his tail, then shifted to human form. "Hello there, I'm Alexander," he said amiably. "Sorry if I intruded on your private territory, but when I found this spot, I just couldn't help myself."*

*Seconds later, a naked woman sat across from him. She had strawberry blonde hair that cascaded down her back, appeared to be in her mid-20s, and had a tanned, athletic body that had obviously spent a lot of time outdoors.*

*"Jennifer," she replied in a gravelly voice. "You're a long way from the city, friend."*

*Alexander chuckled, "Is it that obvious?"*

*Jennifer shrugged. "Can smell its stink on you. Don't get many like you up here." A chuckle escaped her. "Don't get many folks at all up here."*

*"I suppose you don't. That's a shame, though. This part of the country speaks to me."*

*She looked at him sharply. "That so? Where you from?"*

*"Spokane. I've lived there for a long time. You?"*

*"Was born not far from here. Ma lives just across the border." She leaned forward conspiratorially. "If you're from Spokane, then you must have run into the Master at some point. How is it that you're still alive?"*

*Alexander leaned in, too, and whispered into her ear, "I* am *the Master."*

*Jennifer gasped and leaned back, silently appraising him. "That so? I thought you'd be... bigger," she said doubtfully.*

*His laughter echoed off the surrounding area. "Not the first time I've heard that," he told the frowning woman. "So, what happens now, Jennifer?"*

*"Haven't had company in a long time. You hungry?"*

*"I could eat."*

*She stood up and stretched her arms over her head, smiling invitingly down at him. "Got a place not too far from here. Might take a while to make dinner."*

*Alexander stood as well and grabbed his pack. "I'm in no particular hurry."*

*For a long time after that, he treasured the three nights he spent in her cabin....*

***

Wearing a grin caused by Tina's reaction to ambushing him in his own home, Alexander went to his closet and started pulling out the clothes he intended to wear while following up on Melinda's vague lead. He chose based on utility rather than any formal sense of fashion: Stretchy moisture-wicking t-shirt (slightly too big), tactical cargo pants (loose in the waist), black tube socks, boxer briefs (also stretchy), and finally, low-cut square-toed leather boots. Additionally, he ensured the desired contents of the small daypack he grabbed were all there. Freedom of movement was an essential component of his wardrobe selections, as was its ability to survive intact should he need to shift. He had replaced a lot of shredded clothes over the years, and it always sucked to have to do so.

Snagging a set of keys from the table next to the bed, he made his way to the private elevator that Tina had fled through not so long ago. As the doors rumbled closed and he punched the button for the basement, Alexander inhaled deeply. The scent of Tina's bodywash and shampoo were strong within the confined space, as was her arousal. With a wistful smile, he exited the lift when the doors opened, and he made his way over to a matte-black Ducati motorcycle. This was only one of a half-dozen vehicles he parked in the private sub-basement garage. Bright fluorescent lighting ensured that there were no shadows where someone with evil intent could lie in wait, and reflected off the many shiny surfaces of the machines parked within. *It's good to be king*, he decided. Once the helmet that had dangled off the handlebars was in place on his head, he fired up the Ducati and sped up the ramp to street level.

The sun was setting as Alexander rode down Riverside Avenue, the early evening traffic sparse. He raised the visor on the helmet and began to let his senses range out, seeking any anomaly. Scents that one would typically associate with city life assaulted him with each breath: exhaust fumes from all the vehicles and buses, vibrant odors from each restaurant he passed, the smell of hot concrete and asphalt, and the much-less-pleasant aromas from the alleys that ran behind each block of buildings. He cruised in a grid search pattern that took him from east to west and covered the entirety of the city center.

Moving on to Browne's Addition, and its stately Victorian homes, he performed a similar search pattern that also yielded negative results. Alexander finally decided to call it a night after running east out on Sprague Avenue as far as the Walmart, and turned the bike back toward the downtown area. Just as he made the turn onto Washington Avenue, he caught a faint trace of the scent he had been looking for. Slowing slightly, he used his nose to track his quarry to a club on Main Street. Once the Ducati was parked out of sight in the back, Alexander made his way to the front door, entered, and stepped to the right of the entrance, where he stood for a moment. Allowing his vision to adjust to the light level, he used his nose to pinpoint his target location.

His glittering eyes carefully scanned the man sitting at a table near the back. They automatically discounted the two human women seated on either side of him. His quarry was obviously making headway with the charm offensive he was employing on the young ladies. All signs indicated that at least one of them would be leaving with the Millennial douchebag, and fairly soon if Alexander was any judge. Too bad for him, Alexander had other, slightly less-pleasant plans.

He strode over and casually grabbed the last chair at the table, spinning it around, the back facing the surprised-looking object of his attention. Alexander straddled the seat as he eased his weight down.

"Evening, ladies. I hope you don't mind if I borrow my friend here for a few minutes? I

haven't seen him in a very long time, and I just want to get caught up. You understand, right?"

He raised his eyebrows at them, then reached into his back pocket, snagged his wallet, and pulled out forty dollars that he tossed onto the table. "I'd hate for you to get thirsty on my account, so please, drinks are on me." The money disappeared, and with matching smiles, the girls were headed to the bar.

"Hey asshole, what the fuck do you think you're doing?" the scowling face across from Alexander asked.

"*Shut. Up*. I ask the questions, and you get to answer. If I like your answers, you might even walk away from this in one piece," he said matter-of-factly.

"Bullshit!" An attempt to stand was interrupted as Alexander reached across the table and slammed him back into his chair. A startled, uneasy look crossed the man's face. "Who are you, dude? I'm just here to have a good time, I don't want any trouble."

A low growl rumbled from Alexander's chest. "Again, *I* ask the questions. Now, you and I are going to walk out the door together, just like besties. Once outside, you will take a left, then go around the side of the building and stop in the alley. We're going to have a short chat. Got it?"

"Fuck you, man. I ain't going anywhere with you!"

"We can do it *my* way," Alexander cracked his neck as he stood up, "or I can carry your unconscious ass out over my shoulder. Your choice. And frankly, it doesn't really make a difference to me."

The target also stood, mumbling, "Fine, fine." He preceded Alexander out the door, then followed the remainder of the directions he had been given. Once they reached the alley, he was lifted and body-slammed into the brick that made up the outer wall of the club. A lone light provided a low level of illumination that did little to brighten the area.

"What Coven are you? And why are you in *my* city?"

The man struggled against Alexander's hold for a few moments, then relaxed. He sneered and began to morph, and the sclera in his eyes swirled and turned black, while his canine teeth grew larger, more robust. His hands started to change as well, gaining claws, and his overall body structure became denser, stronger, and more muscular. Dark veins stood out as they were pushed to the surface by muscles that grew by twenty-five percent, sharply defined and wriggling into their new configuration. Previously loose clothing now strained to contain the added mass as the transformation neared completion.

Alexander sighed resignedly. "So that's how you want to play it, huh?"

Transferring his left hand to the man's throat, he used his right, fingers curled, to start hammer-striking the lower ribs on the right side of his opponent's torso. With each strike, a muffled *crack* could be heard as ribs shattered. Five times this happened, and on the final blow, the fight went out of the recipient. The breath exploded out of him, spattering blood across the front of his chest.

Alexander shook him, banging the back of his head against the gritty brick with each movement. "Currently, your left lung is shredded and filling with blood. I've fractured the three lowest ribs, and they have perforated said lung. I'm guessing it's a bit uncomfortable, but we both know it won't kill you. Will it, vampire?" he said conversationally.

The answer that was delivered via a gobbet of bloody spit didn't seem to bother Alexander, other than to cause him to tighten the grip he had on the man's throat. His predatory smile as he let the body dangle there for a minute, allowing just enough air through for his target to catch short, wheezing breaths, did little to indicate it took much effort.

He relaxed his grip minutely, but still kept the body pinned to the wall. "Let's try this again, shall we? Simple questions first." Using his right hand, he performed a quick body search looking for weapons. A raised eyebrow when he didn't find any indicated a small amount of surprise.

"What is your name?" A lack of response caused him to tighten the chokehold momentarily, and the vampire's hands rose in response, trying to pry it loose. The effort failed.

Alexander shook his head sadly, long hair blowing in the soft breeze. "Let me be perfectly clear here. The only use I have for you is information. If you refuse to give me that information, then your usefulness drops to zero, at which point I will consider you to be hostile. I only have one reaction to hostility, and it *always* proves fatal. Nod your head if you understand my words."

Still glaring at Alexander, the vampire jerked his head to indicate affirmation.

"Good, good. See, that wasn't so hard, was it? We could have had a simple conversation, but you assumed that this was going to go *your* way. Have I established that this, in fact, is most definitely not the case?"

Another jerk of the head.

Alexander slowly lowered the vampire until his feet were firmly on the ground, and he removed his hand from the man's throat. "Don't try anything, or my curiosity will just have to go unsatisfied…I'll just kill you."

The vampire stood there, rubbing his throat, and glared at him. "My name is Justin."

"OK, Justin, what Coven are you affiliated with? And don't bullshit me, I'm all out of patience."

"No Coven affiliation. I'm an independent."

Alexander leaned in closer, glaring down at the vampire. "You wouldn't lie to me, would you, Justin? Because that would be most unfortunate for you. The reason I ask is that Portland and Seattle should know better than to send anyone here. I'm the Master of this city, and I kill all trespassers. My policy is *You feed, you bleed.* Kind of catchy, isn't it?"

"I swear I'm not lying. I didn't even know Spokane *had* a Master." The fear Alexander saw in his eyes went a long way toward convincing him Justin was telling the truth. He leaned in closer and inhaled deeply. While the smell of fear was present, he did not catch the tell-tale acrid bite of a lie.

"I'll tell you what I'm going to do. You are going to go snack-free tonight." He pulled out his wallet, selected a business card, then handed it to the vampire. "Tomorrow, during daylight hours, you are going to speak to the woman whose information is on this card. In-person, I might add. I'm going to let *her* determine your fate." The careless shrug Alexander gave showed how little that bothered the werewolf. "Most likely, she is going to tell you to leave town and never come back, but *if* she decides to let you stay, you will follow the rules as she lays them out for you."

Alexander's eyes stared mercilessly into Justin's. "Do not fuck with me, or her, or I will *end* your ass." With that, he took two steps back. "Now get the hell out of here before I change my mind."

Justin nodded, then darted around the corner.

***

Instead of going home like he had initially planned, Alexander turned the bike north and drove up Division Street. He was too tightly wound up by tonight's events to sleep, and since it was Friday and he didn't have to be back in the office until Tuesday, he decided to spend the weekend at his place in the country.

Forty-five minutes later, the Ducati pulled into the driveway of a rambling two-story Victorian situated on ten acres along the Little Spokane River. He'd owned the place for quite a while, and no one else, other than Maria, even knew it existed. Alexander only came out here when he needed to clear his mind or get away from the city. He parked the bike, then entered the house, flipping on the lights in the entryway as he walked through the door. Keys and wallet went into the shallow dish on a pedestal next to the door.

Gleaming oak floors and ten-foot ceilings with crown molding retained the sense and style of the original house. Still, he had thoroughly modernized the place when he'd had renovations done. Several interior walls had been removed to open the space up, and a thoroughly modern kitchen was the heart of the first floor. Large windows looked out onto the property, and a pellet insert occupied the former fireplace, more than adequate to heat the home when needed.

The upstairs had also been transformed. Interior wall removal allowed for a spacious master bedroom, en suite master bath with a huge tub and separate shower, and sufficient walk-in closet space for his needs. It was a comfortable escape from the stresses of daily life. Unfortunately, it wasn't centrally located enough to function as his headquarters, not to mention that his antiquities business needed to be in town.

Throwing on jeans and a t-shirt after a long shower, he headed out to the workshop located behind the house. One of several out-buildings spaced around the house, it was one of his havens when seeking solitude. Taking his frustrations out by beating on some metal sounded like just what the doctor ordered. It took him some time to get the forge up to temperature, but he used that interval to determine what he was going to make, sketching out various designs. Alexander lost himself in the process of turning raw materials into a useable bar of Damascus steel. By the time this was complete, the sun was peeking over the horizon, and he decided he had done enough for now. He cleaned up the work area and set aside the steel bar for later.

Alexander took another quick shower then climbed into the comfortable king-size bed. Sleep came fast, but four hours later, he was in the kitchen making himself breakfast. He gazed out the large plate-glass window, amused to see a white-tailed doe making herself at home in the large yard surrounding the house. His gaze went to a large tree that dominated that section of the yard, and the small fenced area and gravestone that sat immediately beneath. A sad smile crossed his face, and his focus turned inward for a few moments, banished all too soon by a small shake of his head. When he had finished eating, he placed the dirty dishes in the sink and made his way back to the workshop.

While the forge was heating up again, he called Melinda to give her a heads-up about his run-in with Justin.

"Alex! Have you come to your senses at last? If so, please don't let me interrupt the groveling that's about to happen. I knew that eventually you would realize I'm the *only* woman for you."

He grinned into the phone. "I wasn't aware that Hell had frozen over yet, Mel."

Her laughter tinkled into his ear before she shot back. "Seriously, Alexander. We both know that no one else could put up with your shit."

He snorted loudly and said, "Uh-huh. My biggest problem with that scenario is that I worry I'd wake up one morning missing several pints of blood, and find you leering down at me as you licked your lips. That's kind of a big hurdle for me."

"Pansy."

"It's true. I *am* a pansy about things like that." He took a moment and checked the time on his watch. "So, I followed up on your lead last night."

"And?" she asked.

"You'll be getting a visit from a guy named Justin." A pause, then, "Let me rephrase that…You had *better* get a visit from him. We had words in an alley downtown."

"I see, and by *words*, you mean…?"

"Hey, he's still alive. That's got to count for something." The silence on the other end spoke volumes.

Alexander sighed ruefully. "According to Justin, he is unaffiliated, but I'm not completely convinced. I told him I was leaving his fate in your hands."

"You, Sir, are a bona fide asshole. Why dump it into my lap?"

"I trust your judgment, Mel. Talk to him if he shows up and let me know what you want to do." His voice took on a much colder tone. "And I also want to know if he doesn't come to see you."

Melinda sucked in an audible breath. "Gotcha, big guy. I'll keep an eye out. I really hope he doesn't decide to ignore your instructions. That would be a less than optimal solution…for him."

"Yes. Yes, it would." His mouth curled up into a smile as he continued. "By the way, how *is* the Brazilian wax business these days?"

The shrieking volume of the cursing he was receiving forced him to pull the phone away from his ear while he laughed, then he deliberately cut her off mid-stride by ending the call. Alexander knew he was going to pay for that later, but it was totally worth it.

***

He finally called it a day and had put his tools away. Alex picked up the mostly finished blade, looking carefully for any imperfections. Satisfied that it was a fair piece of work, he laid it back onto the anvil, then closed up the shop for the evening. Alexander made his way across the yard in the twilight, then entered the house via the back porch. Stretching his arms over his head, he walked into the kitchen to see if the steaks he had pulled from the freezer that morning had thawed yet.

He seasoned both sides of the meat with salt, pepper, and some garlic powder, then set them aside. Exiting the house once again, he put charcoal in the grill and lit it. After the fire was well-started, he went inside and grabbed a tray. A glass, some ice, a bottle of Jack Daniel's Single Barrel, as well as the steaks and tools for the BBQ, all went onto the tray, which he carried outside to wait for the coals to get to the right temperature.

Alexander poured himself a drink and savored the rich taste of the bourbon as the meat seared over the coals. He loved it out here. The night sky was beautiful, and the sounds of nature were soothing to his senses. Sometimes the city became overwhelming, and he just needed to escape.

Once the steaks were cooked to his liking, he pulled them off the grill and set them aside to rest for a few minutes. Cutting into them too soon would only accomplish releasing all of the juicy goodness, and what would be the point of that? His cell started vibrating on the table next to his chair, and he glanced over to see that it was Melinda. He picked it up and swiped to accept the call.

"Pedro's Pizza. Will this be take-out or delivery?" he said in his best Hispanic accent.

A brief moment of stunned silence followed, during which he could almost see her double-checking the number she had dialed, followed by laughter. "Oh, it'll definitely be pick-up. This beating needs to be administered in person...."

Alexander smiled into the phone and said, "Promises, promises. That's all I ever get from you."

"Pffft," she raspberried into his ear. "You can't handle a woman like me, and you know it. I'd have to take it so easy on you that there would be little enjoyment in it for me."

He chuckled before saying, "I'm assuming this call is about Justin. Did the little shit come to see you?"

"He did," Melinda replied.

"And?"

"And what?" Alexander ground his teeth as he pictured her studying her nails, deliberately not answering his question. "Oh, you want details? I really wish you would be more specific about these things, Alex." She sniffed haughtily into the phone.

Holding onto his temper with both hands, Alexander snarled. "Melinda Dearest, would you please be so kind as to provide me with a detailed synopsis of the chat you had today with our pointy-toothed problem?" He concentrated on taking slow deep breaths in an attempt to calm down as he waited for her reply.

"Why, I thought you'd never ask, Alex. But since you phrased that so nicely, I guess I can share."

"Bitch."

"Wrong species, my dear, as you of all people should know." Melinda paused, then continued, "I believe him. According to our friend Justin, he was turned about six months ago by a rogue and has spent the intervening time roaming from city to city in the great Pacific Northwest. Basically, he's been on his own, dumped into the world with no training on how to survive, and no one ever explained the rules to him."

Alexander sighed into the receiver. "What do you want to do with him, Mel? Is he salvageable? Or did you send him packing?"

"I feel sorry for him, Alexander. Remember, when you found me, I was in the same boat?"

"Times were different then, Mel. I could afford to take risks, risks that I'm not sure are worth it now."

"You dumped this problem into *my* lap, mister, said you trusted my judgment," came the quick reply. "Did you really mean that? Because my gut says he can be redeemed."

Exhaling loudly, Alexander said, "Fine, but Justin is your problem from now on. If he fucks up, I'll put him down for good. Agreed?"

"Agreed. I've already explained how things work around here, laid out all the rules, and he says he can abide by them. Plus, you've already put the fear of God into him. You *know* I don't take on this level of responsibility if I don't think I can pull it off."

"I know, Mel, and I'm sorry to be such a dick, but this shit gets old after a while."

He could hear her let out a relieved breath before she said, "Understood, big guy. You sound like you need to relax. We both know you don't handle change very well, and there have been a *lot* of changes in your life recently."

"I'm out in the country for the weekend. For once, I'm doing something *before* you tell me to."

The sound of laughter greeted his response. "Don't let it go to your head, Alex. I'm sure it was accidental."

"You're probably right, but hey, maybe you *can* teach an old dog new tricks. I gotta go, call me if you need anything, OK?"

"I will. Please get some rest, and I'll see you soon." The sound of silence told him she had ended the call.

He spent the rest of the evening polishing off the steaks, and a large portion of the bottle of bourbon, before turning in.

# Chapter 5

*"....The moons of Mars were mined for useable materials, and a small outpost was planted on the surface, enabling resource collection and scientific research into the viability of finding a new home. Several years went by while all of this took place, and the ship was repaired as much as their current situation would allow.*

*Meanwhile, the crew debated what their next course of action should be. While several factions grew out of these conversations, a decision to move operations to the third planet, a water world in the habitable zone, was finally reached via consensus. Leaving behind a skeleton crew to man the outpost on Mars, the rest of the team embarked upon making way to Earth...."*

**Excerpt from the diary of Alexander Matthews**

**May 1931, Surrey, England**

*The clang of the hammer rhythmically beating the hot metal on the anvil had a hypnotic effect on Alexander. The blade he was currently working on was crude—even he had to admit that—but it was a vast improvement over his previous attempts. This apprenticeship had turned out to be much more challenging than he had expected, but was very rewarding in its own way.*

*It hadn't taken him long to realize that quality weapons were extremely hard to come by. And that if he wanted to ensure he had access to them, then he would have to learn how to create them for himself. His search had taken him to Europe, and he had finally found the smith who not only could teach him the craft but would take him on as an apprentice.*

*He had only been here for six months, but he had already learned so much. Obviously, he had much more to learn, but he was a patient man. Alexander had not set any kind of hard deadline for this; the master smith would let him know when it was time to move on. For now, he was happy to work in the forge every day and absorb all he could.*

*Jack was not a young man. In fact, he was in his sixties, and while he was healthy for a man that age, sooner, rather than later, he would die...and a lifetime's skill and knowledge would die with him. Alexander suspected this was the real reason he had acquiesced to his request so readily. With no apprentices, and his craft a dying art, he latched onto the American and was doing his best to pour everything he knew into Alex's brain and hands.*

*Smiling happily, the apprentice continued to work the metal....*

***

Alexander left the house early Tuesday morning and arrived at the office long before Tina. He took the elevator upstairs and spent some time getting ready. When he made his way back downstairs, he stopped at the espresso machine and brewed coffee for two. Then he placed the cups and saucers, and a long, polished rosewood box onto a platter and carried it out into Tina's domain. When he set the tray down, she looked up at him with a puzzled expression.

He placed the coffee in front of her and set the box aside. The tray went onto a cabinet near her desk. Sipping his own coffee, Alexander asked how her weekend was and listened as she talked about spending time with her family. Her animated descriptions of her everyday interactions with her parents and siblings elicited a pang of longing that he quickly suppressed. That part of his life was firmly in the past, and there was nothing he could do about it. When she finally wound down, her eyes returned to the rosewood box.

He followed her gaze and said. "I noticed that you didn't have a letter-opener, so I made you one. Go ahead and open it."

Tentatively, she reached out and pulled the box until it rested just in front of her. Tina glanced up at him curiously, then opened the lid. Nestled in black velvet was something that was about as related to a letter-opener as a tricycle was to a Harley-Davidson motorcycle.

"May I?" Alexander asked, gesturing to the knife that lay within.

Tina inclined her head, speechless.

"Your Aunt Maria also has a dagger that I created just for her. Has she ever shown it to you?" She shook her head. He carefully lifted the sheathed weapon from the box. "I seldom have time to spend in front of a forge these days, but when I do, I find it therapeutic for me to create things of beauty from the raw materials nature provides."

While speaking, he slid the rigid red leather scabbard off, revealing a dramatically patterned blade. "This is an Italian-style Renaissance dagger. They were practical items, as well as effective in either defensive or offensive situations. I decided that a woman whose ancestors called Italy home should have something that speaks to that heritage." Twisting the knife so that it caught the light, he continued, "The blade itself is a Damascus spear-shape, acid-etched to make the multi-layered steel reveal the random patterns of the different metals used. Both sides of the blade are sharpened, so be careful when using it. The guard and fluted pommel are also Damascus, and I used ironwood when I crafted the hilt."

Tina's eyes had widened while she listened to Alexander describe the weapon. She may not have known much about knives or daggers, but she could spot the work of a master craftsman when she saw it.

"Why? Why would you make something like this for me?" she asked him quietly.

He smiled down at her and said, "Do I really need a reason? Making this was rewarding enough in itself. Maybe, I thought you would appreciate it? And hey, some of the mail we get around here is pretty vicious, you can't be too careful." His eyes glittered as he handed it to her. Tina's fingers closed around the hilt, and she realized that it fit her hand perfectly.

"If you like, I can explain how to take care of it later. In the meantime, I need to get back to work."

He strode toward his office but halted momentarily as Tina asked quietly, "Did you make the box too?"

She heard a soft "Yes," but never saw the satisfied expression on his face as he closed the door behind him.

***

Tina marveled at the deadly grace of the dagger Alexander had crafted for her. Truth be told, the rosewood box by itself was a gift that anyone would be happy with. On the other hand, she had absolutely no idea what to do with a knife. She was confident it wasn't something you would toss in the silverware drawer, only to be pulled out to carve a wedge of cheese occasionally.

The more she thought about it, the more confused she became, so she did the only thing she could think of. Tina called her aunt.

"Hello, dear." The mellow voice of her Aunt Maria spoke into her ear. "To what do I owe the pleasure of this call?"

Brow furrowed in consternation, Tina replied, "Alexander gave me a knife this morning. He said you have one too, but what am I supposed to do with it?"

"Oh, dear. You and I need to have lunch …and please bring his gift with you. Why don't we meet at Twigs in Riverpark Square at noon?"

Tina exhaled loudly. "Oh-kaay. I'll see you then.

***

Maria was already seated at a table, overlooking the atrium of the mall when Tina arrived at the restaurant. She dropped her bag on the chair next to her as she sat down. Her aunt said, "I hope you don't mind; I took the liberty of ordering the wine."

"That's fine, I think I can use a drink. Or five."

Maria chuckled as she looked across the table at her niece. She really was a beautiful child, even when flustered.

"We haven't had time to catch up. How is the new job treating you?"

Tina waved a hand in the air. "Good. Mostly. I mean, the work itself is interesting and keeps me busy."

"But?" Maria asked.

Her niece blew a puff of air between her lips and said, "But Alexander is the single most frustrating man I've ever met. Don't get me wrong—he hasn't turned into an octopus suddenly, and I don't get a rape-y vibe off him… But I don't think he even sees me. Is he gay, Aunt Maria?" she asked plaintively.

A sudden bout of coughing followed by laughter was her response to that question. Maria held up a hand as she got herself back under control, tears streaming down her cheeks. "Don't do that to me, child. At least *warn* an old lady before you crack a joke."

Considering her niece for a moment, she chose her words carefully. "You want him to notice you, right? And the fact that he has been a proper gentleman bothers you?"

"Yes. No. Maybe? I'm so confused. He makes me so angry sometimes. Then he does something like this." She reached into her bag and pulled out the box. "What am I supposed to make of a gift like this? I mean seriously, it's not like it's a pair of shoes or something normal like that."

"No, dear, it is a gift far more thoughtful than clothes." Maria set an ebony box of similar size on the table next to the other. She opened it, revealing a beautifully crafted Japanese-style tanto, in a black lacquered sheath with brass cherry blossoms trailing down the length of the scabbard.

Tina sat there, trembling, staring in disbelief at what her aunt had just revealed. "Why a knife? Is it a sign he wants to sever the relationship? I know it's just an old superstition, but still… I just don't understand, Aunt Maria."

"I know you don't, child; that's why I wanted to meet for lunch. As for severing ties with you goes—I think you can put that worry to rest." She took the tanto up from where it nested in white silk, rested it across both palms, and presented it to her niece. "Allow me to introduce you to *Shijima*. That roughly translates to Serenity in English." As she spoke, Maria slowly pulled the blade partway from the scabbard. Shiny metal with a slightly lighter edge that was scalloped in a wave pattern gleamed in the sunlight.

Tina looked even more confused as she met her aunt's eyes. "Why does your knife have a name?"

"Not just a knife, Tina. This is a blade created with a soul, a blade meant for battle, for defense, for my protection. I didn't understand either when Alexander gave this to me years ago. The ass refused to give me a good answer when I asked, too." She smiled in remembrance, then continued, "So, I researched it. I learned more about Japanese sword-making in a week than I had in my whole life prior. This isn't some cheap copy that you can buy on the internet from Amazon. It's the real deal." She leaned forward slightly. "When I was in Japan some years ago, not long after Alexander gave it to me, I took this blade to a master swordsmith and asked him what he thought. Do you know what he told me, Tina?"

Her niece just shook her head.

"That master of his art grunted as he inspected the work and handed Shijima back to me, respectfully. When I pressed him on how he would rate the quality, I was told that he could find no flaw in the blade and furniture. He stated that it was the equal of anything he could produce."

Her niece finally took the tanto from her aunt's hands and pulled the blade entirely from the scabbard. There was no denying its beauty. The metal shimmered like water until it joined an oval brass piece just in front of the hilt, and a wavering line ran along the edge of the blade. Touching the brass with a fingertip, she marveled at the representation of a wolf snarling at a hunter.

"That is called a *tsuba* in Japanese. Westerners would name it a *guard*. It's there to protect the fingers and stop an enemy blade...among other things," Maria told her. "The hilt is wrapped in sharkskin and silk."

"Do you want to know what I did when I discovered this?" Tina nodded mutely again. "I freaked out like you are doing now, and when I calmed down sufficiently, I went to Alexander and asked him to train me in its use. That blade was with me almost every day thereafter. When I had learned enough, and I was comfortable with the weapon, he asked me what her name was."

"Excuse me? Her name?" Tina asked plaintively.

Maria smiled fondly at her niece. "Of course. Alexander forged this weapon for *me*, and since I am a woman, the spirit of the blade is female too. The next morning, I walked into his office and told him that because I felt calm and at peace when wielding this tanto, her name was Shijima."

"What did he say when you shared her name?"

"Alexander just smiled happily and said it was a good name. He then told me he could tell Shijima was happy too. I don't know if he was pulling my leg or not, but sometimes I swear I can feel her satisfaction when I practice." Maria gestured for the blade in her niece's hands and put it away. "Now, let me see what he made for you."

Tina slid the rosewood box over to Maria and watched to see her reaction. Her aunt slowly opened the box and inhaled sharply when she saw the contents. She reached in and quickly freed the dagger, then wasted little time unsheathing it.

"Oh my, Damascus steel. It's beautiful, Tina." She turned the weapon this way and that as she soaked in each detail. "You do realize this is a live blade, don't you?"

"I don't even know what that means, Aunt Maria!" she said with no little exasperation. "He told me I needed a letter-opener."

"Oh my God, he didn't!" Maria laughed heartily at Tina's words.

"He did."

"What an ass. Nevertheless, this is a priceless work of art; please don't use it as a letter-opener."

With a serious look on her face, Tina said, "I'm still confused, though. Why would he give me a knife? I don't even know how to use one."

Maria put the weapon away and reached out for one of Tina's hands. "Well then, that is the first thing you must remedy. Ask him to train you. There is no one better to learn from. Trust me, I know."

"I may not be an expert when it comes to how Alexander's brain works, but I can tell you this. He wouldn't have made this for you if he didn't care about you and your safety." She looked up briefly, then back at her niece. "Very, very rarely, the world of antiquities Alexander operates in can be a dangerous place. He will do everything he can to keep you out of that side of things, but sometimes they trickle through. I'm guessing you haven't gone on a trip with him yet?"

"Not yet. He has taken a couple of flights to China, but hasn't asked me to come along so far. I'm actually a bit jealous."

"Don't worry, dear, our Alexander is just easing you into the life."

Tina sat in silence for a minute, then frowned. "So, does this mean he likes me? I'm so confused. He sends mixed signals, but I get the feeling he would never act on it even if he did."

Maria smiled sadly, then said, "He is a very complex man, dear. That being said, please don't get your hopes up. I'm fairly certain he *has* noticed you, being that he is a man after all."

Her niece peered at her with watery eyes. "But he will never chance hurting you. There are some barriers he just won't cross, and the employee/employer line is one of those. My advice is to enjoy your time with him, and be the friend he needs."

"Friends with benefits?" Tina asked, hopefully. "Never mind, I guess I know the answer to that. I'm just being ridiculous, aren't I?" She used the napkin in her lap to daub at her teary eyes.

"Not ridiculous, my dear, one can always hope. Just don't pin everything on it."

Tina sniffled, then got an angry look on her face. "And who the fuck is Melinda?" She made quotation marks in the air.

Maria burst into laughter again, and then launched into a series of stories about Melinda that took up the remainder of their extended lunch.

# Chapter 6

*"....I joined the Army on April 7th, 1917. A state of war had been declared between the United States and Germany just the day before. My sense of patriotism was as great as any normal American man, and there was no chance I would try to sit this out. My arrival on the Western Front in the summer of 1918 proved to be a sobering experience. Poor tactics and leadership that led to countless unnecessary deaths, horrible mental and physical wounds that many survivors carried until their deaths, ungodly sanitary conditions that contributed to all sorts of sickness and disease, and the sheer randomness of who died and who lived, changed my worldview forever. This is also where I began to formulate a plan to learn more about myself and the others like me. I needed to focus on something more than the horrors of daily life in the trenches...."*

**An excerpt from the diary of Alexander Matthews**

### February 1990, Spokane, Washington

*Alexander tossed about on the sweat-soaked sheets, lost in a fever dream of a past that wasn't his. Eyes writhed beneath quivering lids as REM sleep kept his conscious mind submerged, and ancient events played out in his dreams. The occasional moan or word in some forgotten language was the only sound to break the silence.*

*In his mind, what would become the Yucatan Peninsula stretched out before him, an ice age savannah rich with life and dominated by a glistening city. Step pyramids rose above the lime-plastered walls that protected the inhabitants, and smoke from hearths and temples rose languidly into the air. Farmland surrounded the tall walls, green and verdant, easily enough to feed several thousand people even without the abundant sources of meat that could be harvested not far away.*

*Too bad the army he led was here to destroy everything. He looked behind and raised his hand into the air, then chopped it down, giving the signal to attack. Standard humans, interspersed with his Dire wolf brethren, charged forward, and screams and war-cries rent the very air. The ground trembled as more than three thousand pairs of feet propelled themselves at the enemy.*

*This attack did not go unopposed, however, and the city gates opened wide, disgorging defenders who would meet the invaders on the plain before the walls. Just before the two armies slammed together, volleys of arrows and spears flew through the air, piercing and slicing into flesh. The roars of battle-frenzy, and the cries of fear and pain, reverberated off the walls, adding confusion to an already-chaotic melee.*

*Sabretooth Cats and Dire Wolves faced off, as did their respective hybrid forms, while some of the Weres chose to fight in human form. The general in charge of the attacking force was one who remained human. His attempts to direct the fighting were largely unsuccessful, and things were not going well. His army had been outnumbered from the very beginning and was slowly being pressed back. There were a few bright spots, such as the burning fields, which would deny the denizens of the enemy city food resources, but that was a long-term goal and did nothing for the immediate situation.*

*He looked to a low rise in the west and raised his spear, waving it to and fro, the banner streaming from it whipping through the air. This was a signal to the small force he had stationed there to launch their portion of the attack. They ran forward and began to loft fire-arrows over the wall, hoping to ignite fires that would burn the city to the ground. When the defenders saw this, small groups of skirmishers were sent to harry and destroy the arsonists.*

*Billowing smoke began to rise from within the walls as the battle still raged outside on the plain.* Now we just have to buy enough time for the fires to do their work, *the general thought, and a satisfied smile appeared on his face as he fought and continued to direct his forces….*

***

Tina was preparing to go to lunch, or more accurately, the gym when her boss strode into her office. He seemed excited about something—he was practically bouncing on his toes. She smiled wistfully for a moment then refocused her attention on what he was saying. Something about a buyer for one of the items he'd picked up in China earlier in the year....

Alexander paused. "You haven't actually seen the vaults yet, have you?"

"Is that a trick question, boss? I've seen our business suite, and that's about it." The flush came on rapidly, starting in her cheeks but quickly made its way down to her chest, where it disappeared under the linen blouse she was wearing. "Unless you count a brief glimpse of your living quarters."

He grinned evilly at her as she responded.

"Well, I have certainly been remiss then. Come with me."

Alexander held the door for her, his eyes straying to her shapely bottom as Tina walked past. He shook his head ruefully. *Focus, Alexander, focus,* he told himself as he closed the door and stepped around her to lead the way. They passed a couple of what Tina assumed were empty rental spaces, then stopped in front of a door that looked just as unassuming as any of the others in the hallway. Alexander took out a set of keys and unlocked the entrance, then gestured her in.

Rather than the standard office suite she expected, her eyes were immediately drawn to the definitely non-standard security door that was set into the reinforced metal wall that spanned the entire width of the room approximately five feet from the hallway entrance.

She turned to Alexander with a curious look. He smiled at her bemused expression, then walked over to the keypad on the wall and entered a nine-digit code. With a loud *click,* the locks released, and he swung the door open.

He reached around the entry and put his hand on what she assumed was the light switch, but rather than use it, he stopped and gazed at her with playful eyes. "Do you know what Howard Carter's response was to Lord Carnarvon, who asked, *'Can you see anything?'* when he first peeked into King Tut's tomb?"

Tina shook her head in negation.

"He said, *'I see wonderful things.'*...." Then Alexander flipped on the lights.

She couldn't see much from where she was standing, but what she did see took her breath away. Alexander took her by the arm and led her into a room filled with items on exhibit, shelves filled with artifacts, and bookshelves lined with ancient manuscripts. He paused after a few steps and released her arm. Still grinning, he said, "Take a look around. This is only part of what we have stored here." Then he shrugged carelessly. "Some of it will never be sold…call it my personal collection."

Tina walked to the first display case and gazed down at beautifully carved figurines and amulets. "Those are jades from the Shang dynasty," Alexander's voice said softly from just behind her. "We also have some bronzes that are not currently on display, as well as bronze weaponry from various early Chinese periods."

The next case held Japanese swords of varying sizes. She recognized the shapes and the style of craftsmanship. "The straight, single-edged sword is the oldest. It is Chokuto style, and very delicate. I think it was made in the 7th century, but that's just an educated guess," he said.

Alexander walked over to a different display and beckoned her to come. When she stepped up beside him, he raised a questioning eyebrow. "Have you ever seen an original Gutenberg Bible? This one was printed in the 1450s. Of course, I still prefer the older Illuminated Manuscripts."

He chuckled and said, "Yes, we have some of those too."

As Alexander walked away, he tossed over his shoulder, "Feel free to look around, I have to grab what we came here for. Just remember, if you break it, you buy it." He erupted with laughter when he saw the horrified look on her face. "Just kidding…mostly."

She quickly realized she knew virtually nothing about most of what she was looking at. And if she was honest with herself, she didn't even know what most of it *was.* To be fair, she could say with a fair amount of certainty that an artifact was a coin. Still, she would be at a loss to tell you where the currency came from, its age, or any other identifying information.

One display, in particular, held her attention. Gold, silver, and various gems glittered back at her through the glass. There was no rhyme or reason to the collection, as even she could tell that the artifacts came from different time periods and cultures. But they were all exquisitely beautiful. One necklace had an emerald the size of a golf ball prominently displayed as the central pendant. Tina sighed as she realized that such prizes were far beyond her reach.

Alexander startled her. "I should have known I'd find you drooling over the jewelry."

She elbowed him. "Don't scare me like that! And yes, they *are* lovely." Eyes squinted in a calculating way, Tina asked, "Ball-park figure, what's it all worth?"

"Roughly? I have no way of answering that. Some of what I have here is priceless, one-of-a-kind items that even Sotheby's would be hard-pressed to price."

Holding the box in his hands out to her, Alexander said, "Come on, let's get out of here. I've got to prepare these Warring States period jade stamps for delivery to our customer." He turned out the lights and secured the room before they made their way back to the *Destination Unknown Antiquities* offices.

***

Tina had just finalized the travel arrangements that Alexander had requested. She was happy that he had finally decided to include and introduce her to this side of the business. Travel via a private charter flight from Spokane International Airport to Charles de Gaulle outside Paris, France. They would be staying in the City of Lights for a week, then returning home. She hoped there would be time for sightseeing, as she had never traveled internationally before. Her only regret was that her birthday would fall during their time in France, but she figured it was a fair trade-off.

***

"Excellent. Then I can be assured that the watch will be waiting for me when I arrive on Wednesday?" Alexander asked the man on the other end of the phone as he gazed out upon the grey sky that seemed to crouch down on the city. He could smell the rain that hadn't yet begun to fall but would soon make its presence known. "Thank you, Henri, as always it has been a pleasure.

I will see you in a few days." He wore a satisfied smile as he disconnected and cranked up some music, in this case, *Make Me* by Rail. It really was too bad that they had never made it big, but MTV didn't play their music enough, and thus their popularity never took off.

He picked up the jade stamp that he had set aside when he placed the call to Henri. As his fingers deftly worked the polishing rag into the carved symbols, carefully removing any dirt or dust, his thoughts turned inward.

Alexander knew he was taking a risk by planning the surprise he had in store for Tina. Still, it was only fair that she received some form of compensation for being out of the country on her birthday. A deep sigh escaped him, *not to mention that you really want to get a gift for her, and you can tell yourself all day that it is purely platonic, but that doesn't make it so.* A quirk of one side of his mouth indicated how amused he was. *You never have been very good at lying to yourself.*

All of which was true, and yet, he was still going to go through with it. Tina had been working for him for a couple of months now, and he had somehow managed to avoid any major mistakes that would lead to any sort of unfortunate entanglements.... Still, it was becoming harder and harder to do. Especially so, given the fact that she had been practically throwing herself at him for weeks. Ignoring the offer was wearing on him if the truth were to be known.

Subconsciously, his right hand drifted to the large medallion that he wore around his neck. This odd-looking, yet seemingly ordinary hunk of metal had set everything in motion back in 1903. Of course, he had no real idea as to what it was or the functions it performed back then, because the concepts didn't even exist yet. All he knew for sure at the time was that it had somehow passed a lifetime of memories to his fevered brain, memories that weren't his.

Over the intervening years, he had gained a better idea of its capabilities and the purpose it served, but the truth of the matter was that he was convinced there was far more to be discovered. It was part recording device, somehow scraping experiences out of his brain and storing them internally, ready to be passed along to whoever the next owner might be. And it was also a miniature nano-factory that ensured a constant supply of the nanites that supercharged his body was on hand when, and if, they were needed.

It was the combination of the compiled memories and nanites that made him so different from other Weres. The ability to draw upon other people's experiences and utilize them while in the midst of a decision-loop gave him a distinct advantage in desperate situations; he didn't have to make the same mistakes, nor suffer the consequences his progenitor had. Not to mention, a thousand years of political infighting, warfare, and dealing with both Normal humans and enhanced species gave him a leg up in nearly every situation Alexander could possibly find himself in.

Toss in the nanites that took his already ramped-up body and pushed it to greater heights, and you had a winning combination that couldn't be beaten. The average Were was exponentially stronger, faster, and far more durable than a Normal human. On average, a run-of-the-mill werewolf could manage three times the weight, run faster than an Olympic sprinter, and survive damage that would kill a normal man. Pretty impressive. However, the nanites flowing through Alexander's bloodstream bumped all of these abilities by nearly double the amount. If needed, the nanites would assist with repairing any trauma that was beyond the normal regenerative abilities that the initial virus imparted.

So, if the average werewolf was considered superhuman, then Alexander was in a league of his own. Moreover, the changes made to his body optimized him in all three of his available forms. In addition to keeping him at the same apparent age of twenty-seven that he was the day he became infected, the combination of virus and nanites ensured that his body was at its maximum level of fitness at all times. His optimized wolf form was at the very top of the scales for the species, somewhere between twenty-five and thirty-five percent more massive than average. As for his Battle form, the hybrid of wolf and man, well, it too was much larger than others, towering over a non-enhanced werewolf.

All of this had a purpose. Only the Alpha of any of the enhanced species would have been given these advantages via an amulet, such as the one he wore upon his chest. These were to be the leaders, those who led armies, or managed slaves, for the gods. There were limitations, of course. For instance, his amulet could not be used to upgrade anyone who wasn't a Dire Wolf. If he tried to upgrade a vampire, it would do nothing other than kill them most painfully. This specificity was probably one of the reasons that his was the last functional device on the planet…as far as he knew.

He shook his head, clearing away these random thoughts, and focused once again on the task at hand. These jade stamps needed to be ready and packaged prior to their trip to Paris.

# Chapter 7

*"....Looking upon their new home, the Anunna set about making plans for what would be needed to successfully colonize this new world. It was obvious that no technological society existed, nor even primitive civilizations. The biodiversity of the habitats was amazing and offered vast opportunities for exploitation. Arguments broke out over where their first permanent colony should be located, and when no consensus could be reached, the decision was shelved temporarily. Enough other decisions needed to be made, such as setting up an HE3 mining and processing facility on the moon. This fuel would be needed to keep both the ship and its shuttles fueled over the coming centuries. Advanced 3D printing made the creation of both habitation modules, and the basic equipment needed for mining, to be generated relatively quickly and put into production...."*

**Excerpt from the diary of Alexander Matthews**

## October 1947, Excavations at Eridu in Iraq

*Alexander wiped the sweat from his forehead with the handkerchief he kept in his back pocket for just such an occasion. The desert was always hot, and digging through the layers of compact sand and mud didn't make the job any easier. He was sifting the dirt for any artifacts that might be present but had to admit that, for the most part, this expedition had not yielded much of use to his quest.*

*The amulet he always wore had passed on the knowledge that the Anunna had initially settled in a now-flooded part of the Persian Gulf. He was searching for any indications of surviving technology or culture that might exist in the oldest cities in the area. After all, it would only make sense that as the waters rose at the end of the last ice age, the inhabitants of the region would have migrated up the rivers to higher ground. Considering that several of the oldest cities, Eridu among them, were founded circa 5,400BC, it was entirely possible that at least some of the survivors would have brought their culture with them. Granted, much had probably been lost along the way, and the long span of time between 11,000BC and the founding of the cities was unaccounted for.*

*He suspected that the* 'gods' *of Sumer were the remnants of that earlier society, probably some of the few Anunna descendants that had managed to last that long. It didn't help that the history contained within the amulet abruptly ended with the death of his progenitor circa 13,000BC, and made all his assumptions little better than guesswork.*

*The technology of the ancient space-faring race had already been failing even before that timeframe, and the chances that much would have survived into historical times were slim. Still, some knowledge was not dependent upon machines. Language, including writing, astronomy, agriculture, building techniques, and perhaps even maps of the world could have, and probably did, survive the rising of the seas. He suspected that functional technology would be uncommon, and certainly, it would be fought over as the Anunna attempted to maintain control over the areas within their reach.*

*Sumerian gods were always depicted as being much taller and more muscular than the ordinary people, and this fit in with the fact that the Anunna were a larger species than mankind. Pale skin, red or blonde colored hair, and sensitivity to light were also traits of these people. The distinctive "hand bags" and "watches" that they were often modeled with may have been mythical in nature, but fragments of recollection implied these were real. He discounted the oversized eyes as being cultural because his* 'memories' *did not show that to be the case with the actual aliens. In fact, they were no doubt the origins of the legendary giants that existed in cultures all over the world. Proof continued to elude him, though, as did actual artifacts that he could study and gain additional knowledge.*

*Alexander was seriously considering making a trip to an actual battle site that he had managed to identify from what the amulet had transferred into his brain.*

*The sheer size of the excavations needed would be immense, and the expense ungodly, but it might come down to that to accomplish his goals….*

***

Early morning sunlight streamed in through the window next to his seat, bathing Tina's slumbering form in a soft glowing nimbus. She was reclined in a luxury seat, face turned toward him as she slept, mouth slightly open, and hands tucked under her chin. Alexander reached across the aisle and pulled the blanket up a little from where it had slipped during the night, and resisted the urge to tickle her ear. He looked at his watch and determined that he would wake her an hour before touchdown if she hadn't managed it on her own by then.

Her initial excitement at being on a private jet headed to an exotic location had gradually worn away as the sheer boredom of travel set in. Night had fallen before they refueled in New York, and despite her best efforts, sleep had claimed her not too long afterward.

Now, with the dawn breaking over the Atlantic Ocean and only a couple of hours out from their destination, he pondered the situation he found himself in.

A wry grin passed over his face as he continued to watch the woman who so easily unsettled him on the most fundamental level. What was it that made Tina different from other women he had met over the years? Certainly, he had had affairs, trysts, and one-night stands aplenty. Yet, any sort of long-term connection, much less commitment, had escaped him. If he were completely honest with himself, he would admit that this mostly had been because keeping people at a distance was a defense mechanism. He couldn't be hurt if he didn't let them in.

To make matters even more convoluted, Tina was a Normal, someone who didn't even know his kind existed. On the rare occasions when he allowed himself to indulge in a fling, it was *always* with another genetically modified individual. Such an entanglement was cleaner, far less likely to result in complications.

Sighing heavily, Alexander resigned himself to the fact that he was no closer to solving the problem that slept just two feet away, and he turned to stare out at the sea.

***

Tina stared dully out the window of the limousine that she and her boss were riding in. The trip had been exhausting so far, especially as the initial excitement of flying in a private jet had worn off much sooner than she had anticipated. Oh, it was much better than flying coach as she had on her infrequent trips before coming to work for Alexander, but most of a day cooped up in *anything* gets old fast. Nor did she get much sleep on the flight, and jetlag was hitting her hard, the nine-hour time difference brutal. On the other hand, the smug bastard sitting next to her appeared to be as fresh as a daisy. It should have been impossible. She knew for a fact that he did little more than take a short nap somewhere over the central part of the US, and yet he seemed unaffected by sleep-deprivation.

She got her first glimpse of the Four Seasons Hotel as the limo turned the corner onto Avenue George V. The building was an Art Deco wonder, and typically, Tina would have wanted to spend time exploring it. But right now, all she wanted was a bed. And maybe something to eat, but *definitely* a bed.

Alexander paid the driver as the hotel staff approached, and like magic, the small pile of luggage that had been unloaded disappeared into the hotel. He took her by the arm and led her past the doorman and onward to the front desk. As he approached, the smiling concierge said, "Welcome back, Sir. We have two adjoining suites prepared for you and Miss Ferrante. Your luggage is already on its way up to your rooms. Will there be anything else?"

"Not at this time, Lucien. Thank you."

"Come along, sleepyhead," he said as he gently steered her toward the elevator. When the lift doors opened on their floor, they stepped out and turned left, then continued down the hallway to where one of the hotel staff was standing next to a door. Two keys, and a huge tip, exchanged hands, and then Alexander opened the door and let her into what she assumed was her room. It was gigantic and beautifully decorated. The view from the large sitting area showed the Eiffel Tower not too far in the distance. Tina was confident she would enjoy it more later…after her impending coma.

She made a beeline for the couch with every intention of collapsing face-down into its beckoning embrace, but Alexander intercepted her halfway there. "That is a terrible idea, young lady." The answering growl from her only made him grin.

"You may hate me now, but you'll definitely thank me later." He pointed to her luggage. "You need to unpack and take a nice warm bath. I guarantee you will feel better after that. If I let you go to sleep now, your internal clock will never reset, and you'll feel like this the entire time we're here."

Taking a quick glance at his watch, he continued, "I'll knock on your door in exactly one hour, at which point we will go to a nice Parisian café and get some coffee and a light lunch. Is that acceptable?" Tina scowled at him but nodded her assent. He held up her room key, so she could see it, then set it down on the table in front of the couch.

Once he was gone, she walked into the cavernous marble bathroom and started her bath. Unpacking didn't take very long, and soon she slowly settled her tired and achy body into the almost too-hot water of the tub. She had pinned her hair up to keep it out of the water, as she didn't plan to take the time to wash it. Steam from the hot water rose slowly into the air, and Tina luxuriated in the relaxing heat, letting her muscles unknot one by one. By the time the thirty minutes she had allocated had elapsed, she almost felt human again.

Wearing the robe provided by the hotel, Tina finished applying her make-up. Fortunately, with her skin tone, she didn't require much, and with a final touch of lip gloss, she was done. She wandered over to the closet and perused her choices, eventually settling on a pair of low-cut jeans, a navy t-shirt, and a comfortable pair of flats. A fashionable black leather jacket rounded out the ensemble. She pulled her dark brunette hair into a tight ponytail and called it good.

Since she still had a few minutes before Alexander arrived, Tina opened her laptop and started browsing the news. A story about a particularly gruesome murder in Naples, Italy caught her attention, and she was only halfway through the article when a soft knock sounded at the door. She closed the laptop and set it on the table in front of her, then walked to the door. A small sigh of relief escaped as she took in what he was wearing. Her instincts had been correct as he was wearing jeans also, along with a white long-sleeve button-up shirt, and comfortable-looking brown leather shoes.

"Ready? Paris in August awaits," he said with a slight bow to indicate she should step into the hallway.

"Thank you, kind Sir." She moved into the hall with a giggle. *Gah! I can't believe I just giggled. I hate giggling,* she grumbled to herself.

The next few minutes were filled with small talk as they made their way to a café not far from the hotel. The weather was comfortable, so they sat at a street-side table, and when the waiter arrived, Alexander ordered them coffee and two sandwiches: a jambon buerre and a croque-monsieur.

"I figured I would let you sample each and decide which one you prefer," he said a bit sheepishly. "These are classics, and I would hate for you not to be able to try them while you are here."

Tina nodded agreeably and said, "I didn't know you spoke French. Just how many languages are you fluent in?"

"Speaking or reading?"

She cocked her head to the side and asked. "Both?"

He leaned back in his chair and considered for a moment. "Hmmm, let's say twenty." A short pause. "*Modern* languages, anyway."

"So, let me get this straight, you are fluent in twenty modern languages, both written and verbal?" He nodded reluctantly.

"How many *non*-modern languages?" she demanded.

Alexander looked uncomfortable and muttered, "Another fifteen or so."

Tina sat there, stunned for a minute, shook her head, and opened her mouth to speak...twice. She finally managed to whisper, "Wow."

He shrugged diffidently. "It kind of goes with the territory. I need to be able to authenticate the items we buy and sell, not to mention read through ancient sources looking for something other collectors may have missed."

Their food arrived, the scent of toasted bread, cheese, and meats preceding it and interrupting the conversation briefly. He sipped his coffee as she nibbled on each of the sandwiches. "These are both really good. I think we should split them and call it even."

For a while, they ate in companionable silence, but eventually, she blurted out, "Say something to me in one of the old languages."

"Like what?"

She waved her hand in the air and said with a huge smile, "Surprise me."

Alexander thought for a moment then grinned impishly. "Triúr fear go dteipeann orthu mná a thuiscint: fír óga, fir aosta agus fir mhéanaosta." The words spilled off his tongue with a slight sibilance but were still beautiful to hear.

"What does that mean?"

He used his fingers to count as he replied, "It's an old Gaelic proverb that translates roughly as *Three kinds of men who fail to understand women: young men, old men, and middle-aged men.*" He had to duck quickly as she threw her napkin at him.

"That's terrible," Tina said but was laughing as she did so.

They finished eating, and Alexander paid the bill. Afterward, they spent the rest of the afternoon strolling the streets near their hotel. He filled the walk with outrageous and scandalous tales of the various neighborhoods they crossed through, and imparted some of their rich histories as well. Eventually, the pair ended up back at the Four Seasons, where he asked her to join him for dinner later in the evening and left her at her door.

***

Alexander entered the town-car that the hotel concierge had arranged for, then provided the destination address to the driver. It only took a few minutes before they pulled up in front of the Cartier store on the Avenue des Champs-Élysées, where he requested that the driver wait for him. He entered the store and approached the woman behind the counter.

"May I help you?" she asked, in lightly accented English.

"Yes, please, I am here to pick up a watch. You should have a Silvertone Tank MC, with the alligator strap, waiting for an Alexander Matthews."

"One moment, Sir." The clerk walked away and came back moments later with a box in her hands. She opened the lid and showed him the contents. "Does this look correct, Mr. Matthews?"

He nodded, then pulled his wallet out, removed a credit card, and handed it to the woman. “Would you be so kind as to wrap it for me? It’s a birthday gift.”

“Of course.” She rang up the purchase, and minutes later, he was back in the town-car and headed toward the hotel.

***

Checking herself in the mirror one final time and adjusting her boobs, Tina decided that she looked good enough for dinner. She was still exhausted but was determined to power through the next couple of hours before going to bed. Her curiosity was piqued, but she assumed Alexander wanted to make this a working meal, probably to discuss the particulars of the sale of the artifacts tomorrow.

Her knuckles rapped on Alexander’s door, and he answered almost immediately. He ushered her to a seat at the small dining table and poured a glass of wine.

“I hope you don’t mind, but I thought a private dinner would be more conducive to getting actual work done.” His raised eyebrow and slight smirk made it more of a question than a statement.

“It's fine. I’m still tired from the flight anyway.” Tina sipped from her glass and nodded approvingly. “This is good.”

“I’m glad you like it. A good *Vouvray* is hard to beat, in my opinion. Also, it pairs well with what I had the chef whip up for dinner.” He removed the lids from a couple of serving platters and put food on both of their plates.

Her mouth began to water as the aromas from the meal wafted in her direction. “It smells wonderful. What are we having?”

“Chicken with forty cloves of garlic, haricots verts, and new potatoes in butter,” he replied. The skeptical look on her face amused him. “Don’t worry, the garlic loses its bitterness as it cooks, and adds just a hint of sweetness to the chicken.”

Small talk dominated as they ate, and Tina found herself enjoying this time with her boss. The witty sense of humor that he usually kept well-hidden was evident tonight, and she decided she liked this side of him.... Not that she would ever tell Alexander that.

He poured the last of the wine into her glass and gestured to the comfortable couch. She seated herself at the far end and turned her body so she could face him, pulling her legs under her. Appearing to collect his thoughts for a moment, he then began to speak.

"I don't anticipate any real problems with the exchange tomorrow." He smiled reassuringly at her. "These things tend to go fairly smoothly."

One corner of her mouth quirked up. "But...."

He chuckled. "But on occasion, the buyer is less than honest, and events can get a bit hairy. I have done business with our customer before, and while he's a bit of a prick, he has never tried to rip me off. You might compare him with an especially slimy used car salesman—gross, but essentially harmless."

"What happens if he does attempt to not pay?"

His eyes hardened, and his voice was crisp. "Then, the situation might become more...fluid. If that happens, I want you to immediately get up and leave. Return to your room and wait. Do not open your door for anyone but me. Do you understand?"

"You want me to leave you alone?"

"I do. I can better manage the situation if I know you are out of harm's way."

Tina scowled. "I'm not sure I like the idea of abandoning you."

Alexander sighed. "You'll just have to trust me on this. If you prefer, I can handle the transfer myself?"

"No. I can follow instructions. Doesn't mean I have to like it, though."

"Excellent." They spent the next hour discussing what she could expect and which account the money should be deposited into electronically.

At some point, she fell asleep on his couch, and rather than wake her, he eased her down and covered her with a blanket, gently sliding a pillow under her head and removing her shoes. Alexander spent several minutes just gazing down at Tina's sleeping form, a troubled expression on his face, then made his way to the bedroom, closing the door quietly behind him.

***

Sleep did not come easily to him. Alexander had spent the last hour staring at the ceiling and arguing with himself. Was he doing the right thing? Intellectually he understood that maintaining his distance from Tina was the best choice. Still, he was finding it difficult to do. In fact, as it currently stood, he was half-assing it—neither fully committed to being aloof nor to allowing nature to take its course.

Their banter, where she gave as good as she got, amused him on many levels. Having someone to verbally spar with was fun, and surprisingly, she more than held her own. There was a fully functional brain behind the pretty exterior. However, he noticed that she tried to camouflage that fact as much as possible. *Why* was the question. Alexander understood that some men felt threatened by smart women, but he was not one of them. It was refreshing to be able to have an actual conversation with a woman, and not just talk about nonsense.

Over the last couple of months, he had given up on any pretense of maintaining his regular routines. Maria had been with him long enough that she required very little input from him to handle the day-to-day operations of the business. The same could not be said of Tina, nor did he begrudge having to take the time to instruct her, but the constant interaction was distracting...to say the least. Also, she was far too smart to allow him to provide less than comprehensive information, frequently calling him out on his bullshit when he tried to give her the bare minimum. A stubborn streak a mile wide hid within that shapely body, and she refused to acknowledge that she had a handle on something unless she genuinely *did* understand the material backward and forward.

So...he couldn't pretend she wasn't there, nor could he in good conscience fail to provide the guidance that she needed to get the job done. That would be shooting himself in the foot and potentially damaging to the business. Where did that leave him? *Apparently, it leaves me with insomnia,* he thought, a smile flickering across his lips. *Enough. Stewing on this shit is accomplishing nothing.*

Alexander rolled onto his side and focused on his breathing until he fell asleep.

***

Tina woke to the sounds of Alexander showering and getting ready for the day. She realized she must have fallen asleep on the couch and noticed that he had provided her with a pillow and blanket. She smiled a bit sardonically and thought, *Not quite how you had hoped to spend a night in his room, is it?* Then she grimaced at the horrid taste in her mouth. Chicken with forty cloves of garlic might be excellent going down, but the aftermath left much to be desired. She wanted to go back to sleep but sat up and stretched instead. Verifying that her room key was in her back pocket, Tina exited Alexander's suite and made her way to her room. She stripped out of the clothes she had on, brushed her teeth to get rid of the dead animal that had taken up residence in her mouth, and quickly showered.

Her thoughts wandered as she dried her hair and prepared for the day. Last night was…nice. Definitely not what she expected in regard to how traveling with her boss would be. Rather than treating her strictly as an employee, he had directly involved her in the planning, going so far as to ask for her opinions, even though this was all new to her, and she lacked experience. Tina was beginning to understand why her aunt had loved this job so much.

It was almost mid-morning when she was finally ready to meet the day head-on. Her phone rattled on the end table, and when she picked it up, she saw a text from Alexander. *Ready for breakfast?* She responded in the affirmative and met him in the hallway outside their rooms. They took the elevator down to the main floor and had a leisurely breakfast at one of the restaurants in the hotel.

As she was sipping a perfect cup of coffee, Alexander said, "I almost forgot," then handed her a small box. "Happy Birthday, Miss Ferrante."

Tina gazed at the wrapped package in her hands as though expecting it to explode at any moment, then scowled at him. "How did you know today is my birthday?"

He looked inordinately pleased with himself as he replied, "One of the perks of being the owner of a business is having access to personal data of employees. It's all in your data packet from the day you were hired."

She looked less than pleased by his words, then visibly decided *what the hell* and started to unwrap the gift. There was a sharp intake of breath as she saw the name Cartier on the box. When she lifted the lid, Tina saw a beautiful watch…not just any watch, a Cartier. She puffed her cheeks out, set the watch on the table, and told Alexander, "I can't accept this."

"Why not?"

"Alexander, this had to cost several thousand dollars."

He nodded. "It did. Your point would be?"

Tina's exasperated tone spoke volumes. "Why would you buy such an expensive watch for someone who has only worked for you a few months?"

He sat back in his chair, studying her intently before he replied.

"I *could* tell you that it has nothing to do with how long we've worked together. Or I *could* say that I feel bad about dragging you away from your friends and family during your birthday." He paused. "And it's also possible that our company is going to make a rather large sum of money on the transaction this evening, making the cost irrelevant."

Her narrowed eyes indicated her skepticism.

Alexander sniffed audibly and looked down his nose. "But mostly, a well-crafted timepiece is a necessity for any truly civilized person. I'm just doing my part to ensure you can never use *'my watch is running slow'* as an excuse for being late."

He almost got out of the way of the pastry remnant she threw at him as he laughed loudly. Almost.

***

Alexander and Tina were seated at a semi-secluded table in a restaurant located just a few blocks from the Four Seasons. Each had an untouched drink sitting in front of them, and the waiter had been informed that they were expecting guests. She was fidgeting, fingers idly twisting the new watch on her wrist, her nervousness plainly apparent, but Alexander reached out a hand and rested it on top of hers. "Relax. *Breathe.* Nothing bad is going to happen."

She jerked her head in a nod. "OK."

He continued to let his senses roam, even as his eyes actively scanned the room, looking for threats. Nothing indicated that they were in danger, but it never hurt to maintain low-level alertness in these types of situations. Only a minute later, he saw the person they were waiting for enter the restaurant, an obvious bodyguard following him closely. Their eyes connected across the room, and the two men made their way to the table where Alexander and Tina sat.

Alexander stood and offered his hand. "Jean, a pleasure as always. May I present my assistant, Tina Ferrante?"

Jean shook his hand, then glanced at Tina, appraising her like a piece of meat.

The greasy smile directed at her made Tina's skin crawl. "The pleasure is all mine, Mademoiselle."

He seated himself, while the bodyguard stood slightly to his right, and a step behind, actively scanning for threats. When the waiter arrived to inquire about a drink, Jean waved him off. "No, thank you. We will only be here briefly."

"Do you have the items?"

Alexander countered with, "Do you have the funds?"

Jean opened his arms wide. "That's the problem with this world, no? Where is the trust?"

"I believe it was Ronald Reagan who said, '*Trust, but verify,*' was it not?" Alexander countered drolly.

"Bah." Jean leaned forward, squinting his piggish eyes. "Who can be bothered with remembering what American said what?"

Tina watched as her boss reached down beside him and slowly raised a small metal case, set it on the table, and slid it toward the buyer.

Eyes glittering with thinly disguised greed, the Frenchman rubbed his hands together then opened the top, revealing the five jade stamps nestled within. "How do I know these are authentic?"

"Don't insult me, Jean. If you have any doubts, you should just walk away."

"And these are the correct period?"

"Yes. All from the Warring States era," Alexander replied dryly.

Jean looked up as he closed the case. "My client will be very pleased with this acquisition."

"I'm so glad," was the dry response. "There's just the small matter of payment...."

"Oui, oui." The Frenchman pulled out a cell phone and stabbed at the screen.

Alexander nodded at Tina, who had her tablet on the table next to her. She logged in to the account specified and said, "Transaction verified."

"Excellent. Now, if there is nothing further, Jean, I believe our business is concluded." Alexander stood again.

Hugging the case to his chest, their customer nodded, quickly got up, and with bodyguard in tow, left the way he had come.

The breath Tina had been holding was exhaled loudly. "That was intense."

"Sorry about that. You'll get used to it. Eventually."

"I can't believe we just made $750,000."

"Meh. Jean will charge his client far more than that. But we still made a hefty profit even after what I paid for them." He grinned. "Why don't we order dinner and relax. Our work here is done, and I shall attempt to show you as much of Paris as I can prior to our scheduled departure.

"Alexander?"

"Yes, Tina?"

She looked earnestly into his eyes. "I think I would like you to teach me how to use the dagger you gave me."

He smiled hugely. "It would be my honor, my dear. It would be my honor."

# Chapter 8

*"....My sister died from the influenza outbreak that swept the world from 1918-1920. She was eighteen years old. I was still in France when it happened and only learned of it from a letter my parents sent me. Over 30,000 American soldiers would die from the disease before all was said and done, and three to five percent of the total world population is estimated to have succumbed to it. I never even got so much as a sniffle...."*

**An excerpt from the diary of Alexander Matthews**

**April 1943, On the slopes of Mount Song, China**

*Li Wei casually leaned away from the attack Alexander's Battle form made on him. In fact, his hands were clasped behind his back, but his feet were definitely in play. The werewolf staggered to his knees as the kick the monk delivered to his head stunned him momentarily. Some of the disciples watching from the sidelines snickered, and the glare the abbot shot in their direction promised that there would be retribution for this action.*

*"Balance. Without balance, you will always be vulnerable. Do not commit so quickly, nor so completely," Li Wei told Alexander as he slowly climbed back to his feet. "The ebb and flow of battle must be controlled, as must your own actions. Otherwise, you are like a leaf blowing in the wind that has no power to dictate where it goes."*

*The now-naked man bowed his head respectfully as he received instruction. He had been studying with Sifu for almost a year currently, and while his fighting skills had improved over that time, he knew that even the youngest of the disciples would easily defeat him.*

*Li Wei had found him after a raid on Japanese forces that Alexander had participated in. The rag-tag group of resistance fighters had not fared well in the fight and were on the run. The monk had tended the wounds of his comrades, and during the discussions they had over the course of two days, he had invited the American to study with him. The fact that he was a weretiger convinced Alexander that this would be an excellent way to learn new techniques and gain experience fighting a race of Weres he had no knowledge of.*

*And so, he found himself on the slopes of Mount Song, not far from Shaolin Temple, learning a very specialized form of martial art developed by, and for, Weres. Despite the pain and humiliation experienced daily, he was having the time of his life. To contribute in some way, Alexander had set up a forge and made all the weapons that the monks now used. When he had first arrived, he could not believe the shoddiness of what they had on hand, and he had set about rectifying that situation.*

*The American had spent time in the temple archives looking for anything that might help in his search for the Anunna, and had even gone so far as to ask his teacher. Unfortunately, other than some fragmentary legends and rumors, he had come away with little for his efforts. Li Wei had told him that much had been destroyed as various dynasties had explicitly targeted the ancient writings contained within the temples. Eradication of heretical thought had been the primary goal of these attacks.*

*He was told that perhaps the monasteries in Nepal or Tibet might still have records....*

***

Tina groaned as she eased her aching body into the chair behind her desk. She was nearly certain that if she were to look in a mirror, half of her ass would be black and blue. Of course, that would require that she be *able* to turn her head far enough to *see* her ass...and that was probably impossible. Unfortunately, she only had herself to blame. After all, *she* had asked Alexander to train her. Granted, what that actually entailed was unclear at the time of the request, and had she known, she might not have willingly done so. And what in the hell was he listening to today? Was that Country music? *Whatever,* she grumped.

She swiveled her chair to glance into his office, and he grinned, raising his cup of espresso at her. He may as well have given her the middle finger. *Prick,* Tina thought as she smiled sweetly back. Even the act of placing her purse under the desk caused her pain, and to make matters worse, she knew that the torture would continue tonight. According to the sadist in the other room, her body would adjust to the regimen reasonably quickly, but she had her doubts. Tina opened the drawer beside her left leg and pulled out a bottle of Aleve, twisted off the cap, and dumped two tablets into her palm. After putting the bottle back and closing the drawer, she realized she had nothing to wash the pills down with. She sighed and thumped her forehead on the desk surface, and was beginning the slow process of getting out of the chair when a bottle of water and a heavenly smelling cup of coffee magically appeared before her.

"I thought you might need these," Alexander said cheerfully. "Heimlich Maneuvers involving dry-swallowed pain meds really aren't my favorite activity."

Tina growled at his smug countenance, but even *that* hurt.

"Suck it up, buttercup. It was only two hours." He shrugged indifferently. "I barely broke a sweat."

One bloodshot eye glared balefully up at him, and she mumbled almost inaudibly, "*Gonna kill your ass...just as soon as I can move again...you wait and see.*"

He smiled and patted her shoulder before walking away.

"Ow...motherfucker."

***

Alexander was still smiling as he seated himself behind his desk and started going through the e-mail that had accumulated overnight. One item, in particular, caught his attention, and he was smiling evilly as he called out, "Oh, Tina! I don't suppose you know how to dance, do you? And by *dance,* I don't mean shaking your ass and flailing about wildly."

Her arm slowly lifted off the desk beside her head, rotated behind her, and the middle finger rose until it was pointing at the ceiling. Alexander's laughter echoed as it bounced off the walls, accompanied by the distinctive twang that could only be Hank Williams as he belted out, *I'm So Lonesome I Could Cry.*

***

To say that Tina hadn't accomplished much so far would be a gross understatement. The most that she had been able to do thus far was drink about a gallon of water…slowly. The painkiller had taken the edge off, but she was still very uncomfortable. *I would definitely tell a boyfriend to go to hell if he wanted any nookie tonight. Not that I have to worry about that these days*, she sighed.

And what the hell was Alexander talking about regarding *dancing*? Knowing him, she would get the memo at the last minute, and he would take great pleasure in rubbing her face in her inadequacies. *That's not really fair, and you know it*, she thought. *Any perceived shortcomings are all in your head.* What was it he said this morning? Oh yeah, '*suck it up, buttercup*,' she snorted at the thought.

Still wallowing in self-pity, she was shocked when he walked up behind her, spun her chair around, and scooped her up into his arms. She protested rather half-heartedly and said, "What the hell, Alexander?"

He looked down at her as he strode quickly to the door leading to the hallway and elevators, and locked the door behind them. "It's a surprise. Now quit struggling and relax, or I'll throw you over my shoulder to make it easier on myself."

Once in the elevator, he asked her to push a specific sequence of buttons, then explained it was an override that would take them to the sub-basement. Tina found her head resting against his rather nice chest, eyes closed, and breathing in his scent. A sigh escaped her as she realized that she was enjoying being held by him. *I so need to get laid*, ran through her head.

When the doors opened, he walked over to a newer mustang. He settled her into the passenger seat, fastening the seatbelt around her. She noticed several other vehicles, including a crotch-rocket, occupying some of the available space.

Alexander slid into the driver's side, closed the door, and started the car. The initial rumble as the engine caught settled into a steady rumble, then they were in motion roaring up the incline that would lead them to the street. They barely slowed as he punched the control for the automatic door that secured the garage. Clearing the bottom of the metal door by less than six inches, he hit the gas as they turned left, wheels spinning momentarily.

She got a much clearer look at the car as they entered the sunlight. The body of the vehicle was charcoal-grey, and black racing stripes ran up the hood. Pedestrians on both sides of the street looked up as the Mustang snarled by, and Alexander grinned as he put on the Oakley sunglasses that he pulled off the visor, where they had been affixed. He turned to her and said, "This is one of my babies. A 2014 Ford Mustang GT500 with 662HP of pure *fun*." He shifted as he guided it through traffic with ease. The leather interior still had that new-car smell, and it seemed to her that he didn't use it very often.

Two of the numerous homeless people who made downtown Spokane their home sauntered out into the street. Jaywalking was an art-form in the city, and the fact that they were in no particular hurry was evident as they stopped in the middle of the lane and started arguing.

"Oh, come on!" Tina shouted, her face flushed with anger as she slammed a hand down on the dash in front of her. "Are you fucking kidding me?"

Alexander glanced at her out of the corner of his eye, half amused by her vehemence, and half alarmed. "Are you going to be OK?"

Wearing a sheepish look, she replied quietly, "That kind of shit really pisses me off."

"Noted. Remind me to stay on your good side."

They made a left onto Spokane Falls Blvd after bypassing the people who had blocked their way, and Tina pulled her visor down to block the glaring sunlight. "Seriously, where are we going? I mean, it's nice that you want to take me for a ride in your mechanical penis over-compensator and all, but someone has to staff the office."

Alexander looked to be in pain as she spoke, then leered at her. "I know you aren't talking about *me*, especially since I know for a fact that you've seen the goods."

Tina's face reddened almost immediately, and she glanced away and out the passenger window. What Alexander couldn't see was the evil smile she wore. "I'll grant that I could at least tell you were male, but I've seen better."

"Hah! I doubt that. But whatever lets you sleep at night…." He downshifted and took a right onto Monroe Street, the inertia causing her to slide around on the seat.

Tina had to admit that the car was nice, but she preferred her Bimmer. "Are you in the midst of a mid-life crisis, and this is so you can relive the glory days you never had?" A strange look crossed his face…just for a moment, then was gone.

"Do I look like I'm old enough to have a mid-life crisis?" He thumped his chest and said, "I'm in the prime of my life, darlin', not even a hint of a spare-tire yet."

She had to acknowledge that. He was ripped and not carrying an ounce of body fat from what she had seen as he put her through her first sparring session last night. The car slowed as he pulled into a turn lane, then made a left onto Summit Pkwy. It looked like he was taking her to Kendall Yards…the why was the mystery.

Alexander quickly found a parking spot, killed the engine, and turned to her, batting his eyes innocently before saying, "Would you like me to carry you again? Or can your decrepit ass hobble along for a bit?"

Tina rolled her eyes at him. "I think I can manage…as long as it's not too far, and you keep the pace down."

"Sweet. Let's roll."

They walked less than a hundred feet before he guided her into Spa Paradiso. He headed to the front desk and spoke to the young woman there, who was smiling politely at him. "We have an appointment. Two of the hour-long deep-tissue massages…." He paused, then leaned conspiratorially toward the clerk. "And a full Brazilian for her."

He cringed as Tina took a swing at him, laughing as he ducked away. "I'm guessing that means you don't want the Brazilian?"

"Right. Two hour-long deep-tissue massages it is." He winked at the openly amused receptionist.

***

"That was amazing. I feel so much better."

"I'm glad you enjoyed it. Seemed like the least I could do given your condition this morning. I know you don't believe me, but it *will* get easier. In a couple of weeks, you'll be fine."

She glanced skeptically at him as he drove, but she decided not to comment.

Once the car was parked in the garage, and they were in the elevator headed up, he asked, "Are you hungry?"

Tina thought about it for a second and nodded.

"Awesome. We'll eat in my apartment." He led her to the elevator in his office, and they rode it up one floor in silence.

"Grab a seat, and I'll see what I can scrounge up."

Tina wandered over to the home theater and browsed his movie collection. Mostly action movies like any guy would own, but a surprising number of dramas and foreign films, predominantly Japanese and Chinese period pieces.

He looked up from the food he was preparing and asked, "Do you like Asian films?"

"I can't really say. I've never watched one."

All of the sounds that had been accompanying his efforts in the kitchen suddenly ceased. "Seriously? Well, we shall have to remedy the currently sad state of your cinematic soul."

She laughed brightly over her shoulder. "It's not *that* bad."

"MmmHmm," he grumbled. "I hereby proclaim Friday evenings as '*Educate Tina in the finer things of life*' nights. And you don't graduate until I'm satisfied that you are no longer a heathen."

She chuckled as she sat at the dining room table. "I'm not so sure about that, mister, but I tentatively agree to dip my toe in the waters. No promises, though."

Alexander walked around the island with a serving dish heaped up with a stir-fry in one hand, and a large bowl of rice in the other. He set them in the center of the table and told her he would be right back. As he grabbed two table-settings, he asked what she wanted to drink. The Diet Coke she requested materialized beside her plate, and they dug in.

They bantered back and forth as the food slowly disappeared. She still didn't understand how at ease she felt when they were alone like this. Typically she was on edge, just waiting for someone to say something that would set her off. But so far, Alexander had managed to avoid that particular minefield. Ruefully Tina thought, *it figures that I finally find a guy I could really like, and he's off-limits.*

Alexander cleared his throat. "I received an invitation this morning in my e-mail."

"Oh?"

"Yes, and it affects both of us."

Her brow furrowed in thought, she replied, "How so?"

"You remember how this morning I asked if you knew how to dance? The question with the one-finger reply?"

She grinned at him impishly. "I do, and you so deserved it."

Dipping his head in acknowledgment, he continued. "Well, we have been invited to a gala at the National Archaeological Museum in Naples, a fundraising event that is fairly high-profile."

"Italy?"

"The very one. Anyway, it's a black-tie event and will involve ballroom dancing. I don't suppose you've had lessons?" he asked, his tone full of doubt.

Tina blanched and shook her head in the negative.

"Not to worry. We have until late May to get you up to speed. How fortunate for you that I am well-versed in the art of formal dancing and will add lessons to our training schedule." He patted her consolingly on the hand. "Trust me, it'll be fun."

Tina just stared at him in horror.

# Chapter 9

*"....Eventually, a colony location was agreed to, based upon weather and resource availability, and an advance party was landed via shuttle to begin construction. The settlement was built in what is now the Persian Gulf, but at the time, it was a fertile plain with multiple sources of freshwater. Once the new colony was complete, most of the non-essential residents of the vessel were relocated to the planet-side. For a thousand years, scientists of various disciplines were free to research as they wished, and the rough settlement grew into a city. Population growth was slow as the Anunna were a long-lived race, and childbirth was a relatively rare occurrence. Still, some children were born, and over time what had started out as four hundred castaways grew to over nine hundred...."*

**Excerpt from the diary of Alexander Matthews**

**October 1958, Hidden vault, Alexander's private collection, Spokane, Washington**

*He lit three incense sticks and pushed them into the urn filled with sand that sat before the platform upon which the Dire Wolf mummy lay. Since neither of them believed in the Christian god, Alexander assumed that his progenitor would approve of this sign of respect. The body was protected by a superbly fashioned rosewood case that had glass panes on all sides.*

*He sat in a chair and silently toasted the mummy with the tumbler of scotch he held in one hand. It wasn't often that he made the effort to come to this hidden room, but when he did, he liked to commune with what was left of the man who had made him into who he was today. Alexander's eyes scanned the dimly lit room, cataloging the anomalous artifacts that he had gathered over the years: Gold objects that resembled aircraft, statuary, and ceramics that most assuredly were modeled on non-human subjects, writings on various materials that spoke of the gods, and many other such things. Only the Vatican had a better collection, and the chances of him gaining access to those forbidden items were nil. Unfortunate, really, as he suspected he could learn much from their archives.*

*He was feeling melancholy, not an unusual state of affairs for someone like him. Alexander had read an obituary today, a notice that told him that his last remaining direct family member had died. His brother, Achilles, had lived a long life by human standards, and his children and grandchildren would continue the family line. Alexander had never gotten to know any of them since he had voluntarily broken off contact long ago, and he knew it was for the best, really. He had made peace with the fact that he would never have a family of his own, but today he couldn't help dwelling on the* what-ifs. *Still, a part of him yearned for the normality that he denied himself.*

*He frowned and drank the remainder of what was in the glass.* Monsters don't deserve such things, *he told himself angrily, then strode from the room....*

***

Alexander heard the *ooomph!* as his sparring partner slammed onto the tatami surface of the dojo floor. "You're still telegraphing. Until you learn to hide your intentions better, the floor is going to become your best friend."

He turned slightly and eyed the disheveled form glaring up at him from the mat. "On the other hand, you at least held onto the practice blade this time. Little steps, Tina, little steps."

Extending a hand to help her up, he couldn't help but admire the total package that was Tina Ferrante. Currently, the object of his observations was dressed in tight black yoga pants and a teal sports bra...and covered in a considerable amount of sweat. For a moment, as she glared at him, it seemed she might not accept the assistance, but then she heaved a sigh and took the hand. He easily lifted her to her feet, then tossed her a towel to dry off.

"Let's call it a night. You did well."

"Not well enough." She snorted angrily.

Alexander gave a soft smile and shook his head slightly. "It's only been a couple of months, and I see some real improvement." He strode over to the refrigerator and grabbed a couple of cold bottles of water, setting one on the island in the center of the kitchen. "Granted, you still telegraph your attacks, and over-commit when you launch them, but that will come with time and practice."

"I just get so frustrated."

He nodded and quirked an eyebrow, then placed his right hand on the center of his chest. "And that brings us to the real issue. It might come as a bit of a surprise, but I'm afraid I'm duty-bound to inform you that you have a wee bit of a temper."

Tina blushed and looked away. "I know. Trust me, I know. It sort of runs in the family, but I think I got more than my fair share of it, and I know that's not a real excuse." She twisted the top off the bottle of water violently and took a long drink.

Considering her words, Alexander replied earnestly, "Without control, all you have is passion. Anger by itself is nearly useless. Focused anger, on the other hand, can provide power and strength."

On the verge of tears, she said, "But how? How do I tame it? When it flares up, it consumes me."

"While the old Klingon adage '*Revenge is a dish best served cold*' isn't entirely relevant for your situation, it does contain a nugget of truth."

She rolled her eyes and scrunched her nose at him. "Nerd."

His answering smile and sip of water indicated that her shot had missed its mark. "Seriously. Rather than allow rage to dictate your actions, you need to tamp it down, channel all of that emotion into a cold, dark place...and quietly choke the shit out of it. It doesn't go away, but it puts your logical brain in charge again."

Tina batted her eyelashes at him and said in an overly innocent tone, "I thought you told me once that the words *logic* and *woman* should never occupy the same sentence?"

He stood there, stunned, blinking his eyes owlishly. "Yes, well…." He cleared his throat. "However, I can neither confirm, nor deny, ever actually making that statement."

Gesturing with his bottle of water, Alexander continued. "Regardless, the point I'm trying to make is that until you are able to shake hands with your rage monster and get on with the task at hand, you will be severely limited. Not by actual *ability*, but by not being the master of your own domain. Does that make sense?"

"You make it sound so simple." She sighed wearily and looked down at her feet.

His hand reached out and lifted her chin until she met his eyes. "Don't you think I get frustrated and angry? I do. However, I refuse to let my lizard brain win. It's as simple as that."

Dropping his hand, he wrinkled his nose, looking her over from head to toe, then leaned forward slightly and sniffed delicately. "Good God, woman, you reek."

Tina laughed as she chased him around the island. He was smart enough to not let her catch him.

Hands held up in surrender, he said, "If you would prefer, we can always drop the fight training and focus exclusively on your dance lessons."

She had a horrified expression on her face as she replied, "Nope. Nope, nope, nope. It's all good. I'm just going to take a quick shower before we watch *Zatoichi Meets Yojimbo*."

***

Tina had the multi-head shower in Alexander's bathroom warming up as she studied herself in the mirror. Turning first one way, then the other, she decided that all of the exercise she had been getting lately had gone a long way to toning her body up. She looked damned good, even if she did say so herself. All of the bruises the first couple of weeks had provided were now gone.

Despite how frustrating the lessons she was getting from Alexander could be, she was continually surprised by how much actual fun she was having. Sure, any seven-year-old with a pillow could kick her ass currently, but she *was* improving. He was a good teacher, although she would never admit that to his face, and he was supportive while still pushing her to her limits. God knew that he never allowed the fact that she was a woman stop him from bringing the pain. She appreciated that fact since experience had led her to believe that men would always hold back when teaching a woman. Tina was sure that, given time, she could become a true badass...or close to one anyway.

She lifted her arm in the air and pushed her boob up slightly, then let it fall. *Even the girls are getting firmer,* she noticed with satisfaction. Turning back to squarely face the mirror, she ran her hands over the developing six-pack and froze in consternation as she noticed the Yeti living between her legs. *It's not like it really matters since there isn't anyone likely to see it anytime soon.* The corners of her mouth curled upward as she pictured getting two eyes and a nose tattooed right above the hairline, and growing her bush into the equivalent of a biker beard. She quickly banished the idea and made a note to take care of that housekeeping problem soon, then hopped in the shower.

***

Alexander occupied himself with preparing some snacks while Tina showered. It was always distracting for him, knowing she was just feet away, naked, but he forced his mind onto other things. Sliced meats and cheeses, as well as fruit, were on the platter he set on the table in the home theater area of his apartment. The *Clos du Bois* Merlot was open and should be ready to pour by the time she finished up.

While it would be a stretch to say that he had his emotions in check where she was concerned, he *had* found a middle ground that allowed him to simply enjoy being around her. When she had first asked him to train her in the martial arts, and specifically in the use of short blades, he had panicked. Being in such close and constant proximity was going to be a challenge...and he knew it.

Still, she was like a breath of fresh air for him. Tina's naivete and chaotic personality drew him like a moth to a flame. It had been a very long time since he had looked at the world the way she did, and getting to experience life through her eyes was working wonders for him. To say that she was mercurial would have been an understatement. She flitted about without a thought for how she might be perceived, and he couldn't help but laugh at her antics.

*Have I ever been that young and carefree?* Alexander wondered. *If so, I certainly don't remember it.* That's not to say that she didn't have any negative quirks...she did. It didn't take much to spark that temper she kept barely restrained at the best of times, but those stoked fires also spoke to him since it was something that they shared. His wolf traits meant he was never far from slipping into a rage at the slightest provocation. However, over the years, he had become adept at keeping it under control.

Tina was an inquisitive person, and since she didn't filter herself much, she came across as rude...maybe brash was a better word. Even so, it was genuine curiosity, not just a way to fill in conversations. Alexander could work with that, and her abrasive manner didn't bother him in the slightest. As long as she wanted to know the answer to a question, he would happily indulge it and provide the solution. Too many people these days either were afraid to look stupid or just didn't care enough to ask.

To be honest, he found Tina *interesting* in a very fundamental way. His lifestyle didn't lend itself to much human interaction, and he desperately missed it. Maintaining a safe distance from any form of personal entanglement and ensuring that very few people knew who Alexander Matthews really was, had become a way of life for him...and just maybe, that had been a mistake. He wasn't quite prepared to acknowledge that as fact yet, but he was at least entertaining the idea.

***

The Blu-ray was queued up and waiting when she finally exited the bathroom and made her way to the couch. Her hair was still damp, hanging loose down her back, and she had changed into a different pair of yoga pants and a *Ramones* t-shirt. The fact that she was braless was plain to see, especially considering the shirt was a little on the tight side. He smiled when he saw the logo, and she glanced down at her chest. "What?" she asked suspiciously.

"I was just admiring your taste in music," he said.

Her eyes narrowed a bit. "Are you *sure* it was my shirt you were eyeballing?"

Alexander laughed as he stood up. "Even if it wasn't, I would never admit it. My turn to sluice off, back in a few."

***

*I know you wouldn't,* she thought wistfully. She shook her head to break that chain of thought and wandered over to peruse his bookshelves. Tina was amazed at how comfortable she had become with showering at his place. In the beginning, it had been harder. In fact, the first time he had offered, she had flat out refused, horrified by the idea, but over time had come to accept that it really was just an innocent offer, and not some twisted plot to get into her pants.

Not only did she train in his apartment now, but she also ate quite a few of her meals here, as well as the movie nights like this one. It was nice. Granted, it smacked too much of being in the friend zone, but he seemed to *get* her in a way that no one ever had before. Tina thought she would miss having an active social life, but surprisingly, that really wasn't the case. The time spent with Alexander seemed to more than make up for what now seemed like a fruitless search for *something.* What that was she wasn't sure, but she was positive she wouldn't find it in some random guy met in a club or by swiping an app. Tina was gaining insight into what her aunt had told her that first day of work, and she was beginning to understand how Maria could have dedicated so much of herself to this job. *It didn't do anything to relieve the horniness, though,* she thought and grinned to herself. *Ah, well. Can't have everything, I guess.*

. The first bookcase she came to was filled with hardbacks covering archaeology, anthropology, and interestingly enough, mythology. They were divided into no particular order that she could see, but randomly pulling them out, she found Sumer, Mycenae, and the Celts all represented. She could tell by their fragile condition that some of these books were quite old.

The next set of shelves was exclusively dedicated to languages. She shook her head as she remembered what he had told her in Paris. All seemed well-used, but she felt no need to examine them.

She shifted to another and was amused to find that all of the books contained on these shelves were science fiction and fantasy. Tina recognized several of the books and authors. It would appear that her boss only collected first edition hardcovers, and many of them were signed by the author.

"Would you like to see signed first edition copies of *Lord of the Rings*?" he breathed from just behind her.

Startled, she spun in place and yelled, "Stop doing that! You scare the shit out of me every time you sneak up on me."

Straightening to his full height and glaring imperiously down the length of his nose, he said, "I do not sneak, madam." Then a sniff. "I cannot be held responsible for your failure to take note of your surroundings in a competent manner."

"So, like I said, *sneaking*."

He just stared at her for a few seconds. "You never answered my question. Would you like to see the Tolkien books?"

Tina relented. "Yes, please. I've never seen or held an original before."

Alexander smiled as he reached over her head and pulled three books from the top shelf. His fingers caressed the bindings prior to depositing them in her hands. "I didn't know you liked this type of reading material." He followed a beat later with, "Actually, I didn't know you read *anything* that didn't include a lot of pictures and over-sized type."

"Ooooh, you are so lucky I'm holding books worth more than my annual salary," she growled.

He smirked down at her. "Not quite…individually, but close." Alexander walked over to the bottle of wine and poured two glasses.

"What, no warning to be careful with them?"

He appeared to consider her question seriously for a moment, shrugged, and said with complete sincerity, "No. I trust you."

Tina was stunned. Four simple words, and yet they conveyed so much meaning. She walked to the couch and very carefully set two of the books down while she gently opened *The Fellowship of the Ring* and read the first line to herself. She looked up at Alexander as he set her wineglass on the table, far enough away from the books to be safe, awestruck by it all. "All three books are signed?"

A nod from him. "We can skip the movie tonight if you like." He held up an index finger. "On one condition."

"What would that be?"

"You have to read to me from that book."

Tina grinned at him. "I think that can be arranged."

***

Eyes closed, and head resting on the back of the couch, Alexander listened as Tina read aloud. She was quite good at it, seldom faltering, and adding inflection where needed. He was moderately impressed, to tell the truth. A yawn interrupted her recitation, and he turned his head to glance her way. He could tell she was tired but fighting it.

Alexander picked up the bottle of wine and checked the level of its contents, then poured the majority into his glass, and just a bit into hers.

He reached over and gently removed the book from her hands. "I think you have worked hard enough tonight, young lady. We can continue this another time."

She smiled gratefully at him and drained the remaining wine in her glass. "I'm so tired…but I totally have to pee." She got up and walked to the bathroom.

Alexander picked up the Tolkien books, put them back into place on the shelf, and reseated himself on one end of the couch. When Tina came back, she sat next to him and leaned her head onto his shoulder, pulling her legs up onto the sofa next to her. "Just gonna close my eyes for a minute, OK?" she murmured.

He put his arm around her shoulders and snugged her closer. Within seconds she was sleeping. They sat there for almost an hour, Alexander simply enjoying feeling her so near. It was only when he noticed that his shirt was beginning to get wet as she drooled on him that he decided to move her to his bed. Once he had her tucked in, he took off the shirt with the wet-spot and tossed it in the hamper.

He brushed a wisp of hair off her cheek, turned off the lights, and went to sleep on the sofa.

***

Try as he might, Alexander just couldn't get to sleep. His thoughts roiled around his head like a tornado, troubling him greatly. Why was he so attracted to this brash young woman? Granted, she had a supermodel's good looks, but it was more than that; he had known many beautiful women over the years, and none had affected him this way. At some unconscious level, the two of them just *clicked.* The *why* was what eluded him.

He was conflicted. On the one hand, he wanted to protect her, keep her safe from the world, even lock her up in a gilded cage. And on the other, he was drawn to her, intoxicated by who and what she was. This girl was a danger to him, to everything he had done to isolate himself from ordinary humanity. How could he justify endangering all that he had built? All of his carefully hidden secrets were at risk...and he almost didn't care.

Her pure naïve joy in the world, in making discoveries, was an almost forgotten part of his past. Alexander found himself living vicariously through her eyes, reexperiencing the wonders of the universe. For Tina, each day was to be savored, not endured. It was refreshing to his cynical old soul. He found that he needed that innocence and joy to continue to be a part of his life ...even if it *was* at a distance.

Alexander had spent so long shutting the world out and living in a prison of his creation that he had forgotten what it was like to have a life that was inclusive, and not exclude everyone and everything. And he *craved* it like a starving vampire craved blood.

This girl—and from his one-hundred fiftyish years perspective, she *was* a girl—had destroyed a century worth of brooding isolationism in a matter of mere months. Mentally sighing, he acknowledged that there was little he could do about it short of terminating her employment...and he just didn't think he could bring himself to do that. Like it or not, she was a part of his life now, and one he refused to let go of. Basically, he was fucked, and he knew it.

***

Tina slowly rose to consciousness. Something wasn't right, but she couldn't put her finger on it immediately. As time went by, she realized she wasn't in her bed. In fact, she smelled Alexander. His scent permeated the pillow her head was lying on. She smiled lazily; it was…nice. Her eyes snapped wide open, and she rolled over to make sure he wasn't actually in bed with her. *Jesus Christ, Tina. You're making a habit of sleeping in his rooms,* she chastised herself.

She sat up, curious as to where he might be. At first, she didn't see him, but motion out of the corner of her eye drew her attention. His skin glistened with sweat as he swept through a series of moves, the sword he was using blurred in figure eights, then suddenly lashing out periodically. He was barefoot and only wearing a tight pair of biker-type shorts, his breathing shallow, frequently gusting out as he went on the offensive. The medallion on a chain around his neck slapped into his wet skin as he advanced and retreated across the floor. She watched raptly. It was like a deadly dance, but it was also strangely beautiful at the same time.

It ended all too soon, and he noticed her watching while he was toweling off his face. He smiled at her, teeth gleaming in the bright sunlight streaming through the windows. Alexander quickly wiped down the leaf-shaped blade, which Tina now realized she didn't recognize, before he placed it back onto one of the weapon racks near the dojo.

"Hungry?" he asked as he walked toward the bed she was sitting in, knees beneath her arms, and chin resting on them.

"Starving," she replied.

"Sweet. Let me grab a quick shower, and I'll make breakfast while you rinse off."

She smiled at him as he walked by, went into the vast walk-in closet only to return holding some clothes, and entered the bathroom, closing the door behind him.

***

When Alexander had finished his morning ablutions and gotten dressed, he set out a new toothbrush, still in its packaging, on the surface of the sink, and a button-up shirt just in case she wanted something fresher than the tee she had worn to bed. He grinned ruefully as he thought, *Sorry, kiddo, I don't wear boxers, so you are stuck with the panties you're in.*

He ruffled his still-damp hair into a semblance of order and opened the door. Alexander jerked a thumb in the direction of the bathroom and said, "You're up. I left a new toothbrush on the counter, and a shirt you can borrow if you want."

She raised an inquiring eyebrow at him. "Do so many women pass through your bedroom that you keep spare toothbrushes on hand?"

His cheeks burned in sudden embarrassment. "No. I warned you I was anal. I buy in bulk when I go to Costco."

Laughter trailed her as she passed by him and disappeared into the bathroom.

***

Breakfast was scrambled eggs, toast, coffee, and orange juice. As they finished up and he placed the dirty dishes in the sink, Alexander asked, "Do you have any plans for today? I know it's Saturday, but if you aren't busy, I would like to take you somewhere fun."

Tina gave him the hairy-eyeball and said, "*Fun*, fun? Or Alexander fun?"

"Maybe a little of both?" he answered sheepishly.

She considered that briefly. "OK, fine. But I want to go home and change first."

He allowed that he could work with that, and requested that she wear comfortable jeans and shoes that she wouldn't care about getting dirty.

She gave him some side-eye at that but said she would. They agreed that he would pick her up in front of her apartment building in forty-five minutes, and she bounced over to his private lift and was gone.

Alexander disappeared into his dressing room briefly, only to reappear carrying a large black tactical bag, which he set on top of the bed. He reached behind the headboard and toggled a switch that released secret compartments built into the base of the sleeping platform. The drawer closest to the headboard contained an impressive array of blades and pistols. He selected two of the pistols and several magazines, then placed them on the mattress. The second drawer held several AR-style rifles. He grabbed a short-barreled version with a folding stock and a full-size model with a medium-size scope.

More magazines joined the weapons on the bed.

Re-toggling the switch closed the compartments, and as they were doing so, he went back into the dressing room and walked out holding two inside-the-waistband holsters. The bag was considerably heavier when he was done, and he set it on the floor near the elevator. The last task he performed was to change into black tactical cargo pants, a *SIG Sauer* logo t-shirt, and black jungle boots.

Quickly glancing around to make sure everything was copacetic, he nodded and grabbed the bag prior to entering the lift and punching the button for the sub-basement. Once the doors opened, he quickly made his way to a black BMW 850CSI and settled the tactical bag in the trunk. Seated comfortably behind the wheel, he reached out and patted the dash gently. "Sorry it's been so long, baby, but you get to go for a ride today."

He exited the garage, and within minutes was parked in front of Tina's apartment building. When she opened the lobby doors, she was greeted with the sight of him leaning against the side of the car, arms crossed nonchalantly across his chest, and wearing yet another pair of high-end sunglasses.

Tina was shaking her head as she approached the car. "Are any of your cars normal?"

His quick grin said it all. "Not if I can help it. Besides, this is a classic."

Both strapped securely into the car, and he had them rolling down the street. Simultaneously, Alexander continued to regale her with useless information. "She has a 5.6L V12 engine, a finely tuned suspension, and I'm sad to report that they only made this model for four years, ending in 1996. Consider her to be the older sister to your M4."

Tina patted the oversized brick phone located between the seats. "More like the grandmother."

His face contorted in pain, and he grabbed his chest with one hand. "Don't listen to her, baby, she knows not what she says. I'll have you know that this phone is an original that came with the car. If I wanted to, I could likely still pay for the service."

"Why the hell would you want to? That thing is ginormous."

He sniffed loudly. "Not the point. I could if I *wanted* to."

Alexander turned on the CD player and increased the volume as the first notes of Robert Cray's *Strong Persuader* album filled the car. He turned his head and began singing along with the lyrics, and while Tina pretended to cover her ears and crouch down in the seat, but he could see the small smile of enjoyment that she tried to hide.

He finally relented after the seventh song ended, and he powered off the CD player. "I love that album. I've seen him in small venues three times, and every show was amazing."

"I liked it. What is the name of the band?"

"If you want, I can get you a copy. That was Robert Cray, and this CD is easily his best. Some people will tell you it isn't true blues, but usually, I'd rather listen to him than someone like Muddy Waters or Robert Johnson."

They rode the rest of the way in companionable silence until he pulled the car into the driveway of his country house. As he killed the ignition, he turned to her and said, "No one knows about this place except for your aunt, and now you. As a matter of fact, it isn't even on the list of company assets. I'd appreciate it if it stayed that way."

She nodded her head. "I can do that. Why so secret, though?"

Alexander smirked at her. "It's my zombie apocalypse bolt-hole."

She got out of the car as he went to the trunk and grabbed the bag. He led her to a large metal outbuilding, set back about seventy-five yards from the main house. Tina wasn't sure what it was used for as it was relatively narrow, maybe fifty feet wide, but almost one-hundred yards long. She quirked an eyebrow at him and said. "Bowling alley?"

"Hah! Not quite."

Alexander opened the rugged-looking door and waved Tina in, hitting the lights as he entered behind her. As her eyes adjusted, she realized it was an indoor shooting range. He could feel the intense side-eye as he stood beside her, but he chose to ignore it. "Right this way, Madam."

He could tell that whatever else she had expected to be doing today, this most definitely wasn't it. Her resigned footsteps as she reluctantly followed him, amused Alexander. If he had to guess, she had probably never fired a weapon before.

He opened a locker and tossed her the hearing protection and ballistic glasses she would need. The attractive brunette looked at him skeptically, but slid a band off her wrist and pulled her long wavy hair into a ponytail. Several boxes of ammunition were added to the bag at his feet, then they made their way over to the shooting bench.

He pulled out one of the pistols and held it pointed at the ground. He showed her how to lock the slide back, ejected the magazine, and visually inspected the bore to ensure that no cartridge was present. "This is a SIG Sauer P320 XFIVE. This one is chambered for .40 S&W caliber, and each magazine holds fourteen rounds."

He frowned down at the weapon in his hand for a second then looked up to meet her eyes. "I know that you have probably heard this a thousand times in movies, and maybe even from someone you know, but I cannot reiterate this point enough. You never, ever, point a weapon at anyone, even if it's unloaded. The *only* time it is permissible is when you intend to take someone's life. And if the situation has reached that point, then you don't hesitate, you don't think about your actions, you just aim and pull the trigger. Life or death may depend upon it. Yours. Do you understand?"

A subdued Tina lowered her gaze to the handgun. "I think so. I'm not sure if I could do something like that, though."

"Fair enough. None of us ever do until the moment arises, but if you train hard enough, burn it into muscle memory, then more often than not your subconscious will take over and do it for you."

For the next twenty minutes, Alexander covered range safety, the specific operations and functionality of the handgun, how to load the magazines, and demonstrated the proper stance and grip. In the end, he pointed at the safety glasses and indicated that she should put on the hearing protection. He attached a target and ran it out to twenty-five feet, then gave her one magazine, which she inserted and chambered a round as he had shown her earlier.

Tina nervously took her stance and aimed over the sights as instructed, then pulled the trigger. She was startled as the weapon bucked in her hands, and also at the sheer volume of the discharge. Alexander had her clear and safe the pistol before running the paper target back to where they were standing. She could clearly see the bullet hole in the top right corner of the target.

Alexander pointed to it and said gently, "*Squeeze* the trigger, don't jerk it. This is what happens when you do that." He then explained that she would be going through a process to zero the weapon to her needs. He affixed a red dot approximately one inch in diameter to the center of the target and ran it back out.

"OK, when I tell you to, I want you to pick the SIG back up, insert the magazine, and slowly squeeze the trigger five times, taking time to aim between shots. Try to keep your grip and stance the same as you do so. Aim at the red dot, ensuring that you are looking down the iron sights. When all five shots are fired, clear and safe the weapon, then step back from the firing line. Clear?" She nodded that she understood.

He gave her the go-ahead, and she tried to do as Alexander instructed. This time when he pulled the target back, there was another hole high and to the right, but the rest were closer to the center, although still off by about three inches. He made an adjustment to the sights and had her repeat the process after he covered each bullet hole with a white dot. They did this twice more until Tina was consistently hitting close to the zero mark. However, she still had the occasional *flyer* as he called them.

Once the SIG was zeroed for her use, he had her shoot through a magazine, swap it out for another, and empty it as well. As he replaced targets in between sessions, she could tell that the groups she was creating were getting smaller…still not good enough, as he demonstrated with the other pistol he had brought. But better.

"How are your hands and trigger finger feeling?" he asked after an hour.

"Hmmm, maybe a little sore, but not too bad." Alexander nodded and reached into the bag and pulled out a strange-looking pair of gloves. They had padding on the knuckles and ridged surfaces on the fingers. He handed them to her and said to use them for the rest of the day.

"Let's take a short break. Grab some water from the fridge over by the lockers if you want."

When she wandered back after doing just that, he had put the pistol in what he called an inside-the-waistband concealed carry holster. Slipping it through the belt she was wearing, he adjusted the fit until it was snug in the small of her back. He told her that she would carry it that way for the rest of the session, so she could get used to how it might affect her balance as they performed various exercises.

Tina noted that his handgun was different than the one she was using. He explained that he was using a Walther PPQ M2 .45 caliber. It had fewer rounds per magazine, but compensated with greater *knock-down.* He knew a lot of what he had told her today had gone straight over her head, but she truly seemed to be enjoying the time at the range. Initially, she had been somewhat timid because it was obvious that no one had ever taken the time to teach her how to shoot. Guns were scary and unnecessary, according to a large portion of people in the world. Yet after spending only an hour or so with Alexander, she seemed to be changing that worldview.... As he had told her, weapons had some inherent dangers, but that could be mitigated by using proper safety procedures, and the single greatest threat came from the *user.*

He prepped another target and ran it out almost to the end of the range. Alexander reached down into the bag and pulled out what was obviously a military-style rifle. "This is a SIG Sauer 716 G2 rifle. It fires a 7.62mm round and is extremely reliable."

They once again went through operating procedures, and he explained how the scope worked. One section of the waist-level bench was raised, revealing a yoga mat and two sandbags that were on the floor. He helped her get into a proper *prone* position. Alexander had Tina adjust the sandbags until the barrel of the rifle sat at the right height when she snugged the stock into her shoulder. She observed that the bullets being loaded into the plastic magazines were much larger than what had been used in the pistol.

Again, he had her go through the zeroing procedure. When the scope was dialed in, she fired several magazines while she got comfortable with the weapon. By the time he had her safe the rifle, her shoulder was starting to get sore, but he insisted that she handle one more weapon. According to him, it was an AR-15 set up very similarly to the M4 rifle used in the military. There was a different type of sight called a *Red Dot,* and the stock folded to make the whole thing smaller.

Additionally, there was a handgrip toward the end of the barrel that allowed her to control the rise of the barrel and more easily aim it. She learned that this weapon fired a smaller NATO standardized round in 5.56mm.

Instead of having her fire from the prone position this time, he allowed her to stand. He ran the target out to fifty feet, and she established a zero relatively quickly. Unlike the more massive rifle, this one was light and shorter overall, which made it easier for her to use. While she fired it, she realized there was considerably less kick, which was evident from the look of relief on her face, as her shoulder was almost certainly a bit sore.

Using the red dot sight proved to be almost intuitive, and her shots were hitting very close to where she wanted them to, spanning only a couple of inches on the target.

All too soon, Alexander stopped her and determined that they had trained enough for one day. He took the weapons she had used and put them in an empty locker near the entrance, along with the shooting glasses and hearing protection. "These are yours if you decide you want to continue learning how to use them. If that is the case, I will show you how to clean them next time, along with the proper maintenance each needs to stay in good working order."

She nodded thoughtfully.

"I come out to the range several times a month, and you are welcome to join me if you want."

Once he had locked and secured the building, they got back into the car and headed into town. Twenty minutes into the ride, a visibly troubled Tina asked, "Alexander, why did you take me out to your place and teach me how to use these weapons?"

She chuckled a bit, then said, "Don't get me wrong, I totally enjoyed myself after a while, and I'm feeling pretty badass, but what was the purpose?"

"Other than just for the fun of it?

"Yeah."

He turned to look at her with a level gaze. "The world is not always a safe place, and sometimes a knife just isn't good enough."

Tina rode in silence, left to consider what he had said...and what he hadn't.

# Chapter 10

*"....As time went by, the technology they had brought with them began to wear out, becoming increasingly more difficult to maintain and manufacture. The decision was made to triage what was most essential and to come up with other, less technical, and more sustainable methods to perform day-to-day tasks...."*

**Excerpt from the diary of Alexander Matthews**

**May 1962, Beirut, Lebanon**

*The elusive scent continued to lead Alexander along the Rue de Phenicie. The night air was filled with music and laughter as people enjoyed themselves at any of the many clubs that lined the street. This town was a jet-setter's dream with its five-star hotels, happening nightlife, and cosmopolitan feel. It was difficult not to be drawn into its seductive embrace.*

*Still, he had caught a faint trace of something he had never experienced before, and curiosity pulled him along in its wake. He was getting closer—his nose told him that much—and his target was definitely female. Alexander's eyes scanned the raucous crowd, looking for any sign that would pin down who he was searching for. He stepped into the shadows of an alley and continued to watch. She had to be here...somewhere.*

*"Would you care to explain why you are stalking me?" a melodious voice asked quietly from just behind him.*

*Alexander turned around slowly, hands in plain sight. The statuesque raven-haired beauty who stood before him almost took his breath away. Mediterranean features including olive-colored skin, dark eyes, and strong nose somehow combined perfectly in this woman. She was nearly as tall as he was, and the form-fitting dress and heels accentuated her look.*

*He smiled guiltily. “I apologize if I frightened you, that was not my intent.”*

*Her eyes bored into his, looking for any hint of dishonesty. “Then what* was *your intent, if I may be so bold as to ask?”*

*Alexander hesitated briefly, then shrugged and plunged ahead. “What are you? I’ve never scented anyone like you before.”*

*Her laughter tinkled musically on the air. “I take it subtlety is not one of your strongest suits.” She leaned toward him and inhaled deeply as she closed her eyes. “Wolf…but different. You aren’t like the others. What are* you?”

*It was his turn to laugh. “I could show you, but perhaps a busy street isn’t the best place for such a reveal.”*

*“True. But it* would *be amusing,” she replied. “Still, you haven’t answered my question.”*

*“I’m a throwback.” She looked confused at his words. “Hmmm, are you familiar with the animals that lived during the last ice age?”*

*She shook her head. “Science has never been of much interest to me.”*

*“OK. Let’s just say that a species of wolf lived in America at that time, and that is what I shift into.” He leaned back against the wall of a building. “My turn. What are you?”*

*“I am a Child of the Forest. My kind has not interacted with humanity much, but I found the life of seclusion to be uninspiring.”*

*“Is that like an elf?” he asked.*

*“Pffft, similar in some ways maybe, but no, not an elf.” She wrinkled her nose in distaste as she answered him. “We have always lived in the lands surrounding the Mediterranean, never venturing far from its shores.”*

*“Fascinating. I have never had the pleasure of meeting one of your people before. Thank you.”*

*The Cheshire Cat grin she gave him should have been a warning, but he failed to heed it.*

*The alley was flooded with pheromones generated by the woman, who took his arm companionably. “Would you like to join me? I promise it will be mutually pleasurable.”*

*Dazed and overcome by the chemical cocktail, all he could do was nod in agreement as she led him to her hotel room. She delivered on her promise in every way.*

*Only much later, and after a great deal of research, did he discover that the Children of the Forest had been designed and bred as concubines for the less-bigoted Anunna....*

***

Alexander eyed the inventory spread out before him. Based on Tina's reaction when he gifted her the expensive watch, he would have to be very careful about what he chose as her Christmas present.

Many of the items would be perfect for her. Still, given their value, they would probably send her reeling and cause consternation he'd rather avoid. That being said, he set aside the necklace with the large emerald, reluctantly. Which meant that the sapphire earrings had to go as well. Almost all of the jewelry they had in stock was either antique, expensive due to the materials used, valuable due to the culture and period made, or some combination of all of these.

A growing sense of desperation was building in his chest as he scanned what lay before him, ...and then his eyes settled on a matched set of bracelets. *Yes. Yes, these will do very nicely,* he thought as he picked them up and examined them. Not overly valuable, and an impulse buy on one of his trips to India, they were still antiques and beautiful in their own right.

*Now I just have to find a box and wrap the gift....*

***

Tina was pressed firmly against him as he led her around the dojo. While still not what he would call a natural dancer, she was quickly picking it up, although she spent far too much time thinking about it rather than relaxing and going with the flow.

The floral scent of her shampoo wafted to his nostrils, and he drank it in as he reveled in how nice it felt to hold her. She glanced up at him with a gleeful smile, a slight sheen of sweat sparkling on her skin...and almost stumbled when she lost her concentration.

"Focus, Tina. Focus."

"I'm trying," she responded breathlessly.

"I know you are. Another couple of months and you'll be a pro."

"You think so?"

Alexander pulled her into a dip, grinning at her surprise. "Trust me."

She giggled as he brought her back upright and continued with the lesson. Unfortunately, the proximity, and his inability to ignore the scent of her arousal, got the better of him. A growing uncomfortableness in his pants was indication enough of that.

Tina glanced down, then grinned devilishly at him. "Focus, Alexander. Focus."

***

Christmas was just five days away, and Alexander was getting moody. In many ways, the holidays were the hardest times for him since he had no one to share them with. This year was even worse than usual because of Tina, and he had decided to leave town and spend the next three weeks in Hawaii. At least there, it wouldn't *really* feel like Christmas…it's hard to get into the holiday spirit when you are lazing in a tropical paradise.

He walked through the office carrying his bags and dropped them near the doors, then walked over to Tina and handed her a small, intricately wrapped Christmas present.

"Please don't open this until at least Christmas Eve."

Tina looked mortified. "Alexander, I didn't get you anything…."

He smiled indulgently down at her. "That's OK, it's not like I really *need* anything."

"Still, I feel bad."

"Don't. Enjoy your time off with your family, and if anything comes up, you know my number."

She smiled brightly. "I also know where you'll be since I booked all your reservations. That being said, I'm pretty sure things will be quiet, and I won't have to intrude on you."

"You don't intrude," he said fondly. "Trample well-thought-out plans into the ground, maybe, but never intrude."

She pointed a finger at him, imperiously. "You should leave before you give me ideas. At least *you* don't have to spend quality time with loud nieces and nephews, nosy siblings, and parents who want to know when I'll '*bring a nice boy home*,'" Tina said exasperatedly.

He looked wistful as he replied, "No. I don't have to do any of those things."

***

Midnight Mass was over, and everyone was gathered around the living room talking excitedly about morning when all the presents would be opened after breakfast. The kids had gone to bed reluctantly, and only the adults were still awake. She had been quiet all evening, finding it hard to get into the spirit of the holiday. It just didn't feel right without Alexander being around. She knew she was being silly, but he was part of her daily routine, and there was an Alexander-sized void that had opened up since he had gone to Hawaii.

She idly spun the gift he had given her in her hands as she thought about it. They spent so much time together: morning coffee, lunch nearly every day, whether he cooked it or ordered it, and frequently dinner after sparring. Lately, it had even been Friday night movies and Saturdays at his private gun range. Tina stiffened in her chair as she came to the realization that she missed him, no, she *liked* him, probably more than she should.

Her mother noticed Tina was not mentally with them, and came over to where she sat.

"Are you OK, dear?" she asked as she rubbed Tina's shoulders. "You've been preoccupied all night.

Tina put on a brave smile for her mother. "I'm fine, Mom. Just have a lot on my mind."

"Does the *lot on your mind* have a name?" was the teasing reply.

"Maybe. But I don't want to talk about it. Please?"

"If that's what you want, dear, just remember I'm here if you need to talk," her mother reassured her.

"Thanks, Mom." Tina noticed that her Aunt Maria was looking at her knowingly, a sad smile on her face.

***

The warm sand squishing grittily between his toes as he stood barefoot in the surf only served to remind Alexander that it was Christmas day. Unable to help himself, he had checked the weather in Spokane and was not surprised to find it was a balmy 15 degrees Fahrenheit. Six inches of fresh snow had fallen overnight.

He wondered what Tina was doing at the moment and whether she had liked his gift. Alexander had picked the antique Mughal bracelets up on a trip to India some forty years ago, and they had been sitting in one of the vaults gathering dust since then. Neither piece of jewelry qualified as an antiquity, but they had caught his eye as he perused the wares in the market, so he had bought them. He suspected that they had graced the wrists of some minor nobility in the not-so-distant past, and would look good on Tina. Alexander couldn't remember what he had paid for the bracelets, but he had appraised them as he was wrapping the box. They might be valued at two-thousand dollars on today's market, on a good day. His lips quirked up in a semi-smile; not even *she* could bitch about that, not to mention, the word *Cartier* was nowhere to be found.

***

The tremble in her hands as she held the bracelets nearly caused Tina to drop them in shock. They were beautiful, and she knew that he had put a lot of thought into the gift. Obviously, they were antique, but she had no idea just how old they were. She frowned as she realized it would probably be a good idea to learn more about the business she was now in. No doubt Alex would be more than happy to teach her.

"Those are lovely, dear," Maria murmured from just behind her shoulder. "Seventeenth century Mughal if I'm not mistaken."

"How do you even know this stuff, Aunt Maria?"

A soft chuckle. "I got tired of feeling stupid every time I saw something in the collection, and I decided to do something about it. I was still learning when I retired."

Tina snorted ruefully. "I know, right? I mean, I know a coin when I see one, but is it Roman? Greek? No idea, and it pisses me off. I'm not used to feeling inadequate."

Maria patted her arm consolingly. "You may have to get used to it. Some of what Alexander has in those vaults pre-dates civilization as we know it. The sheer breadth and depth of his knowledge astonishes me to this day."

Tina nodded thoughtfully. "I didn't even get him a gift, you know. What kind of an ass does that make me?"

"Well, it's not like he actually needs more stuff," Maria told her.

"That's beside the point; I should have remembered."

Maria looked at her, speculatively. "Why do I have the feeling that this isn't about you forgetting to get him a gift?"

Tina blew out a frustrated breath. "Because it's not? I miss him, Aunt Maria." She gestured around the house filled with Christmas decorations and excited kids and adults. "I want to enjoy this, all of it, but I can't help but wonder what he's doing right now. It just feels like something big is missing."

Maria whispered, "You've got it bad, kiddo."

Tina's shoulders drooped, and she sagged into the loveseat.

***

Alexander looked up curiously as the knock sounded on the door to his bungalow. He wasn't expecting anyone, and had not ordered room service. He walked over and pulled the door open. His eyebrows nearly disappeared into his hairline in surprise as he looked down at an obviously jetlagged and disheveled Tina.

Her expression was hard to read, but a fear of rejection was definitely part of it. "I thought you were spending the holidays with your family?"

"I was. I did," she blurted out. "Can I come in, please? These bags are heavy."

He stepped out of the way and waved for her to enter. As she walked by, Alexander noticed she was wearing his gift. He smiled in delight.

Tina had stopped partway into the bungalow, standing in the middle of the floor with her bags, back turned to him. "Alexander?"

"Hmmm?"

"There aren't any rooms available. Can I stay with you?" Her voice broke a little on the last words.

He strode over and relieved her of the luggage. "Of course you can, Tina."

"Thank you," she replied in a small voice.

Dragging the bags over to the dresser, he teased, "Judging by the weight of these, I'm going to have to give you most of the closet and at least half the dresser...."

"Alexander?"

"Yes, Tina?"

"Don't be an ass."

***

The private bungalow only had one bed, since he had not been anticipating company. Not that he couldn't sleep on the comfortable couch, although it was too short for his long legs. *Ah well, c'est la vie,* he thought as he strolled along the Maui beach while Tina took a nap. It was well worth the discomfort just to have her here with him. It was amazing how quickly his mood had improved when she surprised him by flying all the way to Hawaii.

He was sure there was more to the story than he was likely to get out of her. Stubborn didn't even begin to describe that girl. He had to admit that her stubbornness was one of the things he found most appealing about her. Once she got her teeth into something, she rarely let go of it until she had beaten it into submission. There just wasn't any *quit* in that woman, and while occasionally it was a complete pain in the ass, it was also a good indication of her inherent strength.

While he was more than pleased that she had cut her vacation short and had landed in his lap, it also presented him with a problem. He was still conflicted where she was concerned. Being in such proximity to Tina certainly wouldn't make things any easier on him. He sighed heavily, but not having her around had been driving him crazy too.

***

Tina was in the shower shaving her legs and armpits, as well as a bikini line. There were times when being Italian truly sucked. It wouldn't do to appear all *nature girl* on the beaches of Maui...especially not with Alexander. Her lips curled into a smile at how horrified he would be if she walked out in a swimsuit, hair poking out everywhere, legs covered in fur, and her armpits looking like a patch of crabgrass. It would totally serve him right if she did just that. Truth be told, though, horrifying him was the last thing on her mind.

She rested her forehead against the cold tiles of the shower and let the water pound against her back. What the hell was she doing? When she hopped on the commercial flight in Spokane, Tina didn't even know if Alex would want to see her, much less allow her to spend the holidays being underfoot. She couldn't even make it for *three weeks*. How fucking pathetic was that? The fact that Aunt Maria understood and was sympathetic only made matters worse somehow.

All Tina knew for sure was that she had been miserable and hadn't wanted to mope around her family, ruining their happiness. He had been gracious about the whole thing, and Alex appeared to be glad to see her today...although perhaps a bit surprised. She hiccupped through the tears running down her face, laughing at the thought that this would make an excellent plotline for the Hallmark channel. Maria was right; she *did* have it bad.

She scrubbed her face angrily and told herself to quit stalling. The fact of the matter was that she was here now and would just have to make the best of it. It was not like he would toss her out on her ass...even if she probably deserved it. No. She would get ready and see what Alex had planned for the evening, and she would let the chips fall where they would.

***

Alexander stood there like a stunned ox when Tina walked onto the lanai. The coral-colored bikini and wrap suited her skin tone perfectly, and the dark wavy hair that she had combed back and to the side gently blew in the steady breeze coming in off the Pacific. She looked at him tentatively, unsure of herself, which was odd because Tina was never self-conscious.

He walked over to where she stood and lifted her chin with his right hand. Her eyes were puffy as if she had been crying, and he frowned at the thought of anything causing her pain. Tina pulled away, refusing to meet his eyes.

"Alexander, I…" she began.

"I understand, you don't have to say anything."

"How can you say that?" she challenged him with a jutted chin.

He thought about it for a moment. "What do you think I've been doing for the last week? If you had to make a guess, that is."

She had her arms crossed over her chest defensively as she responded, "I don't know, surfing maybe? Golf?"

The laugh exploded from him. "Golf? Seriously? I don't even own a set of clubs." His face sobered, and he continued, "Every day, every *single* day, I walked the beach and wondered what you were doing. When I had depressed myself enough, I would come back to the bungalow and sit here, staring at all the people enjoying themselves. I missed having you around, kiddo."

He heard her sharp intake of air at his words, and continued to stare out at the sun setting over the ocean. "I have spent many, many holidays alone, Tina, and it's always been fine…just the way things were, you know?" His shoulders lifted in a shrug. "But this year was different. I totally blame you," he teased.

She laughed. "Sure. Blame the hot girl."

Alexander turned back to face her, obviously troubled. "This is all new territory for me, Tina. I'm not sure how I even feel about the whole thing. Just know that I *am* glad you are here."

She nodded and slid up beside him, bumping his arm with her shoulder. "I can live with that. I missed you too."

His hand scrubbed through his hair roughly. "Let's just go with the flow and enjoy ourselves, OK?"

***

The pain from the crick in his neck woke Alexander early the next morning. The couch simply wasn't big enough for him to comfortably sleep on. He stood and tried to work the knot out as he walked to the service phone sitting on the desk. He placed an order for breakfast to be delivered in half an hour, then grabbed some clothes and headed into the bathroom to shower.

Alexander was exhausted, both mentally and physically. Having Tina here was bittersweet. On the one hand, he was no longer alone, which was a good thing. But on the other, he was facing a situation that he should never have allowed to happen in the first place. It had obviously taken a toll on her as well, and he felt like shit about that.

He stood under the showerhead and let the hot water beat down on him, lost in thought. One thing he knew for sure was that he could never, ever, tell her the truth. If she found out on her own, then so be it. Maria had handled the knowledge well enough after all...but would Tina? No, he couldn't risk it. Couldn't risk losing her. And if that meant keeping her at arm's length, then that was just the price he would have to pay. He knew he was being a selfish bastard, and since he was being honest with himself, he acknowledged that this was going to hurt Tina, but he just couldn't see another way forward.

Monsters were not supposed to have normal lives, normal relationships. He had felt that way from the first moment he realized what he had become. Over the years, he had even come to accept that fact. Unfortunately for him, he had never counted on the train-wreck that Tina had made of his carefully crafted and structured life. She hadn't intended it to be that way, no more than he did, but fate had taken note of them and decided to let the universe have its way. Had Tina been any sort of genetic freak like he was, then he would gladly make the leap, but the fact of the matter was that she wasn't. Nor would he wish that upon her.

Alexander shook his head angrily; no, he would just have to maintain a distance between them. Some things just weren't meant to be, and this was one of them. Heart aching in his chest, he stepped out of the shower and got ready to face the day.

***

Alex was pouring coffee for her when she stepped out of the bathroom. Breakfast was waiting on the small dining table, and it smelled delicious.

Tina smiled at him as she sat down and placed the napkin in her lap. "Good morning."

"Morning," he mumbled back.

She made a face at his response but shrugged it off. Sleeping on that short couch must have sucked. Tina decided to offer to share the bed. After all, this was his bungalow, and he shouldn't have to give it up just because she had crashed his vacation.

Tina tried to ignore the scowl he wore, but it was hard. Had this been a mistake? She was beginning to wonder. God knew she was glad to be here with him, and her family most likely was delighted she had taken her moodiness with her when she left. Her heart had gladdened last night as he had confessed that he had missed her, but she could also tell that it was hard for him to admit. Was he having second thoughts?

After fifteen minutes of tense silence, she dropped her spoon onto the plate that held a mostly consumed grapefruit. She sighed heavily, then decided to confront the elephant in the room head-on.

"Do you want me to leave?"

He looked startled. "What? No, not at all."

She leaned forward and glared at him. "Then what the hell is going on? Last night you seemed happy enough to see me. What's changed?"

Alexander slumped in his chair, groaning miserably, and set his coffee cup gently onto the table. "Nothing has changed…and *everything* has changed." He gazed thoughtfully at her. "You are going to need to be patient with me. I haven't had many people I could consider a friend over the years. Old habits are hard to break, especially for me…. Maria once called me *rigid,* and I guess she was right."

Holding onto her frayed patience with both hands, she replied, "I can do that, Alex, but please don't shut me out, and that's what this feels like right now."

He glanced up at her with anguish-filled eyes. "I'm not who you think I am, Tina. Please don't put too much faith in me."

"What the fuck does that even mean?" she demanded, even more confused.

"It means that I come with a lot of baggage, and the odd skeleton in the closet."

Her snort sounded loud in the room. "And you think I don't come with baggage? Dude, I could open a fucking store…."

Alexander laughed, and while the tension eased, it was still there. His gaze settled on her as if he was seeking an answer to a question that only he knew. After a few moments, he asked, "What is it that you want from me? How does this play out in your mind?"

Actively sitting on her temper, she replied in a dangerous voice, "What do you mean?"

Sensing he was on thin ice, he held his hands up placatingly. "I'm genuinely curious as to how you see *us*."

She blew out a breath, exasperation plain to be seen. "Oh-kaayy. I suppose that's a fair question. But if we're going to play this game, then you have to be completely honest with me, too."

A barely suppressed wince passed over his face. "Fair enough."

Tina leaned back in the chair and dived right in. "It's not exactly a secret that I like you…more than I should, and despite warnings not to let it happen." He started to respond, but she held a palm up toward him, cutting him off. "Let me finish; this is hard enough.

"You get me, Alexander, and in a way that is totally new to me. And I like to think that you have feelings for me, too. The time we spend together is *good*…comfortable. I don't have to pretend to be someone I'm not, and I love that." She paused, gathering her thoughts. "I understand that you think getting involved would be a bad idea, but don't you see? We already are in so many ways.

"I'd love nothing more than for this to become something more intimate, but if that's not in the cards, well, I guess I can live with that. Better friends than to wreck what already exists." Tina sat there, looking extremely vulnerable, and waiting for his response.

Alexander walked around the table and scooted a chair over to her side. He reached out and took her hand in his, then started talking.

"Thank you for that. I know it wasn't easy, and I ask that you let me get through what I have to tell you before interrupting." An impish grin split his face. "And we *both* know how hard that will be for you."

A wry smile and a bob of her head acknowledged that statement.

"I'm drawn to you as well, and it goes against *everything* I believe in. Bosses don't take advantage of their employees, and that is set in stone as far as I am concerned." He looked troubled before continuing. "Or at least that's how I used to think. You confuse me, Tina Ferrante, and constantly push me out of my comfort zone.

"I told you earlier that I'm not who you think I am, and I'm not, but for reasons that are my own, I won't elaborate on that. That being said, I want you to understand that I would like nothing more than to get to know you better.... It's just not possible for reasons I can't go into." His hand squeezed hers gently.

"All I can offer you right now is more of the same, and if you can handle that, then you are more than welcome to become an even bigger part of my life." He paused and let go of her hand. "If not, if that isn't *enough*, then I will understand if you decide to move on."

A rude snort greeted his words. "Like *that's* going to happen." She poked him firmly in the chest and continued. "That's not really what I wanted to hear, Alexander, and I can't claim to *understand*, exactly...but OK. I'm willing to operate under those conditions, for now. Just be forewarned that I will be looking for any chinks in that armor of yours and will ruthlessly exploit any I find."

He laughed in delight. "I look forward to it. Now, if we are done, can we please enjoy the weather and the beach? After all, we *are* in Hawaii...."

They spent the day wandering around the resort and talking about what they should do first. She even managed to talk him into snorkeling with her that afternoon.

***

Dinner was excellent and the two bottles of wine they consumed had put Tina into a mellow mood. Alex was fighting off regular yawns, and she could tell he was tired.

"Why don't you just go to bed?" she suggested.

"I don't want to bail on you like that. I am tired, though," he admitted reluctantly.

"Meh. Just stay on your side of the bed, and it will be fine."

Looking somewhat surprised, he said, "Are you sure? I can sleep on the couch again."

Tina chuckled. "It's fine, quit being a big baby, we're all adults here."

Alex conceded her point and disappeared into the bathroom long enough to change into a pair of pajama bottoms, then climbed into the right side of the bed and quickly fell asleep.

She watched him sleep as she finished the last of her wine, her thoughts taking her places that they shouldn't. Why wouldn't he make a move? Tina could tell he was attracted to her, so it had to be something else. Was crossing that line so hard for him? Maria had told her he never would, but she refused to believe that. No. It had to be something else, something he felt was insurmountable.

She drank the last of the wine, shook her head in confusion, and got ready for bed. When she slid between the sheets, she could feel the heat radiating off him. Tina mentally sighed and shifted over so she could lay her head onto his chest. Alex unconsciously slid his arm around her, and she snuggled into his embrace and drifted off.

***

Alexander was mortified. He had woken up to find that he was spooning Tina. But that wasn't the worst part, oh no, it was so much worse than that. His hand was cupping her breast through the t-shirt she was wearing, her nipple hard beneath his fingers. And as if that wasn't bad enough, he was also sporting morning-wood, which was currently poking menacingly into her backside.

He eased himself out of bed as stealthily as he could and dashed for the bathroom, where he took the first of many long, cold showers that would become routine over the next couple of weeks. What he failed to see was the satisfied grin that Tina had on her face as she pretended to be asleep.

***

It was New Year's Eve, and the fireworks display was in full force. Wailea had gone all out for the show, and people were stacked up anywhere they could find a place to stand. Tina was currently perched on his shoulders so she could have an unobstructed view. His hands gripped her upper thighs firmly, holding her in place even as she squirmed around in excitement. Alexander wished she would settle down…or that she was wearing more than a bikini bottom.

Tina alternately gripped his long hair like reins to stabilize herself, and threw both hands up into the air when she liked a particular set of fireworks. Her heels would thump his chest as she rocked back and forth in her excitement, and it was a good thing that she had taken her sandals off before mounting him like a horse.

The wine they had with dinner seemed to have lessened any inhibitions Tina may have had under normal conditions, and the free champagne that was handed out prior to the show had only added to the effect. Alexander wouldn't say she was drunk, per se, but she was definitely feeling no pain. He was almost jealous, but he had to really work hard at getting a buzz, the wolf metabolism burning it off almost as fast as he consumed alcohol. In most cases, it just wasn't worth the effort.

Providing Tina with a perch that put her over everyone else and allowed an unobstructed view was hardly taxing. Truthfully, she could sit there all night and he would barely notice. That being said, holding onto this squirming bundle of excitement was…distracting. More than distracting if he was honest with himself. The feel of her toned thighs between his hands and the warmth of her crotch that pressed against the back of his neck were practically instruments of torture as far as he was concerned. He just wished the fireworks show would end so that he could safely put her back onto the ground and gain some semblance of control over where his thoughts were leading him.

A final crescendo of explosions and brightly colored bursts announced the finale. The crowd clapped and cheered, then began to disperse into the shadows, no doubt seeking privacy and comfort in each other's arms. Alexander sighed deeply, then lifted Tina easily off his shoulders and lowered her to the ground in front of him. With a quick spin, Tina jumped up and wrapped her legs around his waist, threw her arms around his neck, and pulled his face in for a passionate kiss. For a moment, his body froze in consternation, then he returned the kiss just as forcefully. Tina moaned into his mouth and ground her hips into him, her intentions plain.

Alexander wanted nothing more than to surrender to what he was feeling, but a small, yet vocal part of his psyche reminded him that he couldn't allow this to happen. His hands reached up and gently removed her arms from around his neck as he pulled his head back, breaking the kiss. Her eyes shot open, searching his for answers, and then she sighed softly and slid down to stand on the beach.

Tina looked away, obviously embarrassed. "I'm sorry."

"Why?" he asked softly. "You've been very upfront about your feelings, and I would be lying if I said I didn't enjoy that kiss very much."

Her head turned back toward him. "But?"

"But...I just can't," he told her sadly.

***

To say that Tina was frustrated would be a severe understatement. The two weeks she had spent with Alex in Hawaii were amazing...in every way but one. Even though they had shared a bed the entire time, they hadn't actually *shared* it. He wanted her as much as she wanted him; his body couldn't lie about that. She grinned as she thought about waking up each day, his body pressed up to hers, and the daily erection that he always dashed off to get rid of before he thought she would know about it. She snorted in amusement *as if something that size could be hidden.* Had he even attempted to make a move, she would have thrown herself at him, but he didn't. The man should have joined a monastery; that kind of self-control was almost unheard of...and yet, here she was, completely unsatisfied. It was almost insulting.

Her aunt had warned her, told her not to get her hopes up. But had she listened? No. She had only herself to blame. Why couldn't she seem to be able to find and keep a good man?

Tina took out her phone and stared at it uncertainly. Finally, she jabbed at it and called her aunt.

"Hello?"

"I need your advice, Aunt Maria," she whispered mournfully into the phone.

"What's wrong, Tina?" her aunt said sharply.

"Alexander is pissing me off."

"Oh? How so?"

"I practically threw myself at him in Hawaii and he wouldn't bite."

"Oh, dear," Maria commiserated.

"We shared a bed for two weeks."

The sigh she heard spoke volumes.

"The only action I got from him was while he was asleep," she wailed miserably.

Maria chuckled as she said, "And by *action*, you mean?"

"Some minor groping and major morning-wood pressed into my ass…all while he was asleep," Tina replied. "Is there something wrong with me? Am I broken in some way?"

"No dear, you aren't broken. I was worried this might happen, Tina, and I *did* warn you."

"You did, and I should have listened, but I didn't."

"Did anything he said or may have done indicate why?"

"Not really, just said he wasn't who I thought he was, or some shit like that."

Her aunt was silent for a moment. "He does have secrets, Tina."

"What? Like he's a serial killer? He sacrifices small animals to Satan during the solstices?" Tina growled into the receiver.

Maria laughed freely at those guesses. "Nothing like that, I can assure you. It's complicated, though, and I can't speak about it."

"Jesus Christ, Maria!" Tina said fervently. "That's not very helpful."

"No, I suppose it isn't. But that's what I've got for you," Maria said unrepentantly.

Tina got herself back under control and asked, "What am I supposed to do now?"

"What do you want to do? You know the options as well as I do, dear," Maria stated calmly.

"You mean other than murder the bastard?"

"Yes, other than commit bodily harm."

Tina blew out a loud breath as she considered the question. "What I *should* do is quit."

"But you aren't going to do that, are you, dear?" Maria said knowingly.

"No. If anything, I think that would make me even more miserable. How fucked up is that?" she wondered aloud.

"I understand. So that doesn't leave many other options, does it?"

"I guess not." She thanked her aunt for listening and ended the call.

# Chapter 11

*"....I found that I was accumulating money far faster than I could spend it and had begun investing it heavily. Stocks, bonds, real estate, and even limited partnerships in several promising businesses. All of which meant that my immediate needs were well in hand, and long term, I would have sufficient funds to not only allow for further expeditions, but that would make for a very comfortable lifestyle.*

*There was a building downtown that I had had my eye on for quite some time, and when it came up for sale, I immediately made an offer on it. Structurally it was sound, but the years had not been kind to it, nor had the previous owner spent enough on its upkeep to keep it in any sort of proper condition. Renovation would be neither cheap nor easy. Still, I would be able to make it my center of operations and turn the top floor into a penthouse apartment that would suit my needs nicely.*

*The floor beneath that would house the brick and mortar antiquities business, long-term storage for the artifacts I had on hand (once I could make the vaults secure, of course), and allow for future growth. Everything below that would be turned into offices and business spaces that could be rented out to bring a constant revenue stream...."*

**Excerpt from the diary of Alexander Matthews**

**August 1951, Spokane, Alexander's apartment**

*Alexander lay tangled in his sheets, tossing and turning as yet another foreign vision played out in his head. This particular memory was new, one that he hadn't experienced before....*

*The general's footsteps echoed hollowly as he made his way inexorably toward the throne and the figure that sat waiting patiently for him. He studied her openly as he walked forward. This Anunna was ancient, older than any he had met before, and she radiated authority from her very pores.*

*The raucous sounds of a city being sacked filtered in from the open doorway that he had used just moments ago. "Your armies have been defeated, Lil-it, and this city is now mine," he declared as he came to a stop not far from where she sat.*

*"Yes, yes, a great victory for you, I'm sure," she responded, waving a hand carelessly through the air. "Tell me, when will your Master be satisfied? When all have fallen before his armies? When the world burns and all that we have built is gone? I wonder."*

*"That is not for me to decide," the general stated calmly.*

*Lil-it leaned forward and gazed down at him. "No. I suppose it isn't. What comes next? Am I expected to commit suicide, or do you kill me in En's name?"*

*"The choice is yours, Lady."*

*"I see. Do you know what the greatest part of this tragedy is, human?" she inquired.*

*"I'm not sure I follow. What do you mean?"*

*"When I die, all of the accumulated knowledge that my mother, and her mother, and her mother before, have passed on, dies with me." She snapped her fingers. "Gone as if it had never existed. My life, as such, is no great loss, except to me, but the story of my people will vanish, snuffed out like a candle with my passing too."*

*"I don't understand, Lady."*

*She sighed. "Of course, you don't. You cannot know that my family line has been the lore-keepers, tasked with maintaining the histories of the Anunna, a mantle that we have worn since my people came to this planet so long ago. And now En seeks to destroy that history so that he can re-write it in whatever fashion he desires."*

*"Why must this history die with you?" the general asked, genuinely curious as to the answer.*

*"Because there is no one else to pass it to," Lil-it snarled at him. "My daughter is dead…at your hands. She led my armies into battle, and since you alone stand before me, I must assume she is dead."*

*"For what it is worth, I* am *sorry, Lady."*

*"So you say. I suppose there isn't any use in delaying the inevitable, is there." She pulled a delicate, yet lethal-looking dagger from her belt and placed the point against her chest, fingers of one hand guiding the blade, and the palm of her other hand gripping the pommel.*

*He took one step forward, raising a hand in a gesture for her to stop. "Must the recipient of this knowledge be Anunna? Or would it be possible to pass it to a human?"*

*A thoughtful look passed across her face as she considered his words. "I am not certain. Such a thing has never been attempted, and while the technology is similar to that in the amulet you wear, it is far more powerful." She paused and looked curiously at him. "It is possible that the attempt would kill you."*

*"I am willing to accept that risk if you are willing to take a chance that your family legacy will live on."*

*"Why do you make this offer, human?" she asked.*

*"Some things are more important than individual desires, Lady." He bowed respectfully.*

*A tear glimmered in one eye as she said, "So be it. Come closer that I may touch you. There will be a considerable amount of pain, even if this succeeds."*

*The general knelt at her feet and looked up at her expectantly. Lil-it took up the medallion that rested securely between her breasts and extended a hand, palm forward, and placed the circular disk upon his forehead. Gold and silver wires extruded from the disk and passed between her fingers, terminating in the bracelet she wore upon her wrist.*

*A faint glow sprang to life within the device and she commanded, "Prepare yourself." A moment later, his world became a never-ending sea of agony and blinding white light….*

***

It was an unusually lovely March day—blue skies, relatively warm, and no wind at all. Tina and Alexander were walking back to the office through Riverfront Park, chatting amiably. They had just eaten lunch at *Clinkerdagger's* with a potential renter for one of their open office spaces, and while the meeting had gone well, it was uncertain yet whether a contract would be signed. Only time would tell.

Tina was bombarding him with useless information about people he couldn't have cared less about…as usual, and his attention had strayed. His eyes roamed around, simply enjoying the spring scenery and the thundering water that passed just beneath them as they walked across one of the bridges that spanned both the river and the falls that shared the name. The bridge vibrated from the surging water, a low rumbling roar suffusing the air, and even though he knew it was safe, there was a bit of added spice in the knowledge that not even *he* would survive if the structure collapsed.

A hand on his arm, and the tone of her voice stopped him in his tracks. "Alexander?"

"Hmmm?" he asked, then noticed that six dogs were lying flat in a semi-circle before them. Each animal had its head resting on its forelegs, and their eyes were glued to him. Leashes were held by owners who were baffled by their pets' behavior, and the most urgent of tugs were unable to force the animals to come back to their feet.

He sighed, then knelt before each dog and told them that they were a *good boy*, or *good girl*, depending upon their sex. These simple words seemed to energize the canines, and they sprang to their feet and danced around excitedly, all fighting for his attention. In between petting them, he tried to play off the behavior as something unexpected, explaining that animals seemed to like him…a lot. Skeptical looks greeted his words, but soon he and Tina were standing on the bridge alone once again.

"I don't suppose you'd like to explain just what the hell that was about, would you?" The frown she wore told him just how little Tina believed the line of bullshit he had fed the pet owners.

Alexander thought about it for a moment. "Nope." Then he started walking again, leaving her to catch up as she liked.

***

Melinda looked on as Tina sparred with one of the locals who owed allegiance to Alexander. The woman was another wolf who had lived in Spokane for the last fifty years. She ran a brewpub downtown and had never caused them any trouble, finding his rules easy to comply with. Although the Were was shorter than Tina, she was muscular and had the edge in both strength and speed, but was holding back as Alexander had instructed.

"Your protégé is getting better," Mel conceded. "But Alice would wipe the floor with her if it was a fair fight."

He nodded. "I know. But compared to where she was in September, there is a night and day difference." Alexander couldn't keep the pride out of his voice.

Melinda glanced sharply up at him. "Be careful there, big guy, it's a very shaky tightrope you are walking."

He sighed and bobbed his head. "Tell me something I don't already know, Mel. It gets harder every day."

She experienced a brief twinge of jealousy, then said, "Why can't you ever do things the easy way, Alex? Pining away for someone that you can't ever possess is just wasted energy."

His head slumped and he mumbled, "No kidding, and just like a scab that itches unbearably, I just can't help but pick at it. Fucking pathetic."

Relenting a little, she sympathized. "I get it, really, I do. But you need to shit or get off the pot. The current situation is doing neither of you any good. How long do you think she will wait for you to decide to do something? At some point, she will just give up...and when that happens, Tina *will* leave you."

"I'm well aware of the realities, Mel. You don't need to rub my nose in it."

The misery she heard in his voice nearly broke her heart, and she wrapped an arm around his waist. "Part of my job is to tell you the truth, no matter how hard it is. It's not like I enjoy seeing you suffer...unless it is at my hands, anyway."

He chuckled, "Fair enough. And I *do* appreciate it, but...."

"Yeah," she murmured quietly and turned back to watch the combatants.

***

Tina was leaning over his desk while standing at his side and gesturing at a document she was holding. Alexander was finding it difficult to concentrate on what she was telling him. A combination of the perfume she wore, and the blatantly offered view down her shirt of the lace bra and what it struggled to contain, was robbing him of coherent thought. The wide, knowing grin that she wore told him that she was well aware of the effect she had on him, and there was no sign of repentance that he could see.

"I hope I'm interrupting something," Melinda's voice said from the open door, the mock-disapproval dripping from her words. "You should be ashamed of yourself, Tina, dangling forbidden fruit in front of a starving man like that."

Alexander was grateful for the lifeline Mel had tossed his way, and he struggled to compose himself.

For her part, Tina just smirked at the elfin blonde, and her laughter trailed her as she swept out of the office, closing the door behind her.

"What was that all about?" she asked as she plopped down on the couch.

Alexander staggered to the wet bar and poured an almost full glass of bourbon, and slammed it back. "I have no idea." He gasped, feeling the burn as the alcohol made its way to his stomach.

He held up his now-empty glass and raised an eyebrow.

"I'm good," Mel declined. "I only have a few minutes, but there is a situation that has come to my attention that you need to deal with."

"Oh?" he asked as he walked over and sat at the other end of the couch. "Is it something that will get me out of the office for a while?" He almost begged.

"You know what?" she teased in a slow drawl. "It just might be."

***

Queen's *Fat Bottomed Girls* was blasting through the sound system of the Mustang when Alexander pulled into the private road that led down toward the beach. It had been years since he had had any reason to spend time at Lake Coeur d'Alene, and he had forgotten just how beautiful the body of water was.

The deep blue water surrounded by tree-covered hills provided the perfect backdrop for the mansion situated on a small bay several miles outside the city of Coeur d'Alene itself. He parked the car and was greeted by a sour-looking man as he got out of the vehicle. Alexander extended his hand and said, "Jacob."

Seemingly against his will, Jacob grasped Alexander's hand and shook it. "Alexander."

Pleasantries out of the way, the wolf gestured for his host to lead the way.

"I understand you have a situation."

Jacob stopped and spun to face Alexander.

"I don't have a situation…*you* do."

"Fair enough. Why don't you fill me in while we walk down to the dock," the Master of the city offered.

"She showed up sometime after the holidays, we aren't exactly sure when, and began making trouble almost immediately," Jacob told him. We know that at least three human victims have fallen prey to her during that time, but it may be more." He shrugged angrily.

"When we confronted her and told her to stop her activities, she refused."

"You explained the rules and the consequences for ignoring them?" Alexander inquired.

"We did. The bitch told us that rules are meant to be broken, and she had never agreed to them anyway." His eyes probed Alexander for any reaction to these words. Other than a slight tension in the shoulders, the wolf gave little indication of his thoughts.

"Hmmm, did she indeed?" Spokane's' acknowledged Master leaned his head either direction and loudly cracked his neck. "And did she agree to this meeting?"

"Yes, she's waiting for us now."

"Excellent. Then let's not keep her waiting."

***

The gusting wind off the lake caused the flags on the house to snap and rattle as Alexander made his way to the large dock that jutted out into the bay. As he walked unhurriedly toward the tall woman standing with her arms crossed aggressively, he took some time to study her. The scent he was picking up was similar to, but unlike, the usual Mer marker he was used to. Ranker, more carrion-like, the smell of death personified.

She stood approximately 6'2", and though still lean, had considerable muscle to back it all up. Sea-green eyes stared back at him steadily, and while there was a sense of uncertainty, he could smell no fear. Her long brown hair whipped in the wind, frequently prompting the woman to brush it out of her eyes. The early spring chill seemed not to bother her at all, considering that she was completely nude as she shifted to face him when he drew near.

Mismatched eyes met their sea-green counterparts, neither giving an inch. "Jacob, why don't you do the introductions."

Clearly disgruntled, but unwilling to make an issue of it, the local Mer leader spoke. "Alexander, Master of the city, meet Sandra, independent Siren."

"What brings you to my territory, Sandra?" Alexander asked pleasantly.

She sneered at him. "I fail to see how that is any concern of yours. Count yourself lucky that I even agreed to this ridiculous charade of a meeting."

He tilted his head, a curious look on his face. "Then, why *did* you? Agree to meet, that is."

"I suppose I wanted to meet the man who has this entire section of the country terrified to step out of line." Her expression showed just how unimpressed she really was.

"Well," Alexander said softly. "Here I am."

Sandra snorted rudely. "I suppose this is where you lay down the law and quote your meaningless rules to me?"

His head tilted from side to side, the loud cracks of vertebrae causing Jacob to take several steps back and mutter, "Oh shit."

The Master of the city calmly stepped out of his shoes and slid his jacket off, tossing it at Jacob. "You see, my understanding is that you have already been made aware of those rules and have chosen to ignore my edicts regarding treating Normals as prey."

Fingers unbuttoned the shirt he was wearing, and he shrugged out of it as he continued. "There is only one penalty for breaking my laws, and you have *already* been judged. I'm here in my capacity as Executioner."

Sandra's eyes widened, and he caught the acrid scent of fear for the first time. She glanced over her shoulder at the water, eyes dancing back and forth between him and the lake, seemingly unsure if escape was possible. Tension flowed from her body as some sort of decision was reached, but when she turned back, a self-assured smile greeted the wolf.

"You'll not find me so easy to kill, Wolf." Her hand shot out and latched onto Alexander's forearm, then she dived into the water, dragging him behind.

The shock of the frigid water nearly took his breath away, but he managed to hold onto it. She had already shifted into her Siren form, long muscular tail undulating through the water, propelling them quickly into deeper water. She was much larger in this shape…approximately fifteen feet long, most of it tail. Her tactic was readily apparent, and all she had to do was keep him submerged until he ran out of air. Sandra released him in fifty feet of water, quite some distance from shore. The shark-teeth smile that she turned on him was probably very effective on Normals, but Alexander was not so easily cowed.

He shifted into his Battle form and used his arms and legs to keep him facing her as she slowly circled him. The gills in the sides of her neck fluttered as she breathed in oxygenated water and forced the old out. Clawed hands clenched then released as she played with him, forcing him to hold his breath since he could not entertain the idea of fleeing. If he did, he knew that she would immediately attack.

After a minute of circling him, just out of reach, she shot forward and scored his torso with her claws, and battered him with her powerful tail as she passed. Two more times she was successful with this type of attack, and the water was rapidly becoming cloudy with his blood.

Alexander knew he didn't have much time, and that she held all of the advantages in this fight. If he couldn't come to grips with her, and soon, it would all be over. The very next time she propelled herself at him, he willingly took the hit but managed to latch on with his clawed hands. The skin beneath his fingers was not scaled like a fish, but rather what one felt if they were able to touch a Dolphin. Sandra did not like this at all, and immediately went into what is called a death-roll by those familiar with alligators, clearly hoping to dislodge him.

The Wolf dragged himself toward her upper torso using a combination of his legs and hands, digging his claws deep into her body with each movement. Eventually, he had advanced far enough that his legs were wrapped around her waist, and he had his left hand on her throat, squeezing it to provide purchase. His right hand snaked to the side of her neck and raked claws across the gills there, causing severe damage.

Her eyes were wide now, frightened, and she thrashed about in a panic. Her blood joined his in the murky water, but it was still clear enough for her to see the triumphant grin he flashed at her even as he reached over her head, the claws on his right hand digging into the back of her skull, penetrating deep into the bone and stabbing into her brain. With one titanic effort, Alexander pulled the top half of her head off and dropped it into the depths. The corpse twitched ineffectually as he pushed away from her, watching briefly as it spiraled into deeper water.

The Hybrid thrust for the surface, and when his head broke the water he exhaled loudly, then sucked in gasps of fresh air. It took him a few minutes to swim back to shore, where he emerged, water sluicing off the black fur in torrents.

Alexander shifted back and shivered as he walked to where Jacob stood with a towel.

"Is it done?" the leader of the local Mer asked.

The towel paused long enough for Alexander's head to emerge. "It is."

Jacob jerked a nod at these words. "Good. I expect you can find your way back to your car."

The Master of the city shook his head in wonder as his gaze followed the taciturn little man, then he got dressed and drove back to Spokane.

***

Alexander exited the elevator and poured himself a drink before leaning against the island in the middle of his kitchen. The bourbon burned its way down his throat before settling into his stomach, and suffused his body with a welcome warmth.

He took out his cell phone and dialed a number. As he waited for Mel to answer, he rolled the cold glass across his forehead, eyes closed, and looking weary.

She answered on the third ring. "Is it done?"

A huge sigh escaped him. "Yeah. Not that Jacob seemed to care one way or the other."

"He did. You know how difficult he can be." She paused a moment. "For what it's worth, I'm sorry."

"Couldn't be helped. There was zero chance that she could be redeemed."

"Still...."

# Chapter 12

*"....The fires burned in multiple places around the city, and the flames could be seen clearly from the windows of the penthouse. Smoke blanketed much of the Spokane metropolitan area, and people were unsure as to what they should do. A state of emergency had been declared, and all available resources were being thrown at the fires.*

*October 16th, 1991 would go down as a dark day in local history—two people had already died, and at least a hundred homes had succumbed to the flames. By Saturday, October 19th, the city was surrounded on three sides by uncontrolled fires. There was little danger to the city center, but for anyone living on the outskirts, it was a different story.*

*The emergency responders hoped that at least partial containment would be reached by Monday, but any success was predicated upon the weather cooperating. Sixty-plus mph winds were what had started the crisis in the first place...trees falling across powerlines and sparking the initial fires that had quickly escalated into full-blown uncontrolled wildfires.*

*I sat in the penthouse, lights off, the TV on in the background providing reports, and watched the world* burn...."

**An excerpt from the diary of Alexander Matthews**

**Late August 1970, Spokane Indians stadium**

*Alexander had just returned to Spokane after his involuntary deployment to Southeast Asia, courtesy of the CIA. He was still adjusting to civilian life and had decided to catch a game. The Spokane Indians were a Triple-A farm team for the LA Dodgers and were having an outstanding year. In fact, it looked like they might have a good chance of winning the pennant.*

*A cold beer in one hand and a hot dog drenched in mustard and onion in the other, he cheered loudly as Davey Lopes singled another run in. Alexander was unfamiliar with most of the players since he had been overseas for the last two years, but he could see that this team had some real talent.*

*He chuckled as the short, stout, and rather loud manager, a man named Tommy Lasorda, rushed to get into the face of the home plate umpire when he didn't like a call that had just been made. Highly animated and flailing his arms about in a most Italian manner, he finally felt he had made his point and marched back to the dugout.*

*The warm evening sun beat down on Alexander, but the shadows were beginning to stretch across the field, first base and right field already shadowed as the sun sank in the west. Cheering fans, the smell of popcorn and hot peanuts permeating the air, and a sense of well-being all contributed to making this night feel magical. There was nothing more All-American than a good baseball game on a beautiful night...especially as no one was actively shooting at him.*

***

Tina looked up as the door to the hallway opened, revealing a pretty Japanese woman, maybe twenty years old, and dressed in the latest designer fashion from Tokyo. A bright-white smile flashed as she strode forward and stopped in front of the desk. Raven-dark straight hair was pulled up into a high ponytail that jutted up and back at a fifteen-degree angle, then fell free.

"Is Mr. Matthews in?" she asked Tina in a perky voice.

"May I tell him who is requesting a meeting?" Tina inquired in a slightly icy tone.

"Hai. Please let him know that the daughter of Lady Kitsune is here to pass on a personal message."

Alexander's assistant walked over to the door that led into his office, and she cracked it wide enough to pass the message along, then turned and gestured for the young lady to go in.

"Arigato," she said as she walked past.

Tina closed the door and went back to her desk, confusion evident on her face.

In the meantime, Alexander had walked from behind his desk and greeted his unexpected guest, guiding her to the couch.

"Would you care for something to drink? I'm afraid I don't have tea, but I can make an espresso?" He stopped, then prompted in a chagrined voice, "I'm sorry, but I forgot to ask your name."

"Thank you, but no. I won't take up much of your time," she replied with a smile. "You may call me Tamiko."

He smiled brightly. "Ah, a child of great beauty, indeed." Then he seated himself across from the couch. "My assistant informs me that Lady Kitsune is your mother?"

"Hai. I am attending Mukagawa in the fall, although I have come early so that I may acclimate before my studies begin. My mother insisted that I call upon you and pass on her best wishes."

Alexander chuckled. "While I *am* flattered, I must admit that I am somewhat surprised that she even remembers who I am."

Her answering giggle surprised him. "Apologies, Alexander-sama, but my mother has spoken of you often, and with great respect. Others, those who were with her during her time here, regaled me with stories of your exploits. The great wolf who took on all challengers and swiftly defeated them quite easily. As you can see, your legend is still very much alive."

Turning a bright shade of red, he stammered out, "That's not quite how I remember that night. It would seem that a fair number of liberties has been taken with the facts of the matter."

She leaned toward him, clearly amused. "Perhaps. But the fact remains that both my mother and her attendants hold you in high esteem. I believe you may know how unusual that is for a foreigner?"

"I do, and my esteem for the Lady cannot be overstated. I only regret that I could not spend more time with her."

"How fortunate that part of my visit is to pass on an open invitation to join her at the family estate outside Kyoto. It would seem that my mother shares your regrets."

Alexander leaned back into his chair and expelled a surprised breath. "Please pass along that I will be honored to take her up on her offer, although I cannot commit to a firm date at this time. Additionally, my assistant is a Normal, and completely unaware of our world. I must think about that angle."

"As you say." Tamiko tilted her head slightly, then continued. "My second purpose here is to request that you take me on as a disciple, at least part-time. My mother has made it clear that you have much to teach me, and that learning your unorthodox fighting style will go far to mitigate any flaws that I may have where the martial arts are concerned."

Alexander smiled and paused briefly before responding. "I would be honored, of course, but I do travel quite frequently, so any schedule will be hit or miss." His eyes narrowed as he continued. "Also, I train my assistant as well. Would you have any opposition to sharing my time with her? It would mean disguising your true abilities."

"This is acceptable, and surely, *some* time can be set aside for private instruction so that I can practice at full speed?" she countered.

"Agreed. I will have Tina share our training calendar with you." His eyes twinkled gleefully as he asked, "I don't suppose you need ballroom dancing instruction as well?"

Tamiko looked confused. "Excuse me?"

"Never mind. I look forward to our lessons."

He stood, indicating that their time was up, and walked her to the door. She bowed to him respectfully, and the bow he returned was even more profound. Tamiko grinned and waved at Tina as she headed for the hallway, ponytail swishing in time with her steps.

"Who was that?"

"Royalty, Tina. An honest to God Japanese princess."

***

The scowl on his face showed just what he thought about the situation. "A fucking Ginger. Why did it have to be a goddamn redhead?"

"I don't understand what the problem is, Alexander. Why does the color of her hair have anything to do with it?" Tina asked, curious despite herself.

He turned to her in surprise. "Are you being serious right now? Everyone knows that Gingers are fucking crazy."

"That seems to be a bit broad-sweeping, don't you think?

"Really? Name one redhead you have ever known, who wasn't a complete fucking bitch, I dare you. At best, they might only turn out to be bi-polar and psycho, but I guarantee that all of them have superiority complexes and think that the rest of us only exist to cater to their whims." The last words came out as a growl.

"Now you're just being silly."

"Am I? I guess we'll see." With that statement, he marched into the conference room and sat. Tina followed in his wake, taking the seat beside him and opening up the folder that contained the details of the proposal they were gathered to discuss.

The woman in question was in her late forties and dressed in lawyer-chic. Granted, the cut and material were of the highest quality, but the whole ensemble still screamed ambulance-chaser. The nonchalant aura she was actively projecting was all part of the act, and in no way fooled Alexander.

Her eyes bored into his, probing for any weakness, even as she leaned forward and slid a similar folio his way. "As you can see, my client has made a very generous offer on this property. In fact, too generous, based upon current market value. You won't get anything close to this if you seek another avenue of sale."

Alexander grunted and leaned back in the chair, crossing his arms over his chest. "That's all very interesting, but I'm curious as to where your client got the idea this building was even on the market? Certainly not from *me*." The question posed as a challenge.

The redhead's lips thinned in aggravation at his lack of appreciation of the offer. She turned her dead eyes toward Tina. "Be a dear, and go get us some coffee."

When Tina started to get up, Alexander's hand came down on her arm, stopping her from doing so. "We don't have any coffee."

"Water then." A calculating smirk passed over her face as she looked at him. "In fact, I see no reason your secretary should be present at all."

*Now you've done it,* he thought, highly amused by the situation. A slow mental countdown commenced in his head….

Tina had stiffened in her seat, and he could hear her heart rate skyrocket. His hand patted her arm softly, letting her know that he would handle it. By the way her teeth were audibly grinding, he figured that it was almost time to end this farce.

"We don't have any water, either. Or tea. Or anything else you might ask for." He leaned forward aggressively, and a low rumbling growl could be heard emanating from his chest. "The only reason I agreed to this meeting was that my *secretary* convinced me it was a good idea. In fact, the only thing you have said so far that I agree with wholeheartedly is the fact that my personal assistant shouldn't be subjected to any more of your bullshit."

The woman across from him was gasping like a fish as she processed his words. Tina bumped his leg with her own, letting him know that she appreciated what he had just done.

"I don't think you understand, Mr. Matthews; this property sits in a prime development zone and could be far better utilized than it currently is. Especially if it is replaced by a high-rise multi-use building."

*Damn, she recovered faster than I had hoped.* He sighed tiredly.

"What part of *not interested* is your intellectually challenged state not able to understand?" he asked.

"Excuse me?" she gasped, not used to being spoken to in this way.

"You heard me. I'm going to spell this out in the simplest possible terms. Ones that even you and your *client* should be able to digest." Alexander poked his index finger into the surface of the table with each statement. "This building is currently not for sale. It will still not be for sale next year. Nor the year after that. As a matter of fact, I wouldn't sell this property to your client if I only had a nickel left to my name."

He stood, lifting Tina at the same time. "Is that clear enough for you? Because if it isn't, that's too damn bad. We are *done* here."

Alexander paused at the door to the conference room. "I trust you can find your way out?" Then he made his way to his office, Tina trailing him closely.

***

He had left the door to his office open, specifically so that he could keep an eye on the lawyer and make sure she didn't leave with anything that she hadn't arrived with. Tina walked over to the wet bar and poured herself a tumbler of the bourbon he kept on hand. Her hand shook with anger, and the crystal chimed as the decanter bounced along the edge of the glass.

She gulped half of the contents down, sucking in a hissing breath as it burned its way down her throat, then she lifted an eyebrow at him and gestured with the glass in her hand.

"Yes, please. Two ice cubes in mine, if you will," he told her.

Tina walked over and handed the drink to him. "You were right, she *was* a bitch."

"Yup." Alexander sipped his drink as he watched the lawyer exit the suite in a huff. "Any lawyer is bad enough, but a *Ginger* lawyer is like dealing with the Devil himself."

"Thanks for sticking up for me, by the way," she said softly.

"Of course. This business doesn't work without you at the helm, and *nobody* talks down to my friends. No one."

Tina laughed at that. "She was a real piece of work, alright."

He turned to look down at her. "They feed on fear and weakness, you know? That woman would put the fear of God into a great white."

"Alexander?"

"Yeah?"

She shuffled her feet for a moment, not looking at him. "It was a *lot* of money."

"So?"

Tina shrugged. "I'm just saying."

Alexander walked over and sat on the couch, patting the seat next to him. When she had joined him, he turned to face her.

"It's not just about the money." He held up a hand to forestall her objections. "Money is just a tool, Tina. I don't do this as an excuse to accumulate cash. Having deep pockets allows me to do the things that really matter to me.

"Let's say I sold this building, my home. What then? Can you think of anywhere else that would meet our needs as well?"

"I guess not," she replied.

"And what about all of our tenants? Some of them have been here for decades. Where would they go? Not to mention that all of them would have far more expensive leases—I don't charge market value on any of them." Primarily because they were all genetic misfits like him, and they were assured that no awkward questions would be asked, but also because he *could*...but he couldn't exactly tell Tina that.

"Why is that? I mean, I had guessed that based on the rental income, but why not?" She looked at him curiously.

He raised one shoulder in a shrug. "Are we hurting for money?"

"No. But still...."

"I've known most of these people for most of my life. They may as well be family." One corner of his mouth quirked up in amusement. "Well, maybe some of them are like the relatives no one talks about, or wants to acknowledge, but family, nonetheless.

"This building, with the exception of a few businesses, functions almost as a mini-city. We leverage each other's specialties when we need something. If you need a will drawn up, you go to Mr. Esposito on the third floor. Looking for some temps? Mrs. Summers on the second floor can take care of you. Do you understand what I'm trying to get across?"

Her faced scrunched up as she visibly processed what he had said. "I think so. Selling this building would have an adverse effect on many more people than just you, and money alone isn't the primary deciding factor as far as you are concerned."

"Exactly." He paused momentarily. "That, and I like this building. I can't imagine living anywhere else."

***

Tamiko darted in and latched onto Tina's upper arms, then pivoted and slammed her into the mat. He heard all of the air rush out of his assistant's lungs as she made contact with the lightly padded surface. She lay there gasping, unable to get up, and Tamiko backed away, giving her time to do so.

Once she had regained her composure, Alexander stepped into the arena and gestured for both women to stand down. They knelt and waited for him to proceed. The Japanese girl quickly raised an eyebrow at him and wore a small, self-satisfied smile. He shook his head in exasperation, trying to hide his answering grin.

"OK. What happened, and why?" He looked to Tina for the answer.

Scowling up at him, she sucked in a breath, then answered, "I was looking for an opening and Tamiko beat me to it."

"True. Tamiko?"

"She was overthinking and left herself open. I seized the opportunity."

He nodded his head. "Also true. Tina, sometimes the best defense is a good offense."

Tina leaned back on her heels, frustration clearly evident in her expression. "What the hell does that mean, Alexander?"

"It means that your opponent won't always give you a golden opportunity, and if you hesitate too long, the balance will shift to your foe. Sometimes it is better to simply attack, even if you don't see an opening. Action is better than inaction every day of the week."

"Hmmpf!"

"Let me demonstrate."

***

They had just bowed to each other when Alexander shot forward, sweeping Tamiko's legs, his left hand firmly around her throat. He rode her body down to the mat, knees straddling her hips, and stopped his fist a fraction of an inch from her nose. She tapped the mat with one hand, and he stood, pulling her back up as he did so.

The Japanese girl looked at him with wide eyes, clearly impressed by how easily he had beaten her. Tina stood there slack-jawed, not sure what she had just witnessed.

"As you saw, I never hesitated. Tamiko had no opportunity to effectively defend from the lightning attack I pressed on her. I didn't need to search for an opening because I didn't *need* it. Do you understand?"

Both women nodded their heads, processing his words.

"Don't get me wrong, this is not always the best option, but often enough it is. Especially against an opponent who is much larger and stronger than you." He grinned at his students. "Big men tend to be used to hesitation by others. They have grown used to the fact that their size intimidates people, and it tends to make them slow off the start."

"That being said, if you opt for this attack, you must make it fast, brutal, and effective. Take them out before they can recover because if you show mercy, you *will* lose. Surprise is a tactic that only works once. Understood?"

"Yes, Alexander."

"Hai!"

"Good. Continue sparring then."

***

That Sunday, Alexander and Tamiko had a private session. She currently stood before him in her Fox Battle form, panting heavily from exertion. She was obviously frustrated by her inability to score so much as a single point.

She gathered herself to launch another attack and leapt into the air, one leg extended to kick at his head, and the other curled beneath.

Alexander, still in his human shape, stepped forward, into the kick, and grabbed her by the ankle. He planted his feet and torqued his upper body, tossing her twenty feet through the air to land in an untidy heap at the edge of the mats.

She growled and slapped the floor, then stood up and bowed before walking over and shifting into her naked human form. She knelt down in front of him, sucking in great gouts of air as she tried to get her breathing under control.

He settled into a lotus position and waited calmly. When Tamiko was breathing normally, he asked, "Why am I beating you so handily?"

"I am not sure. My form is correct, my movements smooth and unforced. I can see no reason for my failure." He could tell that it was painful for her to admit this.

"Yes. Your form and attacks are all perfect. Beautiful even." He leaned forward as he spoke. "And that would matter if you were doing kata."

Tamiko cocked her head to one side, clearly not sure what he was hinting at.

Alexander sighed heavily. "In the real world, and in a real fight, one where your life is at stake, there are *no* rules. In the dojo, practicing with other students, the goal is not to hurt your opponent, yes?"

She dipped her head in acknowledgment.

"On the street, your *ONLY* goal is to hurt, or kill, before the same is done to you. Fair play will get you dead, Tamiko. You need to stop operating by a set of rules that has been drilled into you for many years. Your mother understands this, and that is why you were sent to me." He chuckled. "I am a blunt instrument. I fight dirty. I fight to win. I fight to survive. How else do you think I not only beat all challengers that night so long ago, but did so where someone else, someone *fairer,* would have lost?"

The Japanese woman looked thoughtful as she absorbed his words.

Alexander poked her in the breastbone. "The only rule in a fight is to do whatever is necessary to win. Anything less just gets you dead."

He stood up fluidly. "Now, get up and show me what you've got."

***

The head-butt actually took him by surprise, and he released her before she could do it again. Alexander took a step back and watched Tamiko carefully. She was grinning from ear to ear and obviously had enjoyed that very much.

He couldn't help smiling too. It was very well done.

Her fluffy Fox tail was wagging back and forth, even as she kept her guard up. "Excellent. That is not something your sensei would have allowed in his dojo, but as you can see, it was effective. Let me be perfectly clear, any target is fair game. Throat, knees, and even testicles are in play. It's difficult to fight if you can't breathe, if you can't stand, if you can't...well, you get the idea," he told her with a wince.

Her answering giggle let him know she understood.

"Let's call it a day, but keep this in mind: You need to be able to do this in your human form as well."

She shifted quickly, looking confused. "Why would I fight in anything other than my Battle form?"

"It's not always possible to shift if you are in a very public place, for one thing. And another is it will make you a better fighter." He frowned in thought for a moment. "I probably enter combat as a human sixty percent of the time. If you know your opponent's weaknesses, it is not always necessary to shift. Yes, you will be weaker. Yes, you will be slower. But knowledge is power, and frequently Battle form is not needed. Not to mention that losing to someone who can't even be bothered to shift is *way* more insulting."

She laughed again. "I can see that."

"Good. I expect you to think about all of this prior to our next session. Stop being so honorable and try to kick my ass."

"Hai, Alexander-sama."

# Chapter 13

*"....After the war, I visited my parents and my younger brother. The after-effects of the conflict on my psyche made finding any sense of normalcy impossible. On top of that, it was becoming apparent that I wasn't aging as I should be. For all intents and purposes, I appeared to be the same age I was when I had been cursed and turned into a werewolf seventeen years prior. I could see the curious glances that my brother and parents tried to hide, and I decided it would be best if I left home for good.*

*I wandered for months until the railroad brought me to Spokane. Many of the nation's railroads ran through the city, making it a major junction for commerce. The town was a raucous place full of speakeasies, opium dens, and bordellos, all frequented by both locals and transients alike. Crime was rampant, and the police force corrupt. It was the perfect place for monsters of all kinds, and they took ruthless advantage of it. Murder was common, and if you were smart and careful, bodies could be disposed of quite easily into the river that ran straight through downtown...."*

**An excerpt from the diary of Alexander Matthews**

**June 1974, Spokane, The World's Fair**

*So far, this World's Fair had been a complete pain in his dick. With so many nations being represented, and just as many contingents to support this activity, there were bound to be lots of Genetic Underground races wandering around his city. And there were. Unfortunately, there had been incidents that affected the Normal people who lived here, and that was* his *problem.*

*Alexander had finally decided to grab the issue by the balls, so to speak, and deal with it in his particular way. He had spent the last week wandering through the various exhibits and pavilions, identifying the individuals who were definitely not standard humans. Each of these was given a set of instructions on where to be at a specific time, on a specific day, and told that failure to comply would result in their immediate termination. As could be expected, this did not go over well…at all.*

*That was just too damn bad as far as he was concerned. When you came to his town, you followed his rules. Period. The fact that most of them were unaware of his rules, or even that the city* had *a Master, mattered little to him. Besides, he was about to rectify that situation in just a few minutes. Had anyone witnessed the evil grin he was wearing at this thought, they might have decided they had better places to be.*

*Alexander gazed down on the crowd that was gathered below, many of them angry at having been summoned. The Spokane River flowed steadily at this time of year, and the Bowl and Pitcher was the perfect place to have this conversation. Remote enough to provide privacy, yet close enough to the city to make getting here convenient. He had a sneaking suspicion that privacy was going to be necessary, given what was about to happen.*

*He walked purposefully to the center of the clearing and waited for the others to quiet down. A large, belligerent man immediately got into his face and demanded in heavily accented English, "Why have you summoned us here?"*

*Alexander tilted his head back slightly, looking up at the 7'2" tall man. "This is my town, and you were not invited by me, nor were you given permission to be here. Tell me…." He paused. "Excuse me, but what is your name?"*

*A fist thumped against the man's chest. "I am Vladimir Medvedev. Moscow in Mother Russia is my home."*

*"Well, Vlad, I have rules for my city." Alexander stepped forward, bumping the Russian a step backward. "My name is Alexander Matthews, and I am Master of this city."*

*His sharp eyes scanned the faces around him. "Some of you have been very naughty, and some of the people I protect have been hurt…even killed. This is unacceptable."*

*"Bah! Vlad does not care what the puny American wants or thinks." He turned away as if to leave.*

*A hand latched onto his shoulder and fingers dug deep into the muscle, and the big man faltered and went to one knee, pain clearly visible on his features. "I wasn't finished, and it's not polite to turn your back when someone is talking."*

*The fingers continued to dig into the big Russian's shoulder, maintaining a firm grip. Alexander continued, "As I was saying, my rules are simple, and since we are stuck with each other for the duration of this Expo '74, I feel that I must share them with you all to ensure that there is no further confusion."*

*Speculative murmuring broke out amongst the onlookers, and sweat had broken out on Vlad's face as Alexander held him in place with no visible effort.*

*"Rule number one: No killing, or feeding on, the Normals of this city." A finger on his left hand was held up for all to see.*

*"Rule number two: Normals are not to become aware that any of you even exist." A second finger joined the first.*

*"Rule number three: Any violation of rule one, or rule two, will be met with an extremely violent death." The third and final finger rose to join the others.*

*Alexander released his grip on Vlad and stepped back a pace. The big man rubbed at his shoulder and glowered at him.*

*"As you can see, there are only three simple things you need to keep in mind while you are in my domain. Are there any questions?"*

*"Da. Rules mean nothing if you can't enforce them." Vlad shifted into a giant brown bear and rushed Alexander.*

*The smile that flashed across the American's face was nothing less than predatory. Later, many of the onlookers realized this should have been a warning to be heeded.*

*Rather than meet the thousand-pound bear head-on, Alexander elected to dance to the side as he morphed into his Battle form. Some of the onlookers gasped as they got a look at the true form of the Master of this city. While the bear still had a weight advantage, the wolf who wrapped his arms around the bear's neck and proceeded to choke him out was formidable in its own right.*

*Claws raked ineffectually at Alexander's arms, and a worried growl escaped the bear as he realized there was little that he could do. The two Weres struggled mightily for several minutes until the light finally went out of Vlad's eyes. Alexander released his hold, and the bear collapsed at his feet, still alive, but definitely out of the fight.*

*The wolf roared in triumph, then shifted back to the man who ruled this town. He toed the inert form at his feet and spat to the side. "Yob tvoyu mat, Vovochka," Alexander told the unconscious bear.*

*He sighed resignedly. "I had hoped that we could come to an agreement without resorting to violence, but I see that this is not the case. So be it, I will accept all challenges, and if I am defeated, then I will withdraw my objections to your behavior. Agreed?"*

*Thus, began a long night of individual duels in which Alexander beat the mob into submission. Thankfully, he did not have to fight all of them, just a single representative of each contingent. Vampires, Tigers, Lions, others such as Fox people, and even a Hyena all challenged his right to dictate how things would be. The smartest ones of all did nothing but watch this man take on all comers and remain on top.*

*As the sun rose, a bloody and ragged, yet still undefeated, Alexander raised his weary head and glared around him. "Are we done here? I've got other shit to do."*

*Only groans and whimpers greeted his words. A female member of the Japanese Fox contingent approached him diffidently. "A most impressive display, Alexander-sama, most impressive indeed. This one, and those in her party, will obey the strictures as you have laid them out." Amusement glittered in her eyes as she asked, "Could I perhaps impose upon you with a request?"*

*Alexander quirked an eyebrow. "What might I do for you, Lady Kitsune?"*

*She wore a thin, knowing smile as she leaned in and whispered, "We will be here for many months, and this is such a small town, lacking in diversions. I would consider it a favor if you would allow both my Skulk, and the few Vampires who are in attendance with us, to train with you. It would seem that we have much to learn."*

*"It would be my pleasure," he said and bowed as one would to an equal.*

***

They had landed at Fiumicino International Airport on the outskirts of Rome shortly after the noon hour. Tina was feeling better than her first trip to Europe but was still groggy. She hoped, at some point in the not-too-distant future, her body would adjust to rapid changes in time zones. They spent the night at a hotel near the airport, rather than within the central city of Rome itself. Alexander had secluded himself for the day, claiming to be doing research, so Tina took advantage of the spa. A gentle massage and body treatments, along with some time spent tanning by the pool, sounded really, really good.

***

The following morning found the two of them in a taxi heading to a location that Alexander had provided to the driver. It was already hot, and the forecast called for temperatures in excess of ninety degrees. Unfortunately, either the taxi had no air-conditioning, or the driver didn't think it was warm enough to warrant its use.

A short time later, the cab slowed and turned into a long-term storage facility. She glanced at Alexander in confusion, but he just smiled at her and patted her leg condescendingly.

As the taxi pulled away from them, her boss grabbed their luggage and led her to one of the units, punching in a code to open the bay door. He indicated that she should wait, then entered the semi-darkness. A few seconds later, she heard the roar of a sports car, and headlights illuminated the interior. The bright red car eased out, and Alexander put it in neutral while he secured the unit's door.

She slid into the passenger seat while he wrangled their bags into the limited space available in the vehicle. He took his place behind the wheel wearing a satisfied smirk, pulled to the exit, and punched it. Thankfully, he turned on the a/c, so the ride was definitely more comfortable than the cab had been. He kept glancing at her every minute or so, and it was making her uncomfortable.

"What?" she said as she checked her face in the visor mirror on her side of the car. "Do I have something stuck in my teeth?"

"Nope."

She was getting really paranoid at this point. "Don't make me beat it out of you, dude."

"Are you feeling OK?"

"Yes. Why do you ask?" she wondered.

His features took on a very concerned appearance. "Well…we've been on the road for a little while now, and you haven't made a single snarky comment about my car." He shook his head in consternation. "So weird."

"Shut the hell up!" she laughed, punching him in the arm. "I just assumed that you would get around to trying to convert me as to its technical superiority at *some* point during the drive."

Wearing a crestfallen look, he said, "Oh. It's an Acura NSX, in case you wondered." Then he faced forward and drove in silence.

Tina almost felt bad. Almost.

***

Their route took them in a semi-circle along the outskirts of Rome until they got onto the E45, which they would stay on until they reached Naples. According to her phone and Google, it should have taken them a bit over two and a half hours to get there. Alexander did it in one hour, forty-five minutes. She had to hand it to the big guy. He could drive a car.

Traffic inside the city center sucked. She was amazed that anyone would willingly operate a vehicle on a daily basis, anywhere, within the city limits. It was madness. Alexander seemed utterly calm and unconcerned, however, as they listened to The Cars. He said it was the *Candy-O* album, and she was surprised that she recognized a few of the songs, especially as she hadn't even been born when the album was released. It was good, though.

He parked the car, and they walked a short distance to a shop on Via Scarlatti called *Lilith.* He had barely made it inside the door before a shrieking blur slammed into him. "Alexander! Why did you not let Caterina know you were coming?" The slim woman with medium length straight black hair and dazzling blue eyes stepped back while holding onto his biceps with each hand, carefully giving him the once-over.

His laughter as he was greeted by the human equivalent of a hurricane set Tina's teeth on edge. What was it with him and beautiful women anyway? As far as she could tell, he didn't date any more than she did.

He pulled the woman into the crook of one arm and turned her to face Tina. "Allow me to introduce you to my new assistant. Tina Ferrante, meet the one and only Caterina."

"Cat, Tina is Maria's niece."

Caterina stepped away from Alexander, quickly embracing the surprised Tina and kissing her on the cheek. "Maria will be missed. She is a dear friend."

The stunned American could only nod her thanks.

"Why does Caterina suspect that this is not just a social call?" She gave him the stink-eye, pretending to be upset.

"Because it's not. I need a huge favor."

"The Gala at the Museo? You want Caterina to drop everything and perform a miracle?" She sniffed indifferently.

He smiled sheepishly. "You know me so well, dear one. Only a sorceress of your caliber can turn Tina into the best-dressed princess at the ball." Alexander wrung his hands as he continued. "Please, Cat, I never even considered anyone else for this task."

"Rightfully so, you evil man." She looked Tina over carefully. "I don't know why Caterina allows you to impose on her this way. You do realize that you have cut the timing very short?"

He kissed her forehead. "Because you love me, and you know it. Is it possible? Or have I screwed up?"

"Pffft. Caterina will do her best...which is much better than anyone else."

She took Tina by the arm and started to walk off, paused, and said over her shoulder, "Go do whatever it is that Alexander does while he waits for his miracles."

***

The next hour passed in a blur for Tina. Measurements were taken. Samples of various colored cloth made their appearance and just as quickly disappeared, and Caterina muttered under her breath the entire time.

"I don't understand why I can't just wear one of the dresses I brought with me," Tina grumbled.

Caterina glared at her but didn't rise to the bait.

As Tina listened to the woman call her underwear a disaster, she finally lost her temper. "That's it, I'm done. This was a mistake. I'm *sorry* that my lingerie and I don't meet with your approval, and yet I still can't seem to care." She glared around her. "Where's my shit?"

Suddenly the slim woman was in her face, pushing her hard down into a chair. "You shut your ingrate face. I'm not doing this for *you*."

The American sat in stunned silence as the carefully maintained façade that the designer had used was stripped away. For a moment, Tina thought Caterina was actually going to hit her.

"For many years I have known the wonderful man who brought you to my shop. Do you know how many times he has asked me to dress a woman for him?"

Tina shook her head silently.

"Once. You are the first." She spat the words out. "I owe Alexander *everything*. All of this?" She gestured around the shop. "All of my success is because of him.

"Are you familiar with the history of this town? No? It used to be full of what you Americans would call '*bad people*,' Mafioso. When I first came to Naples and tried to open this boutique, I was harassed by such animals. One night, I was closing up this shop when I was attacked."

Her eyes clouded with the memories as she continued. "Alexander was passing by when he saw what was happening. Had he done what most people would have, and ignored it as not his problem, I would almost certainly be dead.

"Rather than do that, he intervened, badly injuring the thugs who were after me.

"*Why would this American do something like this for a woman he didn't even know?* I asked myself as he helped me up from the ground. Do you understand how rare a quality this truly is?"

Tina nodded once again.

"I had some small injuries." Caterina shrugged as if it meant nothing. "He insisted that I come to the home he was staying in at the time, where he cleaned and bandaged what he could. He asked me about the thugs who had assaulted me, and as we talked, I found myself telling him everything I knew about them and their boss.

"Alexander allowed me to sleep in his bed that night, while he kept vigil, watching over me to ensure my safety." Tears welled up in her eyes. "Who does such a thing? Anyway, the next morning he escorted me back to my shop. I tried to work as usual that day, but I was afraid. Afraid that more thugs would come to finish what they had started."

Tina handed her a tissue, which she used to wipe her eyes and blow her nose. "Grazie. Just before closing, that darling man walked into my shop.... This very shop. And told me that there would be no further problems. He handed me his business card and said that if I ever needed assistance again, I should immediately contact him. I could tell that he actually meant what he said." She shook her head in wonder.

"He would check in on me periodically when his travels brought him to Naples, but I never had any trouble after that day. I was curious as to what could cause the local thugs to suddenly leave me alone, so I quietly asked around for rumors and the like."

"What did you find out?" Tina asked, curious, despite herself.

A malicious grin split Caterina's face. "It seems that several of the top leadership, and many of the lower-level thugs, had fatal *accidents* that day. Very coincidental, wouldn't you say?"

Tina was shocked, but somehow not very surprised, by what she had learned.

"The word on the street was that it was very unhealthy for anyone who targeted my shop or me." She glared at the American woman again. "And now you understand why I would do anything for the man you work for.

"Let me ask you a question. Who do you think will be attending the event at the Museo tomorrow night?" Caterina asked.

Tina shrugged. "Rich people?"

A heavy sigh greeted her words. "Yes, there will be *rich people* there. Mostly though, it is for the Elites—the cream of the social crop. Not just anyone gets an invite to such a gala. Big donors to the Museo, as well as powerful politicians and businessmen, will be in attendance. And, of course, their rich snobby bitches of wives will be there too. Everyone will be on display, my dear, and *everyone* will be sniping at any perceived imperfection.

"What do you think would happen if I let you wear your everyday little black dress to a function such as this?" the designer inquired.

"They would eat me for breakfast."

"Dinner actually, but yes, exactly that. Now, shall we get on with it, or are you going to continue to be a brat?"

# Chapter 14

*"....Anunna geneticists realized that the relatively primitive species of Hominids that existed could be modified to become useful sources of labor. Utilizing these creatures for menial tasks such as agricultural work would free up valuable resources that could be put to better use elsewhere. Additionally, the Anunna were not about to perform such tasks themselves, so it made sense to use forced labor to take up the slack. The end result was a genetically modified version of the more advanced Homo Sapiens that came into being around forty thousand years ago. Unfortunately, these humans were not the most tractable of slaves and required constant supervision...."*

**Excerpt from the diary of Alexander Matthews**

**August 1993, A small village in Bosnia**

*Alexander staggered through the streets of the village, assaulted by the stench of death. The only sounds to be heard were the argumentative squawking of the scavenger birds fighting over the dead. Tears ran down his face freely, leaving clean tracks on his dirty skin. Everywhere he looked, he saw death: Men, women, and children. Even the animals had been slaughtered.*

*He had spent a few days with these people prior to heading up into the mountains with a team of archaeologists who were conducting a dig. Nearly everyone in the village was a vampire, and they were good, hard-working people, welcoming him into their midst and sharing their lore. He had planned on returning when his time at the excavations had come to an end.*

*Early this morning, not long after midnight, he had awoken from sleep to the sounds of gunfire. He had rushed to the edge of the ridge they were camped on, and looked down toward the village, where the strobing flashes and sharp barks of automatic weapons fire, faint screaming, and the orange-yellow of buildings on fire greeted him. Alexander immediately started running toward the violence, not caring that he hadn't even put his boots on.*

*They had all been warned, of course, had heard the rumors of ethnic cleansing being carried out at various places in the country, but it was always somewhere else. Not here. The sights that assaulted his eyes as he neared the village had shown that this was no longer the case.*

*The flutter of brightly colored cloth waving in the breeze drew his gaze. A girl, no more than five or six years old, lay sprawled on the ground. Her hand still clutched a handmade doll, the look of terror frozen onto her face, and the sightless eyes looked to the heavens. Her throat had been savagely cut from just underneath her right ear to the other side of her trachea. The blood that coated the front of her dress was turning tacky, and the flies that crawled across her face were already feeding.*

*Alexander leaned against a shot-up car and emptied his stomach. How could anyone do something like this? Death itself was nothing new to him. God knew he had killed more people than he cared to admit over the years…but nothing like this. The sheer savagery on display here was beyond anything he had ever experienced. Innocent lives had been destroyed for no other purpose than expediency: that and a desire to kill that which was* different.

*He walked to where the little girl had fallen, and he gently closed her eyes, then crossed her arms over her chest, ensuring that the doll stayed with her. Alexander picked her up and began walking back the way he had come, no real destination in mind, just a desire to leave this charnel-house. Tomorrow—tomorrow he would do his best to hunt the bastards down who had done this. The dead deserved their vengeance….*

***

The bell rang at the rental property promptly at five the next evening. When Alexander answered the door, Caterina and a heavily weighed down assistant swept into the entryway. "Where is she?" Caterina demanded.

He pointed at a door and quickly got out of their way as they descended upon Tina's bedroom. The entrance to her room slammed shut, and he could hear the lock engage. Much shrieking and shouting of orders ensued.

***

To call what was happening in her room chaos would be doing chaos a profound disservice. Caterina stood at the eye of the storm, imperiously directing the actions of both her assistant and Tina. Soon, three pairs of shoes were lined up on the floor, a beautiful cobalt blue dress hung in the closet, and Tina was completely naked.

Caterina handed her the most exquisite lingerie she had ever had the pleasure of touching. Tina rubbed the material between her fingers and was amazed at the silky texture. She looked up and met the designer's eyes.

"Caterina, of course, prefers to wear nothing under her creations, but if you *must*, then this is acceptable." She waved her hands and said, "Hurry, child, we have much to do and little time."

Tina soon found herself seated in a chair, looking at her reflection as Caterina worked on her hair. At the same time, the nameless assistant was giving her a mani/pedi. It seemed that the designer was going for some sort of formal *updo*, but it remained to be seen how it would finally work out.

Time blurred by, and she found herself wearing the dress as Caterina fussed and adjusted it. A single strap on the right side supported the body-hugging gown, and a long slit ran up the left side. The assistant had her try on the first pair of heels, but the designer simply said, "No. Get that garbage off her feet."

After several trials, they finally settled on the second pair of heels. Tears began to well up in Tina's eyes, and she was quickly handed a tissue and told *don't make a mess of your make-up*. She couldn't help it, though—the woman staring back at her from the mirror was a complete stranger. Never in her wildest dreams had she imagined looking this good.

Caterina nodded her head sharply, then sent her assistant away. "Shall we see whether Alexander approves?"

Tina sucked in a deep breath, then released it. She stepped close to the woman and whispered, "Thank you."

Caterina threw open the bedroom door and announced, "One princess, as desired."

Tina walked out of the room tentatively, her head down, not sure she wanted to know what Alexander thought. She heard a quick intake of breath, followed by the sound of someone plopping into a chair.

She glanced up to see him staring speechlessly at her. His widened eyes raked her from head to toe, and she could tell he liked what he saw. He turned to look at Caterina in disbelief, and the woman barked at him. "Stop imitating a beached fish, it's annoying. Did Caterina not say she would produce a miracle?"

He nodded wordlessly, then stood up. He held a case in his hands and walked over to where Tina stood. "It's perfect, Cat…except it needs accessories." Alexander opened the case, revealing a diamond and sapphire necklace and matching earrings. "I picked these up yesterday while I was waiting for the two of you to finish up."

Tina's hand flew up to cover her mouth, and she took a step backward in denial.

The swat on her ass took her by surprise. "Don't be stupid, girl, *never* turn down jewelry. Especially good jewelry."

Caterina took the case from Alexander and hustled Tina back into her bedroom, closing the door behind them. She reached around and fastened the necklace. Tina's fingers caressed the large sapphire that occupied the central pendant. Quickly the earrings were in place as well.

"I don't understand, Caterina. I can't even hazard a guess as to how much this cost. Why does he do things like this?" She paused. "I'm so confused."

The designer stared at her thoughtfully for a moment. "Do you remember what I said to you yesterday? Specifically, about how many women he has brought to me to design clothes for?"

Alexander's assistant nodded.

"I'm sure you noticed his reaction when he saw you?"

Another reluctant nod.

“Did that seem like a boss who approved of how his employee was dressed?”

In a whisper, “No.”

“No. That was the reaction of a man who is very, very attracted to a beautiful woman.” The wistful look in Caterina’s eye gave way to something much darker.

In a saccharine voice, she continued, “Which is why if I ever find out you have hurt him in any way, I will carve out your heart myself and eat it in front of you.”

***

The drive to the National Archaeological Museum didn’t take long. This was a good thing, given the tensions that existed between the occupants. Neither said a word, though it was apparent that both wanted to.

Alexander pulled the Acura to the sidewalk near the entrance to the museum, and they exited the car. He handed the keys to the valet and accepted a chit in return, which he slipped into the pocket of the slacks he was wearing. Clearing his throat, he said, “Are you ready for this?”

She stepped closer and slightly adjusted his bowtie. “Not even a little.”

Tina smiled tremulously up at him. “Maybe we should have a talk afterward?”

“I think that would be an excellent idea.”

Together they made their way into the museum and the crowd that filled the building. Alexander introduced Tina to several people, and others approached them over the course of the next hour or so. During that time, they nibbled on small snacks and sipped champagne as they mingled.

At 10 PM, several dignitaries, including the gentleman who ran the museum as his personal fiefdom, gave speeches that everyone politely applauded. The announcement was given that the ball portion of the evening would begin promptly at 11 PM.

“And so, the moment arrives when we find out if your lessons took or not. I suspect that all eyes shall be upon you as you rule the dance floor,” Alexander said.

"Only because I'll have tripped and made a fool of myself."

"I would never allow such a thing to happen. And if it did, I would defend your honor to my last breath," he promised.

She looked deep into his eyes. "I know you would, and that means a great deal to me."

He offered his elbow, and they slowly made their way to the area that had been cleared to make room for the ball. A sizeable two-story gallery with a towering, vaulted, fresco-covered ceiling and a patterned marble tiled floor was slowly filling with guests. A small orchestra was arranged at the far end of the long, expansive room. Multiple doors on either side allowed entrance and exit, and foot traffic was taking advantage of this fact.

Alexander guided Tina to a free spot along one wall, and said he would be back with fresh drinks. She nervously nodded at this and told him not to take too long.

He soon found a staff member who was working the crowd, dispensing flutes of champagne from the tray she was carrying. Glasses in hand, he made his way back to where he had left Tina. She appeared to be cornered by two slightly intoxicated men of about her age. Shaking her head at them, she was obviously trying to remain polite despite their unwanted advances.

Alexander walked up beside her, handing the champagne flutes to her, then stepped in front, blocking all access to her. His eyes glittered dangerously. "Thank you for keeping my date company whilst I was gone, boys, but your services are no longer needed."

Seemingly taken aback by his actions, they took stock of the man who had interrupted their attempts to sweep Tina off her feet. The greasier one of the pair sneered up at Alexander. "I think the Donna can speak for herself."

His companion laughed sycophantically, but otherwise contributed nothing to the conversation.

Alexander smirked then stepped forward and between the two men. He took each by the shoulder and turned them to face the other direction, then draped his arms around their necks, pulling them tight. A dangerous rumble emitted from his chest as he growled, "This one is *mine,* blood-sucker and dog-boy. Go find your own."

The final words were spoken as he firmly shoved both of them on their way. The vampire was clearly angry as he glared back at Alexander, but the shifter seemed uncertain. Arms crossed over his chest, Alexander continued to watch them as they slunk away.

He pasted a pleasant smile on his face as he spun and approached Tina.

"I'm sorry about that."

"Don't be. Apparently, ass-hattery crosses national boundaries," she replied. Suddenly a brilliant smile lit her face. "You called me your date."

"Did I? Hmmm, I wonder how that happened." Then he leaned down and gently kissed her lips.

"Is Caterina interrupting anything important? If so, Caterina apologizes." The dark-haired beauty stepped into proximity and beamed at both of them as she pinched Alexander's behind. She was wearing a blood-red gown that hugged her slim figure in all the right places.

Tina laughed out loud. "I'm so glad you're here, you look wonderful."

The designer waved her hand, nonchalantly. "Perhaps."

"Caterina wonders, will the princess allow her prince to have the first dance with Caterina?"

Tina beamed at Alexander and instructed him to fulfill the request. She watched as the raven-haired goddess and the man-candy she worked for gracefully swirled across the dance floor. It was readily apparent that both were accomplished dancers, and she couldn't help a small spike of jealousy.

After the dance ended, and Alexander had escorted Caterina back to where Tina stood, he took her hand and led her straight to the center, where they waited for the orchestra to begin the next waltz.

Tina bit her lip as he gazed down at her. The palms of her hands were damp, and she felt light-headed.

He whispered for her ears alone, "Relax, kiddo. You've got this."

The music started, and he smoothly led her around the dance floor. Once the butterflies in her stomach had settled down, she found that she was actually enjoying herself. She lost track of how many dances they shared, but Tina realized she was slightly out of breath and needed to take a break.

Standing by the wall once again, Alexander entertained her by pointing out various people and telling scandalous secrets about each that any tabloid would give their right arm for. She laughed at his outrageous stories until he glanced at his watch and asked, "Do you want to stay? Or should we go have that chat?"

"I'm ready to leave when you are, but I need to use the restroom first."

He nodded. "I'll meet you outside then. It's sweltering and my shirt is sticking to my back."

***

Tina luxuriated in the cool evening breeze that fluttered around her as she waited for Alexander. She had seen him trying to extricate himself from a particularly insistent couple, and rather than interrupt, she had made her way outside to the steps leading up to the museum entrance. He'd be along sooner or later, and in the meantime, she would soak up some of the ambiance that made up Naples.

"Well, well. What have we here?" a familiar voice cooed unctuously from her left side.

Tina's head snapped in that direction, and she saw one of the boys who had rather amateurishly tried to pick her up earlier in the evening. If anything, he seemed even more intoxicated than he had been.

"You should know that my date will be out any moment now," she warned him.

His leer widened at her words. "Oh, I think not. I made sure that he will be detained for the foreseeable future."

Tina attempted to step past him and make her way back into the museum foyer, but his hand latched onto her bicep painfully, forcing her to an abrupt stop. "And where do you think you are going?" he asked menacingly.

"Back inside. I've decided that the air smells better there than it does out here."

He pulled her close, rank breath washing over her face. "No, I'll not allow it. You and I have a rendezvous to conclude."

She struggled briefly, then felt a sharp impact, followed by a white light flashing behind her eyes, before everything faded to black.

The valet apparently thought nothing of two men, one on either side of an apparently drunk woman, walking across the street and disappearing into the shadows.

***

Alexander finally managed to disengage from one of his regular customers, and had barely made it outside when the ferric smell of blood hit his nostrils. A lot of blood. His head swiveled to follow the scent trail, and he realized he was looking at an alleyway perhaps one hundred yards away and slightly to his left.

He had a bad feeling about this, especially as he looked around for Tina and couldn't find her. His feet led him closer, and he burst into a sprint when he realized that he could smell her distinctive scent coming from that blood-soaked alley. The sight that greeted his eyes when he made the turn was one that would haunt him forever. A form crouched over Tina's body, her torn neck sluggishly pumping blood, as the vampire hissed through gore-covered lips with displeasure at being interrupted. Just behind them was a wolf, snarling loudly as it bared its fangs at him.

Alexander did not hesitate as he charged forward, grabbing the vampire and throwing him directly at the werewolf. Bones broke when the bloodsucker impacted the wolf, and a loud yelp and slurred cursing broke the relative silence of the alleyway.

He knelt next to Tina and raised her just enough that he could brace her shoulders against his thigh. Blood soaked the entire front of her dress and continued to surge out of the large hole that had been ripped into her neck. She reached for his face with one hand as she struggled to speak, bloody foam trailing out one corner of her mouth as a horrible gurgling sounded from where her trachea had been torn open by the bite of the vampire.

Alexander quickly took off his jacket and tried to use it to apply pressure to her wound, but he was losing the battle to keep her alive. "Just hang in there, kiddo, I'll get you some help."

The look of anguish on his face was almost more than Tina could bear. She tried to tell him it was '*OK*' but couldn't get the words out. Her body arched and shuddered as she tried to cough, and her vision was starting to fade when he told her he was sorry, tears streaming down his cheeks.

He knew he was losing her, and at that moment, Alexander decided to do something he had sworn he would never allow. Tearing open his shirt, he grasped the amulet that hung from the chain around his neck and began a partial shift to his hybrid form. He placed the amulet just below her collar bone and bit down on her upper arm, willing with full intent that she be infected as he was. The amulet flared with an internal green light, and the interlocking parts moved of their own accord, forming a new pattern. Four small pinpricks were revealed as Alexander lifted the device away from her body, allowing it to swing freely on the chain.

Even as he watched, the artery and the tissues surrounding the wound began to knit back together. Alexander hoped he had not been too late, but it was out of his hands now. Using the cell phone he had taken from his jacket pocket, he placed a call.

"Cat, I need you. Now."

"Of course. Where are you?" she asked, hearing the desperation in his voice.

"Are you still at the gala?"

"Yes."

"Go out the front door and follow the scent of blood." He ended the call and looked down at the helpless figure in his arms, her eyes closed and chest rising and falling in shallow, rapid breaths.

After what seemed like days, but in reality, couldn't have been longer than two or three minutes, he could hear Cat approaching. She had her hand over her mouth in horror as she walked over to Alexander.

"Oh God, Alexander, I'm so sorry. What can I do to help?"

He rolled his ruined jacket up and gently eased Tina's head down onto it, then handed Caterina a house key. "I need you to take care of her for me, Cat. Can you take her back to my rental and stay with her until I finish what I need to do?"

She nodded her head. "There's no need to worry. She'll be safe with me."

"I know, and I appreciate that. You are the only person in this town I trust right now." He gazed up at her with pain-filled eyes. "When she wakes up, try to explain it to her, please. If she hates me for what I've done to her, I'll understand."

A sob escaped her as she asked, "What will you do now, Alexander?"

When he looked at her, all she saw was death. "I'm going to kill them all."

Without a backward glance, he strode down the alley, following the trail of the two animals who had taken something very precious from him.

Caterina's gaze followed his shadowy figure until it disappeared, then she whispered, "What have you fools done?"

# Chapter 15

*"....Once I had made up my mind that I was going to settle down and live permanently in the Lilac City, I decided that something needed to be done about the Vampires, Weres, and other races that had been treating the ordinary human citizens as their open-air larder. It took three years of constant and bloody vigilante action on a nightly basis to chase the vermin out. From that point forward, I was known as the Master of the city, and my rules were law...."*

**An excerpt from the diary of Alexander Matthews**

**December 1954, Somewhere along the waterfront, Palermo, Sicily**

*The barrel of the revolver was pressed firmly into his temple, the barrel cold against his skin. Alexander stood very still as two more men approached from the front, obviously confident that they had this situation under control.* The world is full of retards, *he thought, fighting hard not to roll his eyes at the stupidity of it all.*

*The goon with the revolver stood to the left of him and was trying very hard to look menacing.... He failed. He was little more than a teenager, and if Alexander had to guess, related to the older man who seemed to be in charge.* All I wanted to do was take a pleasant stroll late at night, *he thought ruefully.*

*The leader barked, "Give me your wallet, and any other valuables you have," in the local dialect. Alexander briefly considered pretending he didn't understand, but decided that he was getting pissed about being on the receiving end of a poorly executed shakedown.*

*"Fuck off," he said, sounding bored.*

*The boy jabbed the barrel of the gun harder into his temple. The American slowly turned his head to look at him. Cold eyes bored into the goon. "You should reconsider your chosen line of work," he said quietly. "This one is likely to end up with you being dead."*

*A hard punch rocked his head, and the third goon was shaking his hand as he backed away from Alexander. The predatory smile that greeted this assault was not what any of the Sicilians expected. "You die first" ground out between gritted teeth.*

*The two men standing in front of him shared a startled glance, then the leader found his courage. "Shoot him."*

*Before the words had even left his mouth, the American made his move. Claws sprouted from his fingertips and he reached up to where the gun rested against his head; he crushed the hand that held the weapon. The sounds of bone splintering and the accompanying shriek of agony echoed along the waterfront.*

*Alexander released the hand and leapt to where the goon who had punched him stood. His left hand went behind the man's head and grasped him firmly, and the strike from his other fist crunched through the nasal cavity and the pars orbitalis. His fist destroyed the entire front portion of his skull and buried itself up to the wrist in the brain behind these structures. A loud squelching slurp was heard as he withdrew the fist and turned his furious eyes on the leader.*

*A knife appeared in his shaking hand—it looked like a cheap switchblade to Alexander—and he weaved it in front of himself as a sort of defense while backing away. The laugh that greeted his actions was derogatory, and when the American opened the hand that had just killed one of the trio, brains and bone oozed off and dropped to the ground, steaming in the frigid air. The man's eyes darted to the long claws that shone wetly in the moonlight, and he tossed the knife at Alexander and tried to run. Two long steps brought the American within striking distance, and the claws of his hand tore into the man's back, spanning the spinal column, and with a jerk, ripped out several inches of the spine. The body dropped face-first onto the cobblestones and continued to twitch for a few moments.*

*Alexander heard the hammer of the revolver being pulled back, and he spun to face the teenager. A single shot rang out and the bullet slammed into his left pectoral muscle. Judging by the lack of penetration, he surmised it was a smaller caliber, like a .38 maybe. He grunted and began to advance on the boy who lay on the ground, revolver held in his off-hand, terrified eyes looking at what was surely his death.*

*The claws on his right hand searched for the bullet that was buried in his chest. Alexander pulled the round out and looked at it curiously before dropping it, the dull clank as it hit the cobblestones the only sound other than the labored breathing coming from the goon who had shot him.*

*He stopped and considered the teenager for a second. "How old are you, boy?" he asked.*

*"Eigh…eighteen."*

*Alexander grunted noncommittally. "Does your mother know where you are and what you are doing?"*

*"No, Signore, she would not approve."*

*"Good. If you want to live, you will need to follow my instructions to the letter…and don't think I won't know. I will, and things will go very badly for you. Understand?" he said menacingly.*

*The boy's head jerked in a nod as he cradled his mangled hand.*

*"You will go home and tell your mother everything. Recount every bad deed you have performed and leave nothing out." He paused meaningfully. "And you will find an honest way to make a living. This one is hazardous to your health."*

***

Even as he loped down alleys and backstreets, his heartbeat thundering in his ears, staying on the trail of his prey, Alexander felt nothing but rage. Tina's lifeblood was drying on his hands, turning tacky as the minutes went by. He kept flexing his fingers impotently, knowing that her fate was now out of his hands. What *was* still in his control, however, was the reckoning that the murderers had earned, and he had every intention of seeing that bill paid in full.

Impotent feelings of loss and sadness threatened to drown out the anger, and he could not afford to give in to them. Instead, he stoked the fires, relishing the rage and hatred that flooded his body with a heady chemical cocktail. His wolf howled deep within the confines of his mind, demanding vengeance, and Alexander fully intended to give his internal companion precisely what he wanted. He cared little about his personal safety. In fact, it didn't even enter into the equation. If he went down under a sea of enemies, it would all be worth it just as long as he could kill those who had wronged the woman he loved.

This situation shouldn't even be possible. There were rules, laws even, that had been put in place to prevent just such a scenario. And these laws had stringent and inflexible consequences attached that were to be meted out to any who would ignore them. Justice *would* be served, and if he took great enjoyment in being the instrument who delivered the punishment, then all the better. Alexander had spent the better part of his life preventing this very thing from happening in Spokane, and he would be damned if it would be allowed here.

Slowing to a halt, Alexander had a decision to make. The trail he had been following split: the wolf going left, and the vampire to the right. Which to pursue first? There was little doubt that both would die this night, but which should he take down now? He shook his head having decided that the vampire would die last, knowing that his doom was soon to call.

***

Alexander was standing in the darkness just across the street from the building where he had tracked the wolf. It was a sizeable multi-level villa, occupying the entire city block, but somewhat isolated. A double gate that was currently open controlled access to the semi-circular drive. There were other buildings nearby, but nothing that directly abutted the property. His entire body trembled with barely contained rage, hands clenching and unclenching with nervous energy. Eyeing the lone sentry guarding the entryway, he decided to make his move.

Streaking across the intervening distance took a fraction of a second, and the guard did not even feel it as his neck was snapped like a twig. Tossing the body aside, Alexander opened one of the massive doors that led into the grand foyer of the residence. His nose tested the air and determined that most of the Pack that was present were located at the back of the building and upstairs.

He ignored the semi-spiral staircases that rose on either side of the foyer, and made his way to the doors that closed off the back of the house. He paused there, listening carefully for any sounds on the other side.

He nodded as he detected the presence of two more guards. Nearly ripping the doors off their moorings, he rushed the sentry on the left and tore his throat out with his bare hand, and before the body could hit the floor, he had struck the second man hard enough that he was unconscious when Alexander caught him mid-collapse. He laid the man on the floor, not taking a great deal of care with how gently he did so, then began stripping out of his blood-soaked clothes.

Once he was completely naked, he grasped the unconscious man with both hands and launched him head-first at the doors he had been guarding. The body exploded through the heavy-oak panels as if they were tissue paper, sending splinters flying in a destructive fan toward the long table currently hosting a large dinner party. The broken body of the guard tumbled down the single flight of stairs and came to an untidy stop about fifteen feet from the last step.

The shocked diners looked up to see a three-hundred-pound black wolf stalk down the stairway, a snarl on its face and a deep rumbling growl emanating from its chest. It paused at the body, pushing it with its nose as if waiting for a reaction, then hoisted its hind leg, urinating on the corpse, clearly showing its disdain. The wolf was the largest any of them had ever seen, easily out-massing any competitor by perhaps thirty percent.

It continued to advance on the table, head lowered and tucked into its chest, nails clicking on the marble tiles, until it was just a few feet from the end closest the doors, then leapt into the air. In the span of less than two seconds, it had transformed into a seven-hundred-pound hybrid form that almost caused the table to collapse as the hind feet slammed down.

It snarled and snapped at the people seated on either side as it arrogantly strode down the length of the table, scattering centerpieces, wine glasses, and dinnerware. The mismatched eyes almost glowed with the hatred that simmered behind them, and no one was foolish enough to try to escape. When the colossal form neared the head of the table, it tipped its head back, throwing its arms wide, and roared thunderously, spittle spraying those unfortunate to be in its path. As the sound still echoed throughout the room, a rapid shift revealed a naked man. If anything, he was more fearsome than his hybrid shape, and death, incarnate, stared at them from his narrowed eyes.

"Where is he?" he demanded in a gravelly voice.

The middle-aged man the question was directed at looked defiantly up at Alexander and shrugged. "You are going to have to be more specific, Signore."

Alexander leaned forward and grasped the sides of the man's head, then easily tore it from his shoulders. Blood fountained, and the corpse fell from the chair to lie twitching on the floor. With a satisfied look, he tossed the head at a servant, who stood frozen, a bottle of wine still in his hands. The gruesome missile struck him in the chest and fell at his feet.

"I am not fucking around here, people, and what little patience I had deserted me a long time ago." He spun in place until he was facing down the length of the table. "Someone in this house attacked a Normal tonight. A woman who was under my protection. A woman I had clearly indicated was *mine*. I followed his scent trail back to this house."

His head swiveled from face to shocked face. "Either you willingly hand him over to me, or I will kill every… last… fucking one of you. Am I clear?"

"That won't be necessary. I'm right here." The quavering voice belonged to the young man standing in a doorway, armed with a rapier and main gauche.

Alexander's head swiveled slowly, and he inhaled deeply. "I recognize your stench, pup. Time for you to die."

He launched himself from the table and rushed at the terrified young man, who tried in vain to defend himself. The rapier hissed over Alexander's head as he ducked under the swing, and the claws that sprouted from his fingertips raked deep furrows into the arm that held the main gauche. The damage was so extensive that it rendered the arm all but useless, and the short blade dropped to the marble floor with a clang.

The youth gasped at the sudden pain and tried desperately to disengage.

The chuckle that Alexander emitted could only be perceived as demonic. "You are going to have to do much better than that, pup." He grinned as he licked the blood off his claws.

"I told you she was *mine*."

Grasping his wounded arm with the hand still holding the rapier, the young man hissed as the wounds began to heal. "We take what we want, *when* we want, and no one tells us we can't," he said defiantly.

A feral grin appeared on Alexander's face. "*Those* days are over, you fucktard. Permanently." His claws ripped through his opponent's abdomen, spilling internal organs and blood onto the already-gore-stained floor. A wail of anguish erupted from one of the women seated at the head of the table. Alexander's left hand grasped the dying man around the throat as the other darted inside the eviscerated torso and ripped the still-beating heart out.

"My son!" shrieked the same voice as earlier.

"What gives you the right?" demanded another.

Alexander crushed the heart between his fingers, then dropped it carelessly. He studied those who remained in the dining room with him, and the cold calculation they saw there did little to reassure them.

"I want the entire Pack here in thirty minutes." He turned his back on them and strode to the servant, who still occupied the same spot as before, and casually kicked the severed head aside. Alexander took the bottle from him with a bloody hand, tipped it toward his lips, and drank deeply. He glanced at the label and said, "This is good. Bring me another bottle."

The servant nervously nodded his head and scuttled away.

Other staff had entered the room and started to remove the bodies.

"Leave them!" he shouted. "I want everyone to see what has happened here tonight."

***

Lounging in a chair that more resembled a throne, one leg casually draped over a padded arm, scowl firmly fixed on his face, Alexander let the dregs of the bottle of wine empty into his mouth. With barely concealed distaste, he surveyed those standing before him.

His audience murmured amongst themselves and nervously eyed the corpses that still lay where they had fallen, pools of blood beginning to clot after being exposed to the air for so long. Most of their attention was focused on the naked man seated in front of them. The half-sleeve wolf tattoo on his right arm and chest stood out in stark contrast to his lightly tanned skin.

Dawn was only a couple of hours away, and Alexander decided to just get it over with. He *really* didn't give a shit at this point. He stood abruptly and took a menacing step forward.

"Some of you are probably aware already, but for those who aren't, I will explain it in the simplest of terms. Last night the gutless wonder over there," he gestured toward the corpse he had eviscerated, "and a vampire friend, decided they could attack and kill a Normal. Unfortunately for them, and by extension, *you*, this Normal was under *my* protection."

The glare he leveled at everyone in the room spoke volumes. "Now, we all know the rules when it comes to Normal humans, don't we? Or am I mistaken, and your Pack leadership has been remiss in explaining the laws to you? Is that the case?" Silence greeted his question.

"IS. THAT. THE. CASE!" he screamed at them.

He heard grudgingly muttered denials in response.

"Excellent. Whilst I was waiting for your slow asses to trickle in, I did a little research via Google." He looked expectantly at them and held up his smartphone. "Do you know what I discovered?"

Silence.

"It would seem that Naples has suffered from a string of gruesome murders over the course of the last year or so. I don't suppose any of you would know anything about that, would you?" His eyes took note of the members of the Pack who wouldn't meet his eyes or didn't seem overly surprised by his statement.

"Now, some of these murders match what I would expect to see if a vampire were to be the culprit, and yet, the remainder indicates a shifter as the killer. What am I to make of this?" he continued in a contemplative voice.

"If you all are cognizant of the rules, and you said you were, one has to wonder what could possibly entice a member, or members, of this Pack to risk the survival of you all." His quirked eyebrow drove home his point.

"I find myself in somewhat of a dilemma. The *only* punishment for breaking the law is death, and much as it would simplify my life to just *end* you all, I find it hard to believe the entire Pack is guilty."

A voice shouted out, "Who are you to judge us?"

Alexander immediately transformed into his hybrid shape, leapt over the crowd and tore the dissenter into multiple pieces. He bent over to pick up his phone, shaking it gently to try to clear as much of the body fluids from it as possible, then calmly walked back through the crowd, all of whom quickly made room for his passage, until he once more stood before them. Transitioning back into his naked human form, he glared balefully at them all.

"I am Alpha. I am *THE* Alpha!" he bellowed. "Does anyone dispute my claim? If so, step forward and challenge."

His glare passed over the crowd, but only one man stepped forward. "I am Enzo Falconi, and I challenge you for the position of Alpha."

Alexander dipped his head in lazy acknowledgment. "Begin when you are ready." He stood stoically, arms hanging at his sides.

They stared at each other for a moment, then Enzo shifted and leapt straight at the Alpha. Alexander stepped into the attack and landed a solid right hand to Enzo's hybrid torso. The air blasted out of him at the impact, and he slid forward face-first on the floor where he had landed. Alexander just stood there, not following up while the advantage was his, then turned his back on the challenger.

Enzo shook his head to clear it as he forced his way back to his feet. He approached Alexander far more cautiously this time, swiping at him with his clawed hands. Enzo had the height and weight advantage, as long as the Alpha remained in his human form. Alexander simply dodged the strikes or redirected them with circular motions of his hands.

Enzo's frustration grew with each failed attack, and eventually, he charged straight in, hoping to take his target by surprise. He failed. Alexander caught him mid-leap and slammed his body down onto the floor with bone-crushing force. His hands had maintained their grip, and he pulled the stunned werewolf closer to his face as he leaned down. "Shift back. Now."

Enzo's form shrank until he was human once again. Alexander's face was only inches away when he growled softly, "I could kill you easily. But I won't.

You were the only one with the balls to challenge, so I'm going to let you live." A pause. "For now."

Speaking in a louder voice, Alexander asked, "Do you submit?"

"I do," was the response.

The Alpha released his hold on Enzo and straightened to his full height. "Anyone else?"

When no additional challengers stepped forward, Alexander said, "So be it. You are now all officially my bitches." Heads were lowered submissively throughout the room.

"Everyone except Enzo… and you." His finger stabbed at one of the staff. "Get the fuck out of my sight."

His eyes pinned Enzo where he stood. "You and I are going to take a ride in a little while, so stay close." He glared at the only other remaining figure. "I need to take a shower and I require new clothes. Strike that, I need two sets of clothes and a backpack. Can you handle that?"

"Yes, Sir. If you'll follow me."

***

The servant led him to what was obviously the former Alpha's quarters, then departed, saying he would return with suitable garments and the backpack. Alexander headed to the bathroom and turned on the shower, running the water as hot as he could stand it. The tacky blood that had been drying on his body was not easy to scrub off. He paid particular attention to his hair and washed it three times before the water ran clean.

Alexander closed his eyes and rested his forehead against the tiles of the shower stall. He was mentally exhausted, and the day wasn't even over yet. He kept seeing the tortured look on Tina's face as she gasped out her final breaths. For all he knew, his last-ditch option hadn't been in time and she had died while he was here dealing with this renegade Pack. He shook himself and forced his focus back onto the tasks at hand. Alexander let his rage grow, stoking the fires until they burned bright and hot. He knew he needed to hold onto the rage until this was done. Only then would he let himself mourn, or, as the case may be, face the consequences of his actions.

He had never wanted this, to be a Pack leader. For the last one hundred fifteen years he had kept himself isolated. Controlling Spokane had been by necessity, not a desire for power. Internal Pack politics, and all the horseshit that went with it, had never appealed to him. For more than a century, he had kept the oath he had sworn the day he woke up in that cave in New Mexico.... Until today. His had been a lonely life, although fulfilling in many ways. Had he made the right choice by infecting Tina? Should he have let her die without even trying? Logically the answer was a definite '*Yes*,' and yet he knew his heart would never have allowed it. From the day she had stepped into his life, Tina had been a disruptive influence. All of his carefully crafted routines that had been so comforting over the years crumbled in the face of her mere presence. He had found himself actually caring what this child of a woman thought of him and his actions. Yet he had barely known her, merely scratching the surface. She'd brought a spark of sunshine into his rather bleak existence, one he had not known was missing. Alexander had walled himself off, purposely created barriers that those around him could seldom penetrate. He could count the number of close friends he had allowed in, on a personal basis, on the fingers of both hands, and only one of them was a standard human. How Tina had gotten around all of his mental fail-safes would forever confound him.

For months he had wanted to tell her the truth, but he was afraid that Tina would leave once she found out what he actually was. That fear had prevented him from opening up to her, but in reality, it had also locked him in a cage of his own devising, with no clear path forward to the happiness he so deeply craved. And so, he found himself where he was today. All his attempts to shield her from this hidden world had been for naught, the control that he thought he had, torn from his grasp by a single act of horror. All that was left to him was retribution, though so far that meal tasted like ashes in his mouth.

Alexander tossed the wet towel onto the gleaming white marble floor of the bathroom, and emerged to find both clothing and a leather satchel set out on the bed. He was moderately surprised to find that the slacks and polo shirt fit reasonably well. The underwear went untouched as there were some lines he simply would not cross, and wearing another man's boxers was one of those, but the socks and shoes would do. He carefully rolled the second set of clothes and placed them in the satchel, which he threw over one shoulder.

His impatient stride quickly delivered him back to the slaughterhouse of a dining room. The house staff froze in place, but relaxed as he saw what they were doing and just nodded. The bodies had already been removed, and the blood was being mopped up even now.

Spotting a now fully clothed Enzo, who had been observing the clean-up process as he leaned against a wall, Alexander gestured for the other wolf to join him. "Take me to the armory."

Enzo raised a brow but motioned for his new Alpha to follow. He led the way down a set of stairs, then along a dimly lit hallway to a heavy steel door embedded in the tufa rock foundations of the house above. He removed an antique-looking key and pulled the door open after unlocking it.

Alexander walked in, perusing the weapons stockpiled within. He grabbed a large pistol whose barrel was extended and threaded externally, along with a silencer. His eyes shifted to the blades carefully arranged on racks, and he selected a functional, but plain, arming-sword and scabbard. Three loaded magazines for the pistol went into pouches on the right side of a tactical belt that also had a holster that fit the weapon.

Looking hard at Enzo, he asked, "Can you shoot?"

The Italian nodded slowly.

Alexander moved to stand directly in front of him with a curious look on his face and said, "Shall I take a chance on you, Enzo? I wonder…."

His nostrils flared as he gazed deeply into the other man's eyes, evaluating what his senses told him. He finally relented and strode past his erstwhile challenger. "You are now my Beta. Grab three wolves you trust and gear up. This operation is to remain quiet, so blades and suppressed weapons only. You have five minutes. At the end of that time, I want to be sitting in a vehicle and on my way to where the vamps live."

***

The toe of Alexander's shoe tapped impatiently on the granite step at the bottom of the house entryway. He had already screwed the suppressor onto the pistol that was now in the holster and strapped to his leg, and once again he shifted the belt to ensure that the weight of the magazines and sidearm was evenly distributed. The hilt of the scabbarded sword peeked up over his right shoulder, strapped for easy access and a quick draw.

He was scowling at the rising sun when a black panel van rushed through the gates and came to an abrupt stop just below where he stood. Enzo jumped out of the passenger side door and took the few steps needed to report to his Alpha. "We are ready, Sir."

"You know the way?" Alexander asked calmly.

"Yes. We can be there in twenty minutes."

"Then let's roll." The big American walked to the back of the van, opened the door, and climbed inside. There were three seats on each side, and he sat in the one closest to the rear and behind the driver.

The hairy eyeball he gave the other occupants did little to reduce the palpable tension in the vehicle, and they rode in silence through the streets of early morning Naples.

The van pulled to a stop not far from another villa that was similar to the one they had just left. The vehicle's occupants all turned to him, seeking further instructions.

"My plan is simple. The four of you will take the exits from the house. Your *only* job is to kill anyone who attempts to flee the building. If you follow me into the house, I will not be responsible for what happens." He sought out each pair of eyes. "I am barely holding onto things as it is, and once I go in there, I plan to let it all out. Either I die, which solves your current predicament, or I kill every one of these motherfuckers. Am I clear?"

Nods from each of them, although Enzo looked like he wanted to protest.

"Your new Beta is in charge of exterior ops. Do you have comms?" Another set of nods. "Excellent. This shouldn't take too long...one way or the other."

Alexander led the way forward once they exited the van. There were two guards at the gate, but a silenced round in each skull took care of that little problem. In a low voice, he told Enzo's team he would allow them three minutes to get into position. After that, he was going to breach.

He spent the time focusing on what lay ahead, playing out various scenarios in his head. At the end of the time he'd allocated, his form blurred across the space and slammed the doors open with his shoulder. Even before his feet hit the floor, his pistol had tracked onto a target and fired a single round that impacted right between the eyes. He could hear multiple pairs of feet pounding toward him from several directions. Rather than wait for them to come to him, he sprinted up the stairs, decapitating a woman with the sword as he ran by, and kicking in the first door he came to. He fired twice but was interrupted as a figure tried to tackle him from inside the room. The pommel of the sword in his right hand came down on the back of the vampire's head, the cranium made the sound of a ripe melon bursting at the impact, and the body slipped bonelessly to the floor. A glance inside confirmed that all targets were down. Alexander slashed the sword through the neck of the one lying at his feet to ensure he would not heal and come after the Alpha wolf once again.

Doors were opening along the hallway, and every time Alexander saw a head or torso, he put a bullet in it. Screams and roars of outrage could be heard, and a grim smile graced his face as he could taste their terror. He crossed the hall and kicked open the next door. A bullet struck his shoulder, throwing his balance off, but he still managed to plunge his sword into the stomach of the vampire who had shot him. Alexander ejected the empty mag and reloaded, leaving the blade jutting out of his latest victim. His hand reached out to the hilt and jerked it from the body as he double-tapped the wailing man, who slipped off the longsword.

The next room was empty, but the fourth suite held a male and a female. He shot the man as he leapt at him, but he realized he didn't have time to line up a shot on the woman. His blade severed one of her arms at the shoulder, her shriek as the sword passed through her flesh sounding loud in the confines of the bedroom. Her momentum carried her past, and the blade flicked out again, this time taking a leg. She collapsed in the doorway, and Alexander gazed down dispassionately as her lifeblood pumped out of the stumps. He stepped over her thrashing body and went from room to room, dispatching every person he came across. Some tried to fight back, some tried to run, but in the end, they all died. Standing at the top of the stairwell at the other end of the long hallway, he realized he was out of bullets. Holstering the pistol, he took stock of his injuries. Most were minor, and the few that weren't mattered little, there would be sufficient time to finish this battle.

His feet did not hesitate as he sauntered down the stairs. He could hear many more vampires still alive on the lower levels, and he fully intended to remedy that situation. At the bottom of the stairs he glanced at the front entryway, and he could see a few extra bodies scattered both in and outside the doors. Alexander nodded in satisfaction, realizing that Enzo and his team were doing their jobs.

He turned toward the back of the house and started walking, dragging the tip of the bloodied blade along behind him. The shrill scraping sound the sword made as he continued forward let the remaining vampires know precisely where he was, and that was fine with him. The house opened up as his footsteps took him deeper into the ground-floor. He was ambushed as he walked into the kitchen and received a deep slash across his upper back. His head swiveled to his attacker, the longsword lashing out to sever the hand holding the blade that had just cut him. He stabbed into the torso at a slight upward angle, piercing the heart, the power of the thrust lifting the body into the air where he held it, muscles bulging in his sword-arm. He examined the vampire's face almost curiously before withdrawing the blade with a flourish. Alexander was already in motion once again before the corpse hit the floor.

There was little of the conscious Alexander left by this point. Bloodlust had taken hold. He had become a killing machine that mercilessly stalked his prey, seeking them out wherever they might hide. The clothes he had borrowed were terribly rent, barely clinging in shreds to his body, and covered in gore, some of it his own. And none of that mattered. Death had come calling, and he was making himself at home.

His nose lifted into the air, seeking prey. Once again dragging the tip of the sword behind him, his steps took him through another doorway. The sound of bullets impacting the wall beside him, and the fleshier *splat* of the round that hit his thigh, indicated that there were still those who would seek to block his way.

Alexander charged forward, ignoring the pain from his leg, and slid on his knees below the firing arc of the SMG wielded by his enemy. His sword described a short arc that severed the feet of the vampire who was shooting at him. There was a cry of agony and the thud of a body hitting the floor behind him. Still on his knees, the Alpha wolf looked over his shoulder to find the vampire struggling to stanch the blood that was fountaining from the stumps where his ankles used to be. He stood up and backhanded the blade, nearly severing the head completely, but just enough remained that when gravity forced it backward, it was still attached by nothing more than skin.

A stairwell leading down beckoned him—more prey hid there, and he could sense their fear. He made no attempt to muffle the sound his feet made on the steps as he walked down them. His heavy tread was impending doom, as inevitable as the stormy surf on a rocky shore. Whimpers and tremulous whispers echoed up from below.

Alexander gazed upon twenty-five or thirty vampires who were cowering against the far wall, children among them. He paused, tried to brush back a lock of hair that kept falling over his burning eyes, but it was so encrusted with blood and other more unspeakable things that it refused to stay put. The shoe on his injured leg squelched with each movement, his blood pooling there with every step he had taken.

His lips curled in a snarl and his body tensed in preparation for one last burst of effort, but a familiar voice stopped him.

"Alexander, no. You have to stop."

He glared over his shoulder, madness in his eyes. "Why are you here? My wrath is righteous, Cat. These vermin have taken from me. Taken the only thing that has mattered in a very long time."

She sighed deeply. "Yes. Some of them did, but not all. Let the killing stop now. Let what you have done be enough."

"Why do you care, Cat? How do you suggest I separate the guilty from the innocent? This very Coven tried to drive you out, kill you even, more than sixty years ago. That's how we met, remember? You are Outcast." He flicked his fingers dismissively.

"I have never forgotten, Alexander. Even so, you would destroy them all?"

The madness in his eyes did little to reassure her. "Why not? They mean nothing to me."

Her hand rose placatingly. "Tina yet lives. I believe she will survive the transformation."

He inhaled sharply. "But at what cost, Cat? She never asked for this, didn't even know about us. I have made her a monster…just like me."

"Alexander, please. Let it be enough."

His eyes glanced over her head to where Enzo stood, his pistol pointed at the back of Caterina's skull. A minimal shake of his head caused his Beta to lower his weapon.

"Fine. I do this because *you* ask it of me." He spun and threw the sword like a spear; the tip entered the chest of one of the vampires at the rear of the room, not stopping until the hilt slammed against the breastbone. The figure dropped to its knees, coughing up blood. Those around him backed away quickly, leaving a clear space.

"That is the one who fed off her. *You* finish him." Alexander's baleful gaze reached out to every surviving vampire. "This Coven belongs to you from this moment forward. It is now your responsibility to ensure I never have to return, because if I do, I will slaughter every vampire in this city. Understood?"

She nodded, squared her shoulders, walked over to grasp the hilt protruding from the figure kneeling in front of her, and twisted it sharply, destroying the heart within. Cat withdrew the blade and cleaned it the best she could on the clothes the corpse was wearing, then walked back to where Alexander and Enzo stood, handing him the blood-covered hilt.

Alexander dipped his head in acknowledgment, then reached out and grasped her shoulder, staining her shirt with the fluids that covered his palm. "*You* lead this Coven, but you are also one of my Betas now, Cat."

Enzo sucked in a breath, surprised by this pronouncement.

"Don't fuck it up." He swept past her and limped up the stairs, leaving her to clean up this mess.

Enzo looked at her guardedly. "That man frightens me, Signorina."

A laughing sob escaped her. "That man should frighten *everyone.*"

She moved closer and whispered, "Let me rephrase my statement. Anyone who breaks his rules, moral code, or harms innocents, would be better served to cut their own throat. He does not tolerate fools, nor does Alexander believe that there is any such thing as overkill."

"Si, I am beginning to understand that."

# Chapter 16

*"....The years between 1925 and the outbreak of WWII were spent mostly in the Middle East and Egypt. I used the money and properties that I had* 'acquired' *when I cleansed Spokane of its unwanted elements to finance several expeditions to dig at various sites. I particularly found Mohenjo-daro to be of interest. Even though I found no trace of the alien technology I was searching for, there were indications in the glassy layer found in the ruins that it was probably destroyed in a continuation of the wars that had been taking place for thousands of years prior to recorded history, possibly by a nuclear device. My intuition told me that there was a link between this culture and the Anunna...somehow...."*

**An excerpt from the diary of Alexander Matthews**

**March 1916, Central Mexico**

*Alexander pushed sweat-drenched hair out of his eyes and plopped down into the camp chair, frustration evident in his actions. He had spent the last nine months slogging through the jungle and examining what little had been excavated of the various cultures who had called this area home. Many days and nights of speaking with tribal elders and shamans had provided very little actionable data, and in truth, about all he could say for sure was that all the cultures shared a belief in the Feathered Serpent—Quetzalcoatl to the Aztecs, and Kukulkan to the Maya.*

*While interesting in and of itself, it did little to solidify his search for traces of the Anunna. He knew that they had been here, in the Americas, because En's city had been in the Gulf of Mexico, somewhere off the coast of Texas. His memories couldn't place the location any more precisely than that, but it was in that general geographic area. En's enemy, the goddess Nin, had a city-state to the south, and his progenitor had attacked it at least once with an army that had traveled by ship to reach enemy territory.*

*Unfortunately, no trace of either city existed on dry land. His hope had been to find clear evidence that when the waters rose at the end of the last ice age, emigres had brought vestiges of their civilization with them when they moved farther inland, integrating into the more primitive peoples who lived there. Hints that they had done so existed in shared ritual beliefs, common pantheons, architectural styles, and other things...but no smoking bullet. To say that he was frustrated would be a colossal understatement.*

*He had decided to wrap the expedition up and go home. Alexander did not feel there was anything to be gained from staying longer. He would just have to look elsewhere....*

***

Alexander limped up the stairs and made his way out to the semi-circular drive at the front of the villa. He sat gingerly on the top step and extended his wounded leg, waiting for Enzo and his crew to bring the van, adrenaline causing his hands to shake. Hanging his head tiredly, he attempted to calm the anger that still burned hotly in his chest. The Alpha knew this wasn't finished, not even close. Alexander would need to spend some time in Naples, not only forging the remaining Pack and Coven members into a cohesive whole, something that went against thousands of years of tradition, but also rooting out the bad seeds that he knew still existed.

He wanted nothing more than to hand control over to his selected Betas, wash his hands of the whole mess, but knew this wasn't fair to Enzo and Caterina. Neither was truly prepared for the leadership role he had thrust them into, but his options were limited. Alexander would stay long enough to establish control, shift most of the responsibilities onto their shoulders, and crush any resistance Pack or Coven members retained. Either complicitly, or through a serious lack of knowledge by their previous leadership, at least one member of each group, but probably more, had felt they could do whatever they wanted to, including feeding on and murdering Normal humans. This should never have been allowed as it not only put them all at risk, but it was fucking *wrong*.

Alexander had spent most of his extended life protecting the people of Spokane from just such atrocities. When he had first arrived in the early 1920s, it was a wild and raucous town. Vampires, Weres, and other varieties of engineered species did pretty much as they pleased. Each morning, horrifically murdered bodies would be discovered and reported to the weak and corrupt law enforcement. Alexander had been sickened by it all…so he decided to rectify the situation. Over the course of the next three years, he had cleaned the city up, either forcing the others out or killing them. There was resistance, of course, but his single-minded focus and iron will prevailed despite this. That was why today he was the Master of the city, and no one, either rogue or affiliated, was allowed into Spokane without his permission. If you could follow his rules—and this included no killing of Normal humans—then you would be granted permission to reside there. Failure to comply *always* resulted in death.

The larger metropolitan areas such as Seattle and Portland still occasionally tested his resolve, but never pushed things too far. The older members of the genetic underworld still remembered what he had done so long ago, and they wanted no part in provoking him to direct action against them or their membership. It just wasn't worth the repercussions. And so, Spokane became a haven for outcasts, rogues, and those who just wanted to live their lives independently.

He was still musing on all of this when the van pulled to a stop just in front of where he sat. Enzo jumped out and hurried to the rear to open the doors for his Alpha. Alexander nodded his thanks as he stepped in and took a seat. When they had been on the road for a few minutes, he asked, "How did Cat get by your team, Enzo?"

To his credit, the Beta did not try to evade the question. "She knocked Giacomo out, Signore. I'm just thankful she did not take his life."

Alexander nodded his head, a rueful smile on his face. "She's a sneaky one. I trust further training for your team is forthcoming?"

Enzo glared at the offending team member. "Si, much more training."

***

When they arrived back at the Pack villa, Alexander reluctantly allowed the in-house doctor to look at his already-healing wounds. He told her not to bother dressing them since he was just going to shower and crash into a bed anyway. The doctor was not thrilled by this, but apparently chose not to aggravate her new Alpha. Enzo tried to take the weapons Alexander had used in the raid on vampire central, but the flat look he received spoke volumes. Instead, he went to the armory and retrieved cleaning supplies and extra ammo, which Alexander took upstairs with him.

The doors to the Alpha quarters were closed, and when he threw them open, he immediately realized he was not alone. His eyes scanned the rooms until they rested on the obviously naked woman sitting up in the bed. He dumped the weapons and cleaning supplies onto a table and strode to the foot of the bed.

As he neared, she let the sheet slip, revealing her breasts. He snorted in disgust. "Why the fuck are *you* in my room? More importantly, why are you in my goddamned *bed*?"

"You are the Alpha. I am the Alpha female. Where else would I be?" she replied haughtily.

A threatening rumble emanated from his chest, and his still blood-stained hands clenched. "You are *nothing*." He spat the words out. "I will give you three seconds to get out of my sight."

"No. It is my right as the Alpha female. You are my mate, as it should be."

Even before the last words were out of her mouth, he had grabbed her by the arm and was dragging her to the door. "Enzo!" he bellowed.

He heard loud footsteps clattering in the hall, then the doors opened, revealing his Beta and two of his TAC team.

Alexander pushed the naked figure at them. "Get her ass out of my sight. I don't give a flying fuck where you stash her, but she is not allowed in these rooms. Clear?"

Enzo nodded almost imperceptibly to his team and they each grabbed an arm. She struggled and was cursing them out in Italian, but they retained their grip.

"Si, my Alpha. Shall I post a guard?"

"I leave that to your discretion." He paused. "However, I need you rested when I wake up. We have much to discuss. Rotate your team and make sure everyone gets some downtime."

Enzo simply nodded acceptance and gestured for the two men to lead the naked harpy away.

Closing the doors, Alexander went to the bathroom and grabbed a towel. He spread it over the table in front of the chair and proceeded to break down the pistol. He noticed that it was an HK45 tactical, and he nodded in approval. His hands went through the motions of cleaning and oiling the parts, then reassembled the weapon and loaded a fresh magazine. Setting it aside for the moment, he reached for the longsword.

It took far longer to remove all of the accumulated gore from the blade and hilt. When he was satisfied, he realized the scabbard would require more attention than he could spare.... Sheathing a dirty blade is never a good idea. The steel itself had survived remarkably well considering the abuse he had given it. There were a few nicks that would have to be ground out, and the edge definitely needed honing, but overall it would do.

Placing the pistol under his pillow, and the blade standing upright next to the headboard, Alexander stripped off the filthy and shredded clothing that had stiffened as the blood dried. He tossed them onto the floor for later disposal, and padded in bare feet to the shower. He scrubbed himself thoroughly until the water almost ran clean; some of his wounds still bled after all, but there was nothing he could do about that. When he had toweled off, he crawled between the sheets and passed out.

# Chapter 17

*"....Five thousand years after creating their first settlement, new colonies were springing up all over the globe, generally along coastlines. Initially, these were small, specialized communities that were either extracting resources only available in specific locations, or were splinter groups that wanted to distance themselves from the primary settlement. Cracks were beginning to appear in the Anunna society, and disagreements were becoming more common. The original colonists were still alive (those who hadn't died in accidents or by other non-natural means) but had become fractured over policies and beliefs. No longer was leadership unified, and the disaffected generally moved to new locations with others of a like mind...."*

**Excerpt from the diary of Alexander Matthews**

**April 2010, Alexander's home**

*Alexander leaned back thoughtfully as he sat on the couch. He had just finished watching the first episode of* Ancient Aliens, *and while he was amused by some of what been presented, some of it matched his own research reasonably closely. It was somewhat refreshing to know that he wasn't the only person on the planet to realize humanity had been meddled with long ago.*

*That being said, it wasn't like he could just walk up to one of the hosts and say,* "Hi. I'm a werewolf, and I can totally blow your mind with what I know." *His mouth quirked up at the corner as he contemplated what kind of reaction that would generate. Still, he suspected that he would be watching this series regularly, if for no other reason than to see if they had uncovered something he had missed over the years—the more eyes on a problem, the better.*

*Truthfully, these types of shows and the plethora of movies that were coming out regularly were probably a good thing. Alexander suspected that sooner, rather than later, people like him were going to be exposed. He already had his doubts as to whether the US government was still in the dark about the various races that shared the world with them. Maybe there would be less panic if the general populace were eased into the idea via shows like this. He snorted loudly and shook his head. Who was he kidding? The world was full of retards, and no amount of prep would keep them from freaking out....*

***

The sounds of furtive footsteps woke him from a deep sleep. The HK was in his hands and leveled at the intruder even before he was fully awake.

"D-don't shoot me, Signore." It was one of the servants, hands high in the air.

Alexander's eyes scanned the rooms for further threats, the barrel of the pistol never leaving its target. "Why are you in my room?"

"I am cleaning up, Sir. Replacing the towels, picking up the filthy clothes, cleaning, just the regular housekeeping tasks." Fear-rounded eyes looked at the barrel of the HK. "If you prefer, I can come back later?"

The handgun disappeared almost as quickly as it had made its presence known.

"No, I'm awake now anyway. Would it be possible to have a meal for two served here? Say, in one hour?"

"That is easily arranged, Sir. Is there anything else?"

"Yes. Ask Enzo to join me here at the appointed time." A small smile. "I apologize if I frightened you, but I'm under a bit of stress."

"I quite understand, Sir. No apology is needed."

"Are you nearly finished? I would like to get ready for the day."

"I will begin out here. The bath can wait."

"Excellent. I will let you get back to it then." He paused at the threshold. "And thank you."

***

Alexander poured coffee for his Beta, then settled back into the chair. "How is the Pack taking the change in management?"

"As you might expect, things are a bit unsettled at the moment."

A chuckle followed a sip of his own coffee. "I suspect that may be a bit of an understatement."

Enzo wore a wry smile as he tipped his cup. "As you say, Signore. Still, things could be much, much worse. I suspect that you may have put the fear of God into them."

Alexander considered how to phrase his next question before taking the plunge. After all, while he was fairly certain he could trust Enzo, there was always the chance he was wrong.

"I'm just going to come straight out and ask, were you aware of the murders? Were they sanctioned kills? More importantly, was it just the previous Alpha's son, or are more involved?"

His Beta stiffened in his seat momentarily, then relaxed. "I was not directly aware of the deaths, but I, as did many others, had my suspicions. Were they sanctioned kills? I don't believe so, although his father and mother definitely looked the other way. As you may already have observed, leadership in this Pack was more about privileges for the few than addressing the needs of the many. My guess is that they knew about his activities but did nothing to discourage them."

"So, you believe he acted alone? At least as far as Pack members are concerned."

"Yes, Sir, I am unaware of anyone else who engaged in such hunts."

Alexander squinted at him. "What role did you play in the Pack? You seem to be a capable sort."

Enzo snorted, amused at his words. "To you, perhaps. I was considered a thorn in the leadership's side. Questioning the status quo was highly *discouraged,* to say the least. Most of the malcontents gravitated to me, and I did what I could to keep a lid on things. It wasn't always easy. As for my role? Whatever scut-work they could come up with to keep me out of the way."

"I see. Their loss is my gain."

The Alpha frowned slightly. "I have a problem, and by extension, that means *'We'* have a problem. I don't know who I can trust within the Pack."

"Including me, I presume?"

"To a certain extent, perhaps, but I find that you are growing on me." He grinned. "If I weren't ninety-five percent sure of your loyalties, we wouldn't even be having this conversation." Alexander leaned forward. "You know these people, and I do not. I anticipate problems moving forward, and well.... You've already seen my usual solution. It tends to be messy for all involved," he stated unapologetically.

Enzo grinned wryly. "If nothing else it is certainly, hmmm, energetic, if I may say so."

Alexander acknowledged this with a wave of one hand.

"I plan on shaking things up, introducing fundamental changes at every level. That will not go over well, especially with the previous power-players." His eyes narrowed. "Tolerating dissent is not part of those plans."

"Understood, Sir. Where do I come into this?"

"I'll just cut to the chase. I don't plan on staying in Naples any longer than I need to. You and Cat will need to work closely together to bind what I put into effect here into a cohesive whole. While I'm fairly certain that I have probably eliminated most of the problematical opposition from the vampire Coven, I was less comprehensive where the Pack is concerned."

Enzo nodded.

"Let me be perfectly clear. *You* will be running this Pack in my absence, and I need to be confident that I am not leaving you holding a live hand grenade. I need you to help me put this house in order."

The Beta thought for a moment about what Alexander had said. "I presume you want my assistance identifying whom we can trust, whom we should keep an eye on, and who the real vipers are in our midst?"

"Predominantly the lattermost, I should think," Alexander replied. "Speaking of vipers, what about my unwanted roommate last night?"

"Ah, yes, Francesca. She will definitely bear watching. You may not be aware, but it was her son and husband you executed, and now that you have made it very clear that she will not be sharing your bed, her status is unclear."

"No. It's not unclear at all. I probably should have just killed her, but she gave me no reason to do so. At least not yet." His brow furrowed thoughtfully. "Who else should I be worried about?"

"None from the lower ranks, but she has allies in the former Pack leadership. Francesca and her friends, along with the late Alpha, had a less than enlightened view on their place within the Pack hierarchy. In fact, there has been dissatisfaction within the rank and file for quite some time. However, open rebellion would not have been an option. Of course, now that you have assumed control…." He lifted one shoulder and waggled a hand back and forth.

Alexander tilted his head to one side. "And so, now they wait to see what I will do, whether I am an improvement. Understood." He leaned back in the chair and crossed one leg over the other. "How do *you* feel, Enzo? If I may ask?"

"For my part, I feel like the change will be positive in the long run. Short-term, it will be difficult. You will need to win them over, show them what it means to be a member of *your* Pack." The Beta tapped two fingertips on the surface of the table, then continued. "Right now, they fear you, and to be honest, you frighten me as well."

"Fear is healthy. It tends to keep one alive."

"Agreed, but it is a temporary solution at best. You will need buy-in for this to work. Especially as you intend to force, for lack of a better term, a marriage with our historical rivals, the vampires."

Alexander raised a palm to stop Enzo. "Will *you* be able to work with Cat and her people? Or is this going to be too large a hurdle for you personally?"

The beta inhaled sharply, then let it go. "For my part, I can see the advantages, and the rivalry has always seemed petty and old-fashioned to me. Our children go to the same schools, make friendships and get along, but when they come of age, they are expected to let all of that go. It has never made sense to me."

He smiled. "Also, Signorina Caterina strikes me as a very capable sort."

"That she is, Enzo, that she most certainly is."

Pensively, Enzo asked, "Do you ever get used to the way she speaks?"

Alexander burst into laughter. "You'll know she likes you when she drops the façade."

"Ah, I see."

"Let's get back on track here for a minute." Alexander ticked items off on his fingers. "The majority of the Pack were less than enthused with prior leadership, but have decided to see if I am any better before taking sides. Francesca and her faction might, and undoubtedly will, cause problems for us either overtly or covertly. And finally, merging the wolves and vampires into a cohesive organization will undoubtedly face opposition. Did I miss anything?"

"That about sums it up, Sir."

"Sweet. There are some other items I want to discuss, but before we get into that, I left my car with the valet at the Museo last night when events transpired. Can you have someone pick it up for me?"

Enzo reached into his pocket and pulled a set of keys out. "I've already seen to it, Sir. One of the staff found the chit in a pocket on your suit. I don't suppose you'd let me drive it?"

"Not today, I'm afraid," Alexander laughed.

Alexander and Enzo talked for another half-hour, and plans were made to inventory the armory to determine what, if any, improvements were needed, what additional training and capabilities Enzo's TAC (Tactical Action Command) team should receive, and various other concerns such as the Pack finances.

***

Alexander wandered the halls of the villa after his meal with Enzo. He observed the staff as they went about their activities. He noticed that while some of the furniture still showed signs of the conflict that took place, at least all the various body fluids had disappeared. His feet led him to the large kitchen and the wonderful aromas coming from that space. A rather short and loud man was directing the junior cooks much as a maestro led an orchestra.

Electing not to interrupt, Alexander made his way back to the front entrance, intending to check in on Tina. He was intercepted just short of the doors by a woman who asked to speak with him. She was dressed in a prim and proper fashion and had an air of authority about her. Everything from the auburn hair put up into a severe bun, to the matronly business suit that did nothing flattering for her, screamed efficiency.

"Excuse me, Signore. May I have a moment of your time?"

"Certainly. And you are?"

She inclined her head. "My name is Julia Acosta. I am the Majordomo for this household."

"I see. What can I do for you today, Julia?"

"It's more what I, and the staff, can do for you. Are there any particular provisions we need to have delivered? Perhaps changes to your chambers? I shall ensure that we accommodate all of your needs." She crossed her hands behind her back and stood waiting.

"How many staff do you have?"

"Twelve altogether. That includes kitchen, domestics, and a few who perform several different tasks, including groundskeeping."

Alexander rubbed his chin thoughtfully. "Is that number sufficient? This is a large house and grounds."

Julia stiffened slightly. "Has Sir noticed a deficiency?"

Hands patting the air placatingly, he said, "No, not at all. My concern is the wellbeing of your team. I don't want to overwork them if a few new hires will make everyone's lives easier. From what I have observed, they are a very efficient and well-organized group."

She relaxed and nodded once. "Thank you. We *are* a little lean, and on occasion, over-extended, which means long shifts, but please don't infer that I am complaining."

"Understood. How many additional staff would mitigate this?"

Julia thought about it for a moment. "Three should resolve the issue."

"Make it so. For further reference, please don't hesitate to come to me with these types of concerns. Is there anything else I should be made aware of?"

"Not at this time, Signore."

"Good, good. As to your initial questions, I do have a couple of small requests." He paused. "Please remove all of the previous occupants' belongings from my quarters, both his…and hers."

"At once," Julia said, signaling one of the domestics hovering close by, and barely hiding a small smile of satisfaction.

Alexander smiled. "Additionally, I would like a new mattress and pillows for the bed. Extra-firm, please."

She nodded.

"As for provisions? Other than a good American bourbon, or decent Islay single-malt whisky, I will eat what everyone else in this house partakes in."

A scandalized look passed over her face. "Excuse me, Sir, but did you say you would be eating…."

A smirking Alexander said, "You heard correctly. Not only will I be eating what you all eat, but I will also be eating *with* everyone. Please ensure that there are enough seats in the dining room to accommodate family-style meals. My expectations are that the Pack will feed as a whole, at least as much as possible. This includes you, Julia."

She quickly suppressed a grin, then replied, "As you wish, Sir."

"Do families live here as well? I assume not, but I haven't been here long enough to know. Regardless, please make sure they are invited as well…including children. It's not required, but I want them to know they are welcome." He smiled. "Especially the children.

"Oh. You may want to warn Chef that I have occasionally been known to actually cook my *own* food when the mood strikes. An appalling thought, I know." He sniffed. "And yet, it cannot be helped. One would hate to be chased around the kitchen by an irate cook with a cleaver. I'm sure you understand."

Julia completely failed to contain the laugh that escaped her lips at his final words, then she bowed slightly and walked away.

***

The Acura was parked where Enzo had said it would be, and it was apparent that someone had detailed it while he slept. Avenged Sevenfold's *Hail to the King* was blasting from the speakers as he drove to his rental property. He was practically vibrating due to the nervous tension that thrummed throughout his body. Alexander was afraid of what he would discover when he got there. After all, the last time he had seen Tina, she had been seconds away from death. Sure, he knew intellectually that if the virus and the nanites had done their jobs, she would be alive and relatively healthy, but her psychological state was the unknown.

It was doubtful that she would have awakened yet—it hadn't even been a full day since the attack—but she was no doubt vividly sharing in the same recorded memories that he had received during his transformation. It was a lot to absorb. Granted, people of this era should be more open to the very idea given the sheer number of books, movies, and tv shows that postulated similar scenarios, but still....

He found parking and slowly made his way up the stairs to the entrance. He knocked since his key had gone to Caterina the night before. Her assistant answered the door and let him in, closing it once he was past.

"How is she?"

"She yet sleeps, but her recovery looks promising."

"Thank you," he whispered. "I'm sorry I never got your name."

A smile greeted his words. "Bettina. My name is Bettina."

"I am pleased to make your acquaintance, Bettina, and thank you for watching over her for me."

"Go to her. Who knows, she may sense you are with her?" She walked to the sofa and sat, picked up a magazine and started reading.

Alexander opened the door and peeked inside the room. Tina lay in the bed, whimpering almost sub-audibly. The door shut softly behind him as he strode to the side of the bed, where he pulled the chair from in front of the vanity so he could sit next to where her head lay on the pillow. Sunlight dappled the room and he could see that the linens were sweat-stained and covered in dried blood. Her blood. There was a large dressing that covered the wound in her neck, and he noticed that the ruined dress she had worn to the gala had been removed. The pinpricks from his medallion had vanished, but the bite he had given her arm still showed, healed, but inflamed. He knew that it would leave no scar, but for now it was an unwelcome reminder of what he had done. A hand to her forehead revealed that she was running a fever, something not entirely unexpected with the changes happening to her body. Tina's hair was matted and filthy with the sweat from the fever combined with the blood from the attack. He slowly, carefully, peeled the dressing from her neck and saw that the gaping hole had closed, even though there was still more healing to come.

He walked into the en-suite bathroom and started filling the tub, then laid out the shampoo and body wash that he found. Alexander could tell they were hers, because he had smelled them on her daily since she had come to work for him.

Going back to the bed, he removed her bra and underwear, tossing them onto the carpeted floor. "Oh my, you *are* a naughty girl." He laughed as he spotted the tiny tattoo of a stick-figure man using a push mower, pieces of grass flying, that was placed just above the hairline on the left side of her crotch. Alexander could cover the entire thing with his thumb, and he suspected that it was a private joke that not many people ever saw. He walked to the door. "I need your help, Bettina, if you would?"

When she entered the room, Alexander was carefully lifting Tina into his arms. He looked up and said, "Can you please change the bedding for me? I'm going to clean her up." He smiled sadly. "I suspect it may take some time."

Caterina's assistant nodded her head and moved in as he carried Tina to the tub and gently lowered her into the water. She moaned and thrashed around a little, then calmed down. Using the loofa he had found near the sink, he slowly began to clean the blood and fever-sweat off her body. Tears ran down his cheeks as he saw the extent of the damage she had taken in the attack.

"I'm so sorry, Tina," he whispered. "I should have been there to protect you."

By the time he had finished, the water in the tub was stained a deep red. He drained the tub and refilled it with clean, fresh water, then began to wash her hair. He was careful detangling the clumps of hair where clotted blood and sweat had created crusty masses that had to be removed before he could apply shampoo. As the once-again-filthy water drained, he opened the music collection on his phone and selected 3 Doors Down's *Seventeen Days* and set it to play.

As soon as the tub had filled again, he wet her long brunette hair and massaged in the shampoo. He took his time and tried to ensure that he got it as clean as possible, and when the play-list got to *Landing in London,* he sang softly to her sleeping form. Her hair wasn't perfect, and she would undoubtedly want to rewash it herself, but it was a night-and-day difference to how it had been. Alexander drained the tub for the last time and used the showerhead to sluice dirty bath-water from her body.

One of the towels was used to dry her now-shivering body, and the other her waist-length hair. He carried her back to the bed; fresh linens had done wonders, and Bettina had pulled the sheet back so he could lay her down.

Alexander slipped his shoes off and sat behind her, so he could comb the damp hair before it dried. He pulled the sheet and blanket up to keep her warm, then spent the next half hour brushing her hair and putting it into a French braid as she lay propped up in his lap.

He slipped toward the center of the bed and leaned against the headboard, nestling Tina into his right arm. Alexander quickly found and purchased Tolkien's *Fellowship of the Ring* on Amazon, and took up the story from where she had left off the night that she had read to him. His voice was low and even, and at some point, he must have fallen asleep.

***

Tina swam in a sea of memories, most not her own. She knew she was dreaming, but she couldn't seem to wake herself. In fact, for a moment there, she thought that she could hear Alexander singing softly to her and...reading aloud? Soon though, it all slipped away as she was overwhelmed by visions of impossible things.

There were visions of tall, cruel people who treated their slaves horribly. She didn't know how she knew they were slaves, but she did. The buildings and cities were unlike anything she had ever seen before, and somehow Tina grasped that what she witnessed had taken place in the distant past.

All sorts of impossible beings paraded before her mind's eye. There were people who were at home in the sea, morphing into creatures with gills and webbed hands and feet. People who turned into wolves, bears, foxes, bulls, big cats, and virtually any other species she could think of. What she could only describe as vampires were present as well, as were elves, satyrs, ogres, and a whole zoo full of other varieties. Some didn't even exist in the fantasy books she loved to read.

These memories were the oldest, but there were also fragments that belonged to Alexander. How she could tell they were his, she did not know, but they *tasted* like him…somehow. There was no other way to describe it. The preposterous thing was that they seemed to span an impossible length of time. Some took place when the country was just exiting what would be termed the Wild West, and others seemed to be during WWI. In fact, the entire 20th century flashed past her eyes in short, fragmentary vignettes. Surely that wasn't possible, was it? And most disturbing of all was that he wasn't always human…she could see fights from his perspective where his hands were fur-covered and had vicious-looking claws. What did that mean?

The last thing she remembered was being stunned by those two idiots and dragged into an alley. The greasy boy grabbed her head and shoved it to the side and grinned evilly at her, then he grew fangs, and the pain she experienced as he tore out her throat was almost unbearable. Tina recalled feeling the suction made by his lips as he drained the blood from her body, and how helpless she felt.

Then there was the sound of a struggle, and Alexander was there, holding her dying body even as he tried to stop the bleeding. The pain and fury she saw in his eyes almost broke her heart as she realized she was the cause. She tried to tell him it was not his fault, but her torn and battered body wouldn't allow it.

She remembered him reaching for the amulet that he always wore, and pressing it to her chest, the slight sting as something pricked into her skin, and the way his face shifted into something bestial…wolf-like…just before he bit her in the upper arm….

***

He was awakened by bloodcurdling screams of terror and Tina beating on his chest and face. Her eyes were wild and fearful, and he could tell she was remembering the attack. Alexander felt helpless, not sure what to do as she continued.

The bedroom door burst open and Caterina flew into the room. She took one look at the situation and pointed her finger at him. "Get out. Now. In fact, go back to the Pack villa and stay there until I call."

He didn't even question her order, just grabbed his phone and bolted out the door, only taking the time to grab his luggage on the way out.

Cat approached the bed and started talking to the panicked woman. "Tina. Tina, it's all right."

Her words had no effect other than causing Tina to back away to the far side of the bed. The screaming continued unabated. Caterina sighed, then slapped Tina's face. Hard.

Bettina poked her head in the door. "Signorina?"

"Bring something to drink. Water. And food, whatever there is."

The shock of the slap seemed to have at least stopped the screaming. Tina knelt on the bed, hyperventilating, blinking her eyes rapidly as she stared at the woman who had hit her.

"Are you done shrieking? Is anyone home?" She snapped her fingers in front of Tina's nose.

Tina's hand flew to her neck, and not finding what she expected there, her expression became confused. "I-I was dying. Wasn't I?" she croaked.

"Yes. You were attacked by a vampire," Caterina stated calmly in a matter-of-fact tone.

Tina stuttered, "That's impossible, those aren't real."

Her assistant walked in with a glass of water and some cheese and meats on a plate, set them on the chair next to the bed, and retreated.

As Tina reached for the water, and nearly drained the contents of the glass, Caterina—the newly designated leader of a Coven she never wanted—considered how to respond. Finally, she shrugged and shifted to her Battle form. As her eyes swirled and turned black, her canines lengthened, and claws tore out of her fingertips. She hissed at Tina and awaited her reaction. She didn't have to wait long.

The young woman began screaming again, terrified eyes bulging out of their sockets as she saw what Cat had become.

The designer let the Battle form go and rapidly transformed into her standard human shape. She sighed again, then slapped Tina a second time.

"I really hope you are quite done with the theatrics." Her tone indicated what she thought of all this.

"What are you?" responded the young woman.

"Hmmm," the designer said. "I suppose I'm impossible and not real. At least according to *you*." She considered Tina for a moment. "If you can cease the histrionics for a while, I will attempt to explain. Agreed?"

Alexander's assistant jerked her head in a nod.

"Good. Please don't make me slap you again." She paused, then continued, "Vampires are *real*. Werewolves are *real*. Many other creatures you think impossible *do* exist, many living right alongside humanity. As you saw, I am a vampire."

Tina blinked and held her hand up to the sunlight streaming into the room. "But, I thought the sun…."

Caterina snorted. "Just one of the many things Normal humans have gotten wrong over the centuries. I go to the beach, love garlicky food, and use real silverware when I eat at home. Vampires are just like anyone else…except better." She grimaced then said, "Perhaps *better* is not the word I should use. Yes, *different* is a better term. We are stronger, faster, tougher, and we live much longer. The primary downside is that we need fresh blood to stay healthy. Let me rephrase that. We need some of what is *contained* in fresh blood. If we don't receive it semi-regularly, we sicken and die."

Tina looked thoughtful. "How long has it been since I was attacked?"

"Almost a full day."

A haunted expression dominated her face. "I remember standing outside the museum when suddenly there was a blow to the back of my head and two sets of arms dragging me into that alley." She rubbed the back of her head. "Then a horrible face leering down at me before tearing into my throat. It hurt so bad, and I couldn't get away no matter how hard I tried…not being able to breathe, choking on my own blood."

Tears were streaming down her cheeks and she was sobbing as she continued, "Then, Alexander was there. I guess he chased them away?"

Caterina smiled thinly. "Something like that."

"He was crying as he tried to stop the bleeding, but I knew I was dying. Then he said he was sorry and his face...changed. Not like yours, though. Different. He bit my arm." She grabbed her arm and saw the faint remaining marks there.

Her eyes narrowed, then she bellowed, "He fucking bit me! I can't believe it. What kind of sick bastard would bite a dying woman?"

"The kind who is trying to save the dying woman. And make no mistake, you *would* be dead. It was a close thing as it was."

"He should have just let me die." The tears were running freely at this point. "Am I a vampire now too?"

"No. You are a wolf...of some sort. I'm not entirely certain what Alexander is, but he is not your typical werewolf."

"I don't want this," she sobbed. "I don't want any of this. Better dead than to be turned into a monster. How could he do this to me?"

"You stupid, stupid girl!" Caterina snapped. "The only reason you have the opportunity to wallow in self-pity like you are is that a good man could not stand by and watch you die. You, the woman he doesn't even realize he is in love with. When I saw the way he was cradling you after he gave you his gift, I knew. Never have I witnessed such grief as what I saw last night. I am two-hundred years old, girl, and have never been loved the way that man loves you."

Tina's eyes widened in shock at Caterina's words.

"Would you like to know what he did after he called me to look after you?"

Silence greeted her words.

"Alexander went to *war*...with two races, both of whom were responsible for your current condition. He tracked the wolf who had assisted in attacking you back to the local Pack villa. That man who you so easily blame for saving your life single-handedly attacked a house filled with werewolves. Think about that for a second.

Tina sucked in a shaken breath.

"I heard all of this second-hand, you understand, but the source is reliable," Caterina explained. "Shall I continue?"

"Do I really want to know?" Tina asked sarcastically.

"What *you* want is irrelevant. Alexander armed himself with sword and pistol, and then attacked a house full of vampires." Caterina sighed. "It is my belief that he wished to die, perhaps subconsciously, perhaps not. At the time, we thought there was an elevated risk you might not make it. The only thing he was focused on was taking as many of them down as possible. And he was *pissed.* Alexander only wanted to be by your side, but retribution was called for, and most assuredly would be delivered.

"It was a slaughterhouse, Tina."

Tina was crying again as she listened.

Caterina glared down at her. "There was no quarter shown, nor asked. He was determined to cleanse those he felt were responsible for your condition. When I found him in the basement, he was preparing to kill every remaining member of the Coven. Every. Single. One. I saw madness in his eyes, Tina. What he had forced himself to do went against everything he has ever stood for, and his actions were eating at him, but he had to do it. Had to avenge *you.* Somehow, I managed to convince him to spare the last of the vampires, and with one exception, he did. That exception was the one who had fed on you. Alexander was covered in gore, slashed, torn, and had more than one gunshot wound…and he didn't even seem to notice."

"That's horrible," Tina whispered, staring at Caterina.

"You stupid bitch," growled Caterina. "Alexander brought *Armageddon* to those who had dared harm you. He was willing to watch the world burn as long as he made his enemies suffer and die. And for what? A silly little girl who feels sorry for herself.

"Quite frankly, I don't understand what he sees in you." She grabbed Tina's face and forced her to look into her angry eyes. "I know of at least three women in his life who would give everything for him to look at them the way he does you. I am one. Unfortunately, he sees me as a friend, and I am, but I have loved him since that day in 1956 when he saved my life." Caterina spun on her heel and prowled through the bedroom door. "Clean up and get dressed. It's time for you to grow the fuck up."

# Chapter 18

*"....By 30,000 BC, disagreements grew amongst the various factions and resulted in actual limited-scale warfare. While these conflicts were generally localized and fairly low-intensity, they did occur with some regularity. The numbers of genetically modified humans had grown, and escaped slaves had begun to push out, breed with, or exterminate native populations of other species such as Neanderthals, Denisovans, etc. Soon there would be just one type of humanity...."*

**Excerpt from the diary of Alexander Matthews**

**July 1925, Whidbey Island, Puget Sound, Washington**

*Alexander emptied the last of the bourbon into Joseph's glass and sighed. The two men had sat on an overturned boat that was resting on the beach, and were drinking the former contents of the three empty bottles that lay at his feet. He had met his new friend late in the afternoon of the previous day, and they had immediately hit it off. Alexander knew right away that Joseph wasn't a Normal, but couldn't pin his nature down enough to identify his exact race.*

*It turned out that he was a Mer, one of the Sea Peoples, and his clan lived in the waters of Puget Sound. Alexander was fascinated, as he had never actually met a member of the race. Fortunately, Joseph was a gregarious type and was willing to answer all his questions...as long as the bourbon lasted.*

*"If I'm lying, I'm dying," the Mer was saying. "The gold blankets the seabed for miles."*

*A skeptical Alexander narrowed his eyes. "If that's the case, then why aren't you and your clan living in luxury?"*

*"Well now, recovering it would require...." He gulped in horror. "Work." A shudder passed through his body.*

*"You realize that with a little effort, you would have enough money to buy your own bourbon, right?" Alexander prodded.*

*The Mer sat up straight and looked down his nose at the wolf. "It's the principle of the matter, Sir. My kind don't sully our hands with any sort of physical labor." He hiccupped delicately. "No, Sir, we fish when we are hungry, salvage the odd shipwreck if we need clothes or such, but we never* work. *It's just not done, you see?"*

*Alexander shook his head, marveling at how different the ways of the Mer seemed....*

***

Alexander parked the Acura and retrieved his luggage before making his way to the quarters he was calling his own. At least for now. Satisfied that his requests had been taken care of in his absence, he flagged down one of the ever-present staff.

"Is there a dedicated conference room on the grounds?"

"Yes, Sir, on the main floor," she replied.

"Would you let Enzo and Julia know that I would like to meet with them in fifteen minutes? Also, please ensure that there are refreshments. I'm not sure how long this meeting will last."

She bobbed her head at him. "Of course, Sir. Will there be anything else?"

"No, that should do it." He smiled at her. "Thank you."

That task completed, Alexander quickly took a shower and changed into one of the few outfits he had packed for the trip to Italy. *I'm going to need to remedy that situation sooner rather than later.*

Tina's reaction when she woke up had left him shaken. The pure fear and panic that he saw in her eyes did not bode well for how she would adjust to her new reality. Hopefully, Caterina would be able to calm her and explain enough of the facts that Tina could begin to rationally approach the changes in her life.

And there was still the little matter of whether she would forgive him for what he had done. The fact of the matter was that he would do it all over again, no matter the consequences to him personally. There was simply no way he could have watched her bleed out and not do something about it. Even if she ended up hating him, it was still the right thing to do.

Alexander sighed. *Well, what's done is done*, he thought as he made his way to the meeting he had called.

***

He had just seated himself at the table in the conference room when both Julia and Enzo arrived. His Beta closed the door and took a chair.

"Coffee?" Alexander offered his subordinates before pouring a cup for himself.

When everyone had their preferred beverage sitting in front of them, he started the meeting. "Enzo and I have already had a one-on-one, Julia, and some of this may be a bit repetitive for him, but I have some things I want to cover."

She tipped her head in acknowledgment.

"First of all, we will be meeting like this fairly frequently…at least initially. I hate to be so hands-on, but I think you both will agree that circumstances warrant it. As time goes by, you will notice that I will leave most of it to each of you. Secondly, as I mentioned earlier, Julia, please don't hesitate to make me aware of any issue that impedes your ability to get tasks done. That goes for you as well, Enzo. I am not averse to spending funds where they are needed."

Enzo nodded thoughtfully.

"Additionally, I will be including the new vampire Coven leader and anyone she chooses to invite, in future meetings. One of the reasons is that both this Pack and Caterina's Coven will be functionally joined at the hip. I plan on making everyone operate as a single entity. Am I clear?"

Julia cleared her throat. "There may be push-back on that, Sir."

Alexander chuckled. "I suspect that may be just a wee bit of understatement. Be that as it may, it *is* going to happen.

"I see that the dining room has been reorganized to accommodate the new eating arrangements. You have my thanks for that, Julia. Has the chef been made aware of my plans?"

"He has. Chef's exact words were, '*Good. That simplifies things.*'"

"Enzo, I want all available Pack members onsite and gathered in the back of the residence before dinner. I will have some announcements to make."

The Beta pulled out his phone and sent a text to his team. "On it."

"I want to run a couple of options by the two of you, and I desire input. As I mentioned, I want the Weres and Vampires to be a cohesive team here in Naples. Generally, the easiest way to go about that would be to force everyone to live together, but neither residence is large enough for that. Can we put out feelers and see if any properties meet the requirements? You would both need to be involved, considering the impacts on both of your departments. Staffing levels specifically for you, Julia, and security needs among others for you, Enzo."

They looked at each other, then nodded.

"We can do that."

"Alternatively, can we buy the properties surrounding this estate? If we had those, we could probably get by," Alexander said. "It isn't the preferred solution as far as I am concerned, for various reasons, not least of which is that I would prefer that the new housing not have belonged to either us, or them, prior to today."

Alexander held up his hand and began ticking items off. "I want room for an indoor shooting range. I noticed that we currently don't have one.

"We need a large auditorium or courtyard for training and conditioning. Everyone will be required to participate, whether they live onsite or not.

"I want a large quiet space with copious amounts of bookshelves. The library will be open to everyone. And, I want art scattered throughout the entire property.

"And the final item, a home theater with seating for forty, as well as a gaming room."

Both of his subordinates had thoughtful looks on their faces, but no objections were raised.

"That is about it for today. I do have a couple of final questions for you, though, and I will want the answers tomorrow. Does everyone have a job? If so, what are they? If not, why not? And what would be your recommendations if we need to assign them?"

***

Alexander stared out at the crowd gathering in the large courtyard at the rear of the villa. It was taking some time for everyone to arrive since some had jobs in the city, and many of the families had their own housing. *It can't be helped, I suppose, but I'm not going to wait much longer,* he thought.

As expected, there were a lot of speculative conversations being had, and more than a few concerned looks directed his way. Francesca, and a small group of her allies, stood near the front glaring at him and whispering amongst themselves. Impassively he stared back, impervious to their implied threat. He knew that sooner or later, they would make a move, and then he could act. Until then, Alexander would just ignore them.

He nodded at Enzo, and his Beta shouted for silence. When the crowd noise had dropped to a level that would allow his words to be heard by all gathered, he started to speak.

"I'm sure you are wondering what this is all about. It's really quite simple," Alexander began.

Spying movement at the rear of the crowd, he saw that Caterina and Tina had just walked in. The latter did not look all that happy to be where she was. He mentally shrugged. There wasn't much he could do about that at this time anyway.

"Not much time has passed since the actions by one of your Pack members forced me to take the Alpha position. I am aware that some of you are not too happy with that." Alexander looked pointedly at Francesca. "Others are simply waiting to see how it will all shake out."

"I'm fine with that. However, I also want you to make informed decisions. Let there be no doubt that changes are coming. One of those changes will be implemented tonight. You may have noticed that the dining room now has seating for most, if not all, members of this Pack. We will eat our meals together, as a family. That includes me."

"That's ridiculous! I refuse to dine with the lesser Pack members," Francesca shouted, her cronies lending their support.

Alexander sneered at her and her group. "Then you don't eat. This is non-negotiable. Of course, you may elect to dine at a restaurant, but that will be on your own dime. No Pack funds will be used in such cases. Before you say anything else that will jeopardize your general health and wellbeing, I would merely point out that your current status in this Pack is Omega as far as I am concerned."

She blanched at his words but remained silent.

"Where was I? Ah, yes. Another major change will be the integration of this Pack with the remainder of the vampire Coven that also forced my hand. This is not open for discussion or debate. It *will* happen. I will be meeting with them tomorrow and making them aware of this situation. I suspect they will also not be overly enthused.

"Regardless, the one certainty in all of this is that much of what has been considered traditional, or normal, will be changing. I am not asking for permission to make these changes. You *will* adopt them."

Alexander held up a fist and began counting off. "If you cannot accept this, you have limited choices. Number one, you can challenge for the Alpha position." The confident grin on his face showed what he thought of that.

"And number two, you can get the fuck out of my city." He glared balefully at them all. "Exile does not mean leaving this Pack and going on about your business. If you choose to leave, you will need to relocate at least as far away as Rome. Let me be perfectly clear. If I find you living anywhere within an hour of Naples, I *will* kill you."

Alexander relaxed and said, "Please consider carefully before making any decisions, but don't take too long, or the choice will be made for you.

"Now, let's eat the meal Chef has prepared."

***

Alexander stayed in place as the crowd filtered back into the villa, his eyes on the two women pushing against the tide and walking toward him. His palms began to sweat, and he rubbed them against his pantlegs. Caterina prowled toward him, head held high. On the other hand, Tina slouched along reluctantly.

"Caterina approves of your speech, although perhaps Caterina should have been made aware of some of it prior, yes?" Her smile softened the words.

"Agreed. Although I'm not sure when we would have had the time."

He stared expectantly at Tina, but she just stood there, eyes down.

Cat sighed heavily. "This one is now your problem. Caterina has explained that she needs to learn how to be a wolf, and that this can only happen in a Pack environment."

He nodded.

"Caterina also wants Alexander to know that she mostly just wants to choke the shit out of the little brat...but will leave that up to him." She sniffed and turned to leave.

"Thanks, Cat. I owe you one." His words were only loud enough to carry to her ears.

He stared pensively at Tina, her arms crossed defensively across her chest, still not looking at him, then he sighed. "Come on then, dinner is waiting. Please sit wherever you like."

Alexander walked away, leaving her to decide what she was going to do.

He caught Enzo's eye as he sat down at an open spot at one of the tables, specifically *not* choosing to sit at the head where he usually would.

His Beta leaned down. "Signore?"

Alexander spoke barely above a whisper. "The woman who arrived with Cat is very important to me. She isn't thrilled with me right now, but I would appreciate it if you could look out for her? Obviously, I cannot."

"Ahh, this would be the cause of the late unpleasantness?"

A faint smile on his face, Alexander responded, "You could say that she was the catalyst, yes. Help her settle in, guide where you can, and be a friendly face. Tina has much to learn and little time to do so."

"As you say, Sir. It will be done."

"Thank you, Enzo, now please eat, let Chef know you appreciate his efforts."

***

Tina took a seat as far away from Alexander as possible. Her emotions were churning, and she just couldn't stand to be in his presence. Part of her knew she was being unreasonable, but she didn't care. He had made a decision without consulting her that would now impact the remainder of her life. Any choice she may have had was taken from her with the bite that infected her and changed her into a monster.

There he sat, across the room, smiling and laughing as he spoke to those around him. For their part, they responded positively, seeming to enjoy his company. She knew very well how charming he could be when he wanted to, but this didn't seem to be an act. How could any of them stand to be around him after what he had done? At least five members of their Pack had died at his hands...and yet it all seemed so normal. Even the children responded to his magnetism, some shyly saying hello, while others brazenly climbed into his lap as their parents beamed at them all. Tina had to admit that he was good with them. Which confused her even more.

Which Alexander was the *real* Alexander? The murderous monster who had bitten her? Or the charming rogue who had cast a spell over most of the people in the room? She had listened to his speech and thought it pretty harsh. Caterina had told her to not be stupid, Pack dynamics were different than human norms, and she would need to figure them out quickly. She also had said that being Alpha came with a lot of responsibilities.

"Excuse me, Signorina, may I sit here?" a faintly Italian-accented voice asked.

Tina glanced up at a man who was a few inches shorter than Alexander. Dark hair, solid build, but not too muscular, and a serious face, worry lines etched deep. She gestured for him to sit.

He offered his hand and said, "I am Enzo Falconi."

She shook his hand. "Tina Ferrante. I'm new here, but I guess you already knew that."

He took a bite of the pasta on his plate. "I did. It can be a lot to process all at once." He smiled fondly at the rest of the room. "I am the Pack Beta, what you might call the second in command, although I share that title with Caterina now."

"I see. Are you here to babysit me, Enzo?" she asked sardonically.

He gazed steadily at her for a moment. "No, Tina. Part of my duties as Beta includes assisting new Pack members with getting settled in, acclimated if you prefer. For instance, I will assign you a room within this residence and ensure you have everything you need. I will also assign any tasks that you may be qualified for, and aid in your continued training as necessary." He paused meaningfully. "I wouldn't have the time to babysit you even if I wanted to."

Her cheeks flushed dark from embarrassment as she realized she had gone too far. "I'm sorry, Enzo, I was out of line. This is all too much to process. Yesterday I was just a normal person, and today…?"

"I understand. It will be a change for you, but it isn't so bad, really. You will see."

She turned to him, eyes blazing. "How is it that I look around me and see happy, smiling faces, when the man who did this to me, the man who killed so many of your Pack sits amongst us?"

Enzo considered her words. "The son of the previous Alpha, and his vampire friend, attacked you in a very public place. The fact that they felt free enough, safe enough, to do so, should give you some indication of what things were like before Alexander took the leadership into his own hands. Not everyone in this room is happy about that change, but I can assure you that many more *are*. Or at least are hopeful it will be a good thing."

He gestured around. "Last night this room held but one table, and only a select few were allowed to dine here. The so-called elite members of this Pack lorded it over everyone else, basking in privilege. No input from the lower members was allowed, much less sought out. Now, look around you…. This looks and feels more like a family. This is how it should always have been.

"Alexander leads, as is his right, as Alpha, but more importantly, he doesn't set himself apart, or act as if he is better than anyone else. I have been a member of this Pack for forty years and I have never seen the like. My visits to other Packs have only reinforced that how I was treated by the former leadership was normal. Expected."

He nodded his head to Alexander. "Does that look like a man lording it over his serfs?"

Tina scowled, but had to acknowledge that it didn't. "I guess not. But even so, does might really make right?"

Enzo chuckled. "It most certainly does in Pack society." His face grew thoughtful and he continued. "But if you are very, very lucky, the mightiest is also the leader you *need*."

She frowned at the Beta. "You sound as if you admire him?"

"I do, Signorina, and I would follow him straight into the mouth of Hell. He is an honorable man, and quite possibly the most powerful Were on the planet." He paused, then said, "Are you finished eating? I have something I want to show you."

***

Tina followed Enzo upstairs and to what was obviously a security office. At least twenty LCD monitors were mounted on the wall above the long desk. He offered her a seat, then took one for himself.

"What I am about to show you has been watched by fewer than a dozen people, and all of them are part of my security team. Other than that, only the actual participants can say that they witnessed even part of it. Do you understand?"

She nodded her head.

"This is the actual footage taken the night Alexander came calling. I will have to switch between feeds because it starts outside, then transitions to a few different zones within the villa." He busied himself with the equipment in front of him, bringing up a view of the outside of the house, which he paused.

"As you can see, there is one guard stationed at the front entrance who provides perimeter sentry activity." Enzo placed his finger toward the bottom of the screen. "I want you to watch here."

The video started to roll, and Tina noticed a blur accelerating across the screen, a brief scuffle, and Alexander tossing a body aside. "Let me replay that at a slower speed; most of the detail is lost because it happens so fast."

Enzo started the video again, but at a much-reduced rate. "You can clearly see the expression on his face as he moves to take out his target. What do you see, Signorina?"

"He looks…calm. Focused, I guess."

"Exactly. This is not a mad animal rushing to destroy his prey." He took another breath. "Do you see any weapons, other than the sentry's?"

"No," she replied.

"No. Many of my team were surprised to note this. An unarmed man should be at a severe disadvantage in such a situation. Let us continue."

She watched as Alexander opened the doors and walked inside. Enzo had to switch to a different feed, this one monitoring the foyer. It clearly showed her boss pausing just inside, dismissively glancing at the stairs, then raising his nose into the air. "He is getting a scent picture of where the Pack are, deciding upon his next course of action. Soon, you will notice that your own sense of smell is greatly improved, as are other things."

Alexander paced over to the set of double doors centered underneath the second-floor landing, cocked his head, then nodded. "He has identified the location and number of the next set of guards just beyond those doors. They are protecting the dinner party that is taking place in the dining room."

Tina looked questioningly at the Beta. "He could hear them. Breathing, shifting of feet, perhaps even their heartbeats. Nothing would surprise me about our Alpha." He switched to another feed.

Alexander grasped the doorknobs and practically ripped them off their hinges as he burst through. The guard on the left was down and bleeding out via a throat that had been clawed open. The other was either unconscious, or dead, as he was lowered to the floor.

"What is he doing?" Tina asked incredulously.

Enzo chuckled. "Ahhh, we are approaching my favorite part. Whenever possible, we will remove our clothing before shifting, either into our wolf form, or our hybrid Battle form. As you might imagine, we tend to destroy whatever we are wearing at the time when transforming."

"I guess that makes sense."

On the screen, a now-naked Alexander picked up the unconscious sentry and launched him head-first through the doors. Even as the body was still in the air, he shifted into a large black wolf. Tina gasped loudly, but Enzo simply paused the video and said, "Magnificent."

She glanced at him, curiously, before asking in a quavering voice. "What do you mean?"

He raised his eyebrows briefly, then seemed to realize that she would not know. "That is no ordinary wolf. He is probably at *least* thirty percent larger than a normal werewolf. The shape of his head and muzzle are wrong, though. Flatter, more powerful, designed for crushing bone. His body is stockier and more muscular than mine, for example."

She still didn't appear to understand, so he continued.

"Every wolf I have ever met, or heard of, is descended from modern analogs: Timberwolves, Eurasian wolves, gray wolves, etc. What you see before you is none of those. It would seem to be a more primitive species." He shrugged. "Regardless, absent identification, he may be one of a kind, or perhaps there are now two." Enzo looked pointedly at her.

She glanced at her arm where Alexander had infected her, and she was not sure what to think.

Enzo switched the feed again, this time showing the dining room. Tina watched as the wolf prowled, snarling down the stairs and over to the body lying on the floor. He pushed at it with his nose, then lifted his hind leg and peed all over him.

The Beta seated next to her was roaring out laughter, and she didn't understand why.

Wiping tears from his eyes, Enzo paused the video again. "Well-played, Sir, well-played. I can see that you are confused; let me try to explain." He spun his chair to face her.

"What do you know about wolf behavior? Normal wolves, not Weres."

"Not much. I know they are hierarchical and that there are dominance fights as members try to move up in ranks. I think."

"That's part of it, but far from a complete picture. Now imagine those same behaviors backed up by a human intellect. What you end up with is mind games at a whole new level. Alexander just simultaneously showed his disdain for the capabilities of the Pack as a whole, as well as disrespect for those *actually* in charge. Look at their faces. Do you not think his arrow struck home?"

"Ok, I can see that. You have a strange expression in this video. Why?" she said.

He smirked. "Well, I was in the process of getting dressed down by the Alpha and his cronies. And since my place in the Pack was at a considerably lower rank than I now hold, I was more curious to see how this was going to play out than I was personally insulted."

The video began to roll once more. The wolf stalked toward the table then jumped. Alexander transformed into the classic Hollywood depiction of a werewolf even before landing on the table.

The video paused again. "This is called our Battle form. It is a hybrid mix of our human and wolf selves: all the benefits and none of the negatives. I should mention that not everyone attains this ability. Again, his is different. Much larger for one, but also bulkier, far more powerful. You will see what I mean in a bit when he and I fight."

Alexander stalked down the middle of the table, snarling and snapping at the diners until he reached the end where the former Alpha sat. He flexed and seemed to roar, but without sound it was hard to tell.

"I almost wet myself when he did that." Enzo chuckled. "It was truly terrifying."

As he shifted back to a naked human, it was apparent that Alexander asked a question...and didn't like the answer. The demise of the former Alpha was quick and unpleasant.

"I'm afraid that having a decapitated head tossed at him was almost more than poor Mario could handle. He still won't talk about it," her Beta said. "You must understand that this was once again a calculated dominance action. Not one single thing that Alexander does from start to finish is random, all is clearly thought-out.

"Ah, yes...and now we come to where your erstwhile attacker decides to make his presence known. Unwise, perhaps, but it did show more courage than I thought the boy had in him. Still, a shotgun might have been a better choice of weapon."

Tina watched as Alexander executed the boy. That was the only word that would fit what she saw. "Did he really have to toy with him? Why not just kill him quickly?" Distaste was evident in her voice.

Enzo looked thoughtful for a moment. "I suspect two reasons. The first was to impress upon the Pack that there were repercussions for their behavior. And secondly, I believe he wanted that boy to *suffer* for the part he played in hurting *you*."

Tina looked uncomfortable as she digested what she had just been told. The worst part of it was that she was responding to the actions that she had just viewed, and the response was not what she expected. There was a side of her that was excited by the violence and how powerful Alexander was showing himself to be. These were foreign feelings for her, and she could only assume that what she was experiencing was related to the changes her body was now going through.

Not too long after that, she watched as Enzo challenged and was easily defeated by Alexander. He was right; she could see the differences between them in their hybrid forms.

"Why didn't he shift? I mean, you had, so why didn't he?"

Enzo smiled at her. "Did it look like he needed to shift to defeat me? I was man-handled from start to finish. That fight established his total dominance over the Pack, and the fact that he did so in human form just added credibility to the act."

He shut down the video replay and turned to her. "I'm sure you have questions, so please, ask them."

"I appreciate you showing me this, Enzo, but I'm not sure what I am supposed to think. His actions were brutal. If you are trying to make me feel better about all of this, I think you failed."

He sighed. "You think that was brutal? Let me ask you something. What do you think would have happened if he had simply walked out after killing that boy?"

"I'm not sure," she admitted.

"Well, I am. There would have been a civil war within the Pack. Each faction pushing for their pick to take over the Alpha position. Blood would have flowed, and many would have died." Enzo leaned forward earnestly. "Alexander knew this. Do you have any idea how difficult it must have been to put his vendetta on hold, even temporarily? That he did so, just to ensure the wellbeing of a Pack he had no ties to, says a great deal about the man. Most would have simply walked out the door and carried the fight to the Coven...all without a backward glance."

Tina's brow furrowed as she processed this information.

"He saved lives by doing so. I have not known your Alexander for very long, but I can tell you this, he thinks of others long before he considers his own needs. That is the sign of a true leader, and only one of the reasons that I, and many others, respect him. In doing so, he has added a considerable burden to his shoulders." Enzo snorted loudly. "Yet even that is not enough, he takes underwing the very Coven of vampires whose member almost killed you. Granted, their membership is much-reduced thanks to him, but he includes them in what he is creating here in Naples. Who does such a thing?

"Come, Tina, let me show you to your room so you can get settled in."

"Enzo?" she whispered.

"Yes?"

"Can you make the room as far away from Alexander as possible?"

***

Having unpacked what few belongings were in her suitcase, Tina glanced around the room she had been assigned. There was a bed, a dresser, the beautiful oak wardrobe along the wall, and a window that looked out onto the courtyard where Alexander had given his speech earlier. A shared bathroom and showers were just down the hall.

She flopped down onto the bed and pulled the pillow to her chest. Her emotions were all over the place, and her mind was racing. It was apparent that Enzo had tried to make her understand...something. But if anything, watching Alexander kill those people only reinforced her feelings that he, and by extension she, were monsters. Ordinary people just didn't do things like that.

Oh, she knew intellectually that humanity had the capability of great cruelty. One only had to watch the news to understand that. But how do you justify what she had just watched? The really fucked-up part of the whole thing was that the Pack seemed to not only accept such behavior, but to admire it. Even Caterina, whose Coven Alexander had decimated, seemed to respect what he had done...no, not just respect, but *approve* of it. How messed up was that?

Was she just being unreasonable? Could everyone else be wrong? That didn't seem likely to her either. And yet, she just couldn't reconcile the man who performed such acts with the man she had spent the last several months with.

Tina acknowledged that she was being a bit childish about the whole thing, but it wasn't like she was given a choice. And truthfully, that was the root of her problem. Would she have elected to become what she now was, if she had been offered it? Maybe. But now she would never know, because that choice had been taken from her.

She continued to struggle with her thoughts until she fell asleep.

# Chapter 19

*". . . . With conflict came the need for soldiers. The Anunna were not about to risk their own lives on such activities and so, once again, utilized their genetic and nano-technologies to create human-derived weapons for use against one another. Many of the creatures of human mythology were based on what came of this wartime R and D. Anunna scientists looked around for inspiration, and began mixing predator species, as well as large aggressive plant eaters, with the already-modified humans. Naga, r, Ogres, Giants, Weres, what would eventually become the half-human/half-animal pantheons of nations such as Egypt, and even Mer variants utilized in water environments were created through trial and error. Other scientists looked to create terror weapons such as what would become Vampires, Demons, and Angels. Many of these creations were not viable and had to be terminated, but a fraction remained functional enough that they became a part of humanity's race-memory, and thus entered our mythology. The only limitations were the creativity of the scientist and the viability of the end-result.*

*Vast armies of these living weapons were created and pitted against one another. The Anunna mostly reserved the role of generals for themselves and cared little for the welfare of their armies. More could always be created as needed, and some were fertile and could breed, thus creating new generations for use in the wars that were being fought. . . ."*

**An excerpt from the diary of Alexander Matthews**

## April 1905, Mesa Verde, Colorado

*The drunken idiots who had been desecrating one of the ancient Puebloan sites near Mesa Verde had a massive bonfire going. A fire that was composed of roof-beams ripped from the structures themselves. They passed around bottles of whiskey as they inspected the day's finds, shouting, laughing, and arguing as they did so. The whole thing disgusted Alexander, and he was determined to do something about it.*

*He was observing the looters from a rock outcropping less than two hundred yards from where the fire blazed. His own camp was half a mile distant, and he knew they had no idea he was there. Alexander had stumbled across them during his explorations of the area, explorations that had been negotiated with and approved by the local Ute people. The same could not be said about the morons he was currently watching.*

*There was no moonlight, so the darkness was nearly complete, and the idiots across the way had ruined any night vision they might have had, by building such a large fire. Alexander swiftly removed his clothing and shifted to his wolf form, and made his way silently closer to their camp. He stopped about one hundred yards out and howled, a deep, mournful sound that echoed off the canyon walls. Startled shouts of consternation could be heard, and the metallic sounds of weapons being readied came to his ears. The wolf grinned and padded closer to his destination.*

*Alexander changed back to his human form and began tossing rocks randomly around the area. He also began moaning and chanting low, nonsense words and sounds that were meant to unnerve the looters. It seemed to be working for the most part, as he could hear several of them arguing that they should leave immediately. Others were determined to stay.*

*He shook his head at their stupidity and turned wolf once again. More howls from different locations, along with more rocks tossed around, added to the general confusion of the looters. Alexander decided they were primed enough, and he shifted to his Battle form. Deliberately loud in his approach to their location, he also maintained a low rumbling growl and loud heavy breathing, all to add to the menacing effect he was going for.*

*All eyes and weapons were pointed in the direction he was coming from, and it was apparent that many of the men were terrified. Suddenly the canyon was blanketed in silence, broken only by loud whispers amongst the men, and the occasional* pop *from the burning wood. Frightened eyes peered into the darkness as heads swiveled on necks, frantically searching for what was stalking them.*

*The lupine demon that sprang into their midst from an unexpected direction, roaring and tossing men and equipment around, was the last straw. The smell of urine was strong on the air as grown men frantically ran in all directions, screaming like little girls, madly scrambling to escape their perceived fate. Alexander continued to roar and toss equipment until the last faint sounds of the fleeing looters had faded away. His mocking laughter echoed off the canyon walls, only heard by the wildlife that had gone to ground as the giant predator had made his way through their territory….*

***

Francesca scowled as she paced the cubby-hole she had been assigned after that man had tossed her out of the quarters she had until recently inhabited. This situation was not to be born, and the interloper must be gotten rid of so that she could put things to rights once again.

Who did he think he was to change the traditions and ways of this Pack? A mere nobody from America. She snorted at the thought that such a pedestrian person would dare to steal the leadership. No, something would need to be done…and soon. Her eyes fell on the cell phone that sat on the vanity, and she made up her mind.

She quickly dialed a number and waited impatiently for someone to answer.

"Francesca," a deep voice spoke into her ear. "Why are you calling me?"

"I have news, Lorenzo, and it is not good," she replied.

"Oh?"

"The Alpha position in Naples has been usurped…by an American."

A moment of silence greeted her words. "How is this possible?"

Francesca sucked in a deep breath, trying to decide how much to tell her brother. "Alessandro and his vampire friend attacked another woman, but this time they were caught."

"I told you that you needed to put an end to those activities, sister. It was always a risk that they would be discovered, putting us all in harm's way," he told her sharply.

"Yes. Well, it won't be an issue any longer," she growled back. "My son and my husband are both dead."

"I...see," Lorenzo said softly. "But that doesn't explain how it happened or why you called me."

"The woman who was attacked was under the protection of an American, a Were, and he took exception to this and tracked my son back here." Francesca paused a moment. "He goes by the name of Alexander. This man executed my husband and son and assumed the Alpha position after issuing a challenge."

"Did anyone take him up on this?" her brother asked with genuine curiosity.

"Only that fool, Enzo," she ground out between clenched teeth.

"No one else?"

"He is quite fearsome, brother."

"Bah, your Pack always was weak," Lorenzo shot back. "All of which was the fault of its leadership...including you."

"Yes, well, that is no longer an issue either. Alexander publicly shamed me by tossing me out of my quarters and declaring me Omega."

A sharp intake of breath could be heard through the phone. "Did he indeed? And what do you plan to do about this, sister dear?"

"I have a plan waiting to be implemented, but this situation cannot stand, brother. If he is allowed to shape this Pack the way he wants to, it will cause nothing but trouble for the other Packs...including yours," Francesca told him.

"We shall see. Keep me advised on whether your plan succeeds."

***

To say that Enzo was less than pleased would have been a gigantic understatement. Alexander grinned at the memory of his Beta's extensive and creative profanity when his Alpha had refused to take any additional security to the meeting with Caterina's Coven. His argument had been that if any of them were stupid enough to attack when he got there, Caterina would take care of it, and if she couldn't, then Alexander was undoubtedly more than capable of doing so. Besides, there was a lot to be said for placing one's head directly into the lion's mouth without the slightest hesitation or fear. Showing weakness with either the Pack or Coven, at this juncture, was not a winning proposition.

No. Of far greater concern was what was going on with Tina. It was evident that she had not forgiven him for turning her into a Were, and even worse, she actually seemed frightened of him. Long-term, this was not a tenable solution, but for now, she needed to learn what it meant to be a wolf. Especially if he was going to release her and send her home. The last thing he wanted was to let a half-trained shifter loose within Spokane because, at some point, she would screw up, and he would be forced to deal with it...and he wasn't entirely sure he could do it.

So that left him with keeping her here until he felt comfortable that she had a good grasp on her new reality, as well as all of the rules that applied. For now, he would just keep his distance and let her work things out on her own. It was going to be rough on her, but it couldn't be helped. He shook his head ruefully as he parked his NSX in front of the Coven villa. *Focus, Alexander, you need to be on your 'A' game for this.*

The sentry at the front entrance eyed him warily as he approached, but the man opened the door for him anyway. The Alpha appreciated his professionalism and nodded at him as he passed. Caterina was waiting for him in the foyer, several unknown members of her Coven arrayed behind her. She stepped forward to meet him.

"Caterina welcomes Alexander, Alpha of both the Pack and Coven of Napoli." She spoke formally.

His eyes surveyed the tense bodies behind their Coven master, coolly appraising each.

"Obey your mistress in all things, and you and I will have no further difficulties. It is only through her will that any of you yet live today," he said evenly. "As for myself, I have already put the past behind me, and am only concerned with moving forward. Hopefully, as we work together, any remaining animosities can be dispelled."

It was difficult to tell by their guarded expressions whether his words had any effect. Mentally shrugging, he looked back at Caterina expectantly. She gestured him to follow and walked to a small side room that held a table and enough chairs for six people.

Alexander seated himself at the head of the table and waited for Caterina and two of her people to sit down. "I'm hoping this meeting will be fairly short, but I will want to speak to all Coven members afterward."

Caterina looked pointedly at a young woman, who immediately used her phone to begin sending texts.

"Cat, are there any immediate needs that are a priority for you right now?" he asked.

"Caterina cannot think of anything other than personnel shortages. The Coven is stretched thin trying to cover all staffing needs."

"Understood. I wanted your thoughts on attempting to bring in unaffiliated vampires and offering them a home. Might that help alleviate your shortages?"

She turned to the man sitting stiffly to her right. "Caterina would ask her head of security. Stefano?"

He nodded, then said, "I have some concerns regarding such an action. They are unaffiliated for a reason, after all."

"Perhaps. And yet, not all of them, I am thinking," Alexander said. "Cat herself was unaffiliated prior to assuming leadership of this Coven. A thorough vetting should eliminate most of the bad apples, and those who don't make the cut will be told to leave this city."

"Sir?"

"I have already put a similar edict in place for the Pack. Now is not the time to have rogue elements in play within Naples. We need to stabilize the situation before considering loosening the restrictions." He paused. "It's something to think about at any rate.

"Let me ask you this. How many Normals who are in the know would be willing to be infected?"

Caterina and Stefano exchanged a glance, then the head of security said,

"Somewhere between seven and ten. However, that would cut into our donor pool, so I'm not sure that is viable."

"OK, let's shelve that idea for now. But something needs to be done fairly quickly." Alexander looked at Stefano. "Do you have sufficient staff for normal security duties?"

"Barely, and that's only because we are all working long shifts," he responded, leaving the *thanks to you* unspoken.

"Cat, I can make some Pack security available if you would like. They would be supplementary forces only and would report to Stefano while they were here. Would that work?"

She raised an eyebrow at her head of security, and after the barest hesitation, he nodded. "Caterina accepts your offer."

"Excellent. I'll have Enzo contact Stefano directly to coordinate efforts."

Alexander cleared his throat. "There is something you all need to be aware of. I have Pack resources looking into a couple of different options that would allow all of us, both Coven and Pack, to live at a single property, rather than separate as is now the case. I have several reasons that I would like to see this happen, but chief among them is the ability to consolidate and share our resources. From a security standpoint alone, this is advantageous. We could merge both teams and share the load. I envision Enzo and Stefano sharing leadership. Would this be a problem for you, Stefano?"

"Would I only lead the vampires?"

"No. We'll mix the members up. Enzo is my Beta and will have less and less time to run the department as I shift responsibilities to him. At some point, you will be the head of security for our combined houses. I should warn you, my expectations are high."

Caterina coughed loudly into her hand, mumbling, "That is an understatement."

Alexander grinned at her. "I am hoping we can find a property with several buildings that will house everyone, provide a training facility, and whatever else I can think of. If either of you knows of such a property, please let either Enzo or Julia know. My long-term goal is to merge the two houses into a stronger cohesive whole. As I am sure you are aware, this has never been done before, and I expect a certain amount of opposition." His gaze hardened, and he met the eyes of each. "This *will* happen. No dissent will be tolerated. Please make sure everyone knows that."

"Finally, some last housekeeping items. I want an audit of all Coven finances, as well as the current state of your armory." Nodding at Stefano, he continued, "If we need to modernize, or beef up what you have, it will be addressed when you give me the formal report.

"Cat, I am having daily meetings with Pack senior staff. Please attend these with whoever you feel needs to be there. I'd rather have just one meeting than have to come over here only to repeat myself." He smiled at her as he said this. "Not that I don't appreciate spending time with you, but…."

She lifted her nose and sniffed dismissively. "Caterina is well aware of the effect she has on males such as Alexander. It is but one of the many heavy burdens she has to bear each and every day."

Laughter filled the room as everyone heard her words. Alexander then adjourned the meeting, and once he was assured that the Coven was assembled, he gave them a slightly modified version of the speech he had given the Pack the day before.

***

Tina was feeling lost. She had awoken to the sounds of people moving about the halls, and then she'd showered. It was a little awkward since she hadn't shared a bathroom like that since high school, but she managed. The aromas of breakfast drew her to the dining room, where she ate far more than she normally would, but she was starving. Her eyes scanned the crowd, taking in the smiling faces and loud companionable chatter that filled the room. Staff were busy refilling platters and drink containers almost as fast as they were being emptied. There were several children present, and their harried mothers tried to keep them focused long enough to actually eat.

Enzo nodded to her from a table near the front of the room, but she didn't see Alexander. She felt guilty about being happy about that fact, but just couldn't help it. Tina still had mixed emotions where he was concerned, and she needed some time to work it all out. Intellectually she knew he had done what he felt was required, but the resentment she harbored would not go away any time soon. Still, seeing the Pack interact with each other, and him, made her doubt herself. If he truly was the monster she thought, then why didn't anyone else seem to see it that way?

Additionally, she had worked and trained with him for months. Could he have hidden that from her so successfully, and for so long? She didn't think so, not really. The genuine attraction she had felt for him during that time also suggested he was exactly what he had appeared to be. Was it merely the fact that he was a werewolf that was clouding her emotions right now? Or was she just being vindictive because he made a choice without consulting her? Granted, it was a choice that had a significant impact on her life, but would she truly have preferred him to let her die? She was so confused.

Tina drank the last of her coffee and made her way back to her room. She threw herself onto the bed and took out her phone, staring at it unsurely for a moment. Her fingers dialed her Aunt Maria.

"Tina, I thought you were in Italy," her aunt's voice said.

"I am. Not sure when I'll be back either," she said morosely.

"Oh? Is everything all right?" Maria asked in a concerned tone.

Tina hesitated, not sure how to broach the subject. "How well do you know Alexander?"

Her aunt replied, "In what way, dear?"

"Like, does he have any secrets?" she probed.

Maria sighed into the phone. "Why don't you just ask the question you are hinting at, Tina."

Her niece ran her hand through her hair exasperatedly. "Fine. You'll probably think I'm crazy anyway. Did you know he is a werewolf?"

The silence on the other end was deafening. "I did. I want you to tell me exactly what has happened."

Tina spent the next few minutes bringing her aunt up to date. Not once did Maria interrupt or ask for clarification. When Tina had finished, her aunt was still silent.

"Aunt Maria? Are you still there?"

"Give me a second, please," was the terse response.

Maria started speaking in a measured, even tone. "So, let me see if I have this straight. You were attacked by a vampire and his wolf partner. As a result, you were dying, and Alexander did the only thing that would save your life…and you are shutting him out?" The last words were hissed into the phone. "*Are you fucking insane?*"

Tina was shocked by the venom-laced words. This was not what she had expected to hear.

"I would have given anything to be in the position you find yourself in. Stop being a selfish brat!" Maria snarled. "My jealousy is killing me at this moment, and while I really want to be happy for you, I just don't have it in me."

Sudden realization struck Tina, and she said, "You never worked for his '*father*', did you? It was Alexander the whole time, wasn't it?"

"Yes. We were attacked in Egypt and he had to fight off a Pack of Werejackals. I witnessed the whole fight, so it wasn't like he could pretend it didn't happen. Not long after we returned to the States, and I had thought long and hard about it, I begged him to infect me." Maria's voice broke on the final words. "He wouldn't do it. Alexander thinks he's a monster and refused to curse anyone else. Do you know how many others he has turned?"

"No. How many?"

"None. Not a single one. Remember when I told you he was the loneliest man on the planet?" Maria asked.

"Yes."

"Alexander is one-hundred forty-six years old. He has watched his entire family grow old and die. He admitted to me that he deliberately lost contact with them because it was too hard, not to mention the difficulty of explaining why he still looked so young. Can you even imagine what that must have been like?" Maria continued relentlessly. "He swore he would never curse another soul the way he felt he had been cursed. And he kept that promise until you were attacked."

"You love him, don't you?" Tina whispered.

"Yes. God help me, I think I always have," Maria hiccupped. "He never let it be anything other than a friendship though. I understand why, but it wasn't easy. Not for either of us. He was attracted to me as well, but he knew the day would come when I'd grow old, and he wouldn't. Now you know the real reason I never married or had children. It wouldn't have been fair to love one man and marry another. So, I stayed a spinster and enjoyed my time with him."

She blew her nose and sniffled a time or two. "But you don't have to follow that path, Tina. If you want a relationship with him, Alexander no longer has an excuse to deny you. Is that something you want?"

Tina sighed. "If you would have asked me even a week ago, I would have said yes. But now…? I'm just not sure."

"Why? Because you think he took the choice away from you? Grow up. You were dying, and he did the only thing he could to save your life." The anger was back in her aunt's voice. "You would be dead right now if it weren't for him."

"It's not just that. He killed so many people. How do I let that go?"

"Yes, he killed a lot of people. Alexander has killed before, and he will no doubt kill again," Maria said matter-of-factly. "I *can* assure you he never does so lightly. You grew up in a town never knowing that other types of humans even existed. Why do you think that is?"

"I don't know," her niece responded.

"Because Alexander controls the city. The formal term is that he is the Master of the city. He kept everyone in line. For almost a hundred years, he has kept the peace and ensured that Normal people were safe. You can't do that without breaking some heads."

Maria paused, then continued relentlessly. "He didn't go to war with the Coven and Pack just because they nearly took you from him. That was part of it, clearly, and probably even a big part. But what *really* pissed him off was that something like that could occur at all. Regular people are to be protected, not fed upon. So, he did the only thing he felt he could—he rectified the situation in his own special way. Wolves and Vampires may seem human, Tina, but their very natures dictate certain behaviors. Dominance has to be clearly established and firmly maintained. Might makes right isn't just a saying to them…it's fact."

A moment later, Maria spoke again. "He took control of both houses because the previous leadership was defective. There was no way he could ignore the lack of control they had over their people, nor could he just walk away and let the same thing happen to another innocent person. People talk about honor like it's a dead thing. I can tell you it is *not*. Alexander just doesn't have it in him to not fix a situation when he knows he can. So, he did. Do you understand?"

"Not really. It's so weird watching him interact with the Pack. They should hate him for what he did, and yet they don't. He is making major changes to the way things work, and rather than chafe at it, they seem to be embracing them. Don't get me wrong, the old elite aren't happy, but everyone else seems to be taking it in stride."

Maria snorted. "That's because he established his dominance quickly and ruthlessly. They respect that. Unlike Normal humans, the Pack has enough wolf in them that a clear hierarchy and a strong leader are comforting, even necessary. Those poor bastards have no idea what they are in for. Alexander won't leave until he stabilizes both the Pack and Coven, but make no mistake, he has zero intention of sticking around to run things forever."

"I think that he has already chosen Enzo and Caterina to lead in his absence," Tina said.

Laughter belted from the phone. "Caterina? Oh, that's too funny. I suspect she isn't entirely pleased with her new position."

"Probably not, but he named her his Beta over the Coven."

"She can handle it. That is one tough lady, my dear."

"Enzo said that had Cat not intervened, at great risk to herself, Alexander would have killed every vampire in the Coven, including children," Tina said.

"I doubt that Caterina was really in danger, but it sounds like Alexander was furious. My guess is that a lot of that rage was because they had forced his hand. He will kill when it's necessary, and he obviously felt it was, but that doesn't mean it was easy for him to do so. At heart, Alexander is a gentle man who just wants to be left alone." She sighed. "I can't imagine what releasing the monster he truly believes he is must have done to his psyche. I'm sure it was devastating. And just so you know, those children were never in danger.

Alexander would sooner die than see a child harmed."

"I've seen the videos, Aunt Maria. He was fucking scary. An emotionless killing machine, like some sort of wolf Terminator."

"I'm sure it seemed that way, Tina. Alexander can be very focused when he is on task. I would venture to guess that during sparring sessions you may have let your emotions get the better of you?"

"Yes, and he always tells me that I need to control them. So annoying."

Another laugh. "Well, what you saw was him practicing what he preaches."

An uncomfortable silence reigned for a time.

"What am I going to do, Aunt Maria?" Tina asked.

"You need to let go of whatever resentments you have. He didn't steal your choice from you. There was no other option. Period. Embrace the gift he has given you, because it *is* a gift. You have the opportunity I always longed for." A deep breath. "If not, then when he feels you are ready, he will let you go. And you will have to figure out what to do with yourself after that."

The sound of gunshots suddenly rang out from the front of the building. Tina sat up and said, "I have to go, Aunt Maria, something is happening." Voices were shouting, and footsteps thundered down the hall. Tina ended the call and ran down the stairs, only to find utter chaos.

***

Alexander's foot had barely touched the first step leading to the entrance of the Pack villa when the large caliber bullet struck him in the left shoulder blade. Blood, meat, and bone sprayed the doors in front of him, and the deformed bullet buried itself in the wood. The impact spun him 180 degrees, and the second round took him in the solar plexus. His body collapsed to the ground, face to the sky. The sentry on duty immediately pulled his weapon and scanned for the shooter.

Enzo and two more security burst through the doors. Enzo rushed to where Alexander lay, the Beta yelling for medical assistance while the remaining guards sprinted to where the sentry was pointing. The shooter managed to get off another shot before being taken down and disarmed, but no one else was hit.

When Tina reached the top of the steps, the Pack doctor was already trying to stanch the flow of blood from Alexander's wounds. Blood was everywhere, so *much* blood, and time slowed down for her as she tried to take it all in. There was a ringing noise that dampened all other sounds, and she could feel her pulse pounding furiously. At the same time, everything took on a clarity she had never experienced before.

Enzo was shouting commands and attempting to get control over the situation. The medical team struggled to hold Alexander's body down as he went into some sort of convulsive spasm; blood gurgled and foamed from his mouth and his hands clenched against the hard driveway, fingers digging deep. His back arched, then relaxed. Somehow his eyes found hers, and a sad smile remained on his face even as his body slowly deflated. She knew the exact moment when he died.

Stunned, all she could do was stand there as the medical team rushed his lifeless body past her and into the villa. *He can't be dead*, she thought. *I never even got the chance to say good-bye.* It was at that moment that she realized she had already forgiven him. Stupid, really, because she should have been asking him to forgive *her* for being such an ass about the whole thing. The nails of her fingers were biting into her palms, drawing blood, though she didn't feel it. Her body was shaking from the sudden burst of anger and adrenaline that flooded her system.

*This must be what he felt that night*, flitted across her consciousness as she finally understood how he could have done what he did. A part of her carefully filed that thought away to be examined later, but for now, her focus was on the figure being dragged between the security team to stand before Enzo. She tilted her head curiously as she studied the man. Maybe early thirties in apparent age, 5'8" in height, slicked back black curly hair, and five o'clock shadow. He was cursing at Enzo in Italian and struggling against his captors as he was halted just in front of the Beta. Enzo's right arm launched forward, and a fist landed in his gut, folding the perpetrator over from the force of the punch. Tina smiled a little at that, but it wasn't *nearly* enough. No, not enough at all. Her wolf was insistent, howling with rage, and she consciously surrendered to it. Tina pondered appropriate punishments for a moment, then calmly descended the steps, gliding up behind the Beta. Her right hand reached down and tugged Enzo's pistol from the holster at his hip, then she gracefully pirouetted around him, right shoulder and arm facing Enzo throughout the motion, stopping only when she was squared up with the assassin. She raised her arm and when the pistol sights aligned on the prisoner, she fired two rounds into his heart and one into his head, at point-blank range. Warm blood splattered the front of her body and face, but if Tina noticed, she gave no indication. The look of shock on the shooter's face as she executed him was priceless.

She turned ninety degrees to her left and took a step back, placing everyone within her peripheral vision, unsure of how they would react. Tina automatically ejected the magazine to ensure she still had ammo, then reseated it into the butt of the pistol. When she looked up, Enzo was signaling his team to stand down. She had an ice-cold, stoic look on her face when she asked, "Do we have a problem here, Enzo?"

"No, Signorina, although it perhaps would have been best had I been able to question him first."

Tina shrugged dispassionately, then tucked the weapon into the small of her back, the waistband of her pants holding it in place. "I'll be keeping this."

She walked past him, never even glancing at all of the shocked faces that looked at her as she made her way back into the villa. Behind her, Enzo and his team shared stunned looks with the Pack members who had witnessed what had just happened.

To Be Continued....

# Author's notes

Wow. I can't believe I'm actually writing this. How I got here is all due to a strange series of events.

Flash back to June 2017. I had just been laid off from a job that was not only slowly killing me, but was also crushing my soul. And of course, I was let go the day before my family and I were to fly out for a three-week vacation in southern Italy, a vacation that we had been planning for almost two years.

Strangely enough, my new status of being unemployed didn't really bother me, and while I spent the first week just decompressing, the second found me asking myself—what now?

One evening, as we lounged around after a full day of sightseeing, I expressed my dissatisfaction with the book I was currently reading. My wife, evidently fed up with listening to me bitch about how I could do better than a lot of what passed for literature these days, rolled her eyes and said—Do it. Or shut up (I'm paraphrasing, but you get the idea). Challenge accepted! I sat down and began to write my first short story.

Which brings us to my first novel, the book you have just read...hopefully. Urban Fantasy/Paranormal was not something I spent much time on. Not really my cup of tea, you see. Or so I was convinced. That all changed one evening after we returned to the States and I was channel-surfing. I ended up watching a couple of episodes of Ancient Aliens on the History Channel. At first, I was amazed that it had survived for so many seasons. Then I was horrified by the thought that people actually believed this was a thing. And finally, I decided to see if I could come up with any premise that might hold up given that some of what was presented were true. The vast majority of it was utter bullshit, but I picked over what they offered and selected a few nuggets to build a story around.

At this point it was merely a thought exercise…a way to amuse myself while watching a man with the worst hair-do I have ever seen present this BS as fact. Eventually though, I had pieced together a story that wasn't horrible. And actually, it was pretty damned interesting (as long as you could suspend dis-belief).

When I realized that it would have werewolves, vampires and other cryptids, my one absolute criterion was that there would be no magic. None of my characters would sparkle, thank you very much. It had to be based on science. Granted, the science was so advanced that much of it would seem like magic, but still, science.

Basic premise in mind, I sat down to write the story. Three months later, the book was done. Less than a year after that and I had two follow-on books making up a trilogy (and a shit-ton of ideas for associated shorts and additional novels). They practically wrote themselves.

Now I just needed the money to pay for proper editing, artwork, etc.… Which meant going back to work, at which point my writing speed quickly dropped. Funny how that works. Anyway, in a nutshell, that is the story of how this book came to be.

Thanks for reading, and if you enjoyed it, please leave a review on Amazon, preferably 4 or 5 stars. The more the better for a new author such as me. If it does well enough, books two and three will follow in short order.

L. D. Albano, November 2020

For those who are curious, or just have an excess of time on their hands, I have a blog that I use as a forum for things that interest me…and where I discuss my writing process, challenges, etc. Just hop on over to: https://inadvertentconsequences.com

Made in the USA
Columbia, SC
15 October 2022